PRAISE FOR

A Dark and Stormy Murder

"I can't remember when I've been so enthralled in a story and its characters. This is a book that Phyllis A. Whitney and Mary Stewart would have loved, not to mention Elizabeth Peters and Victoria Holt. And what's not to love? Writing that flows beautifully, suspense that builds slowly and almost unbearably, and a setting that is perfectly beautiful and mysterious, yet also menacing. I think fans of Susanna Kearsley and Deanna Raybourn will devour this book like I did."

—Miranda James, *New York Times* bestselling author of the Cat in the Stacks Mysteries

"Julia Buckley's new *A Dark and Stormy Murder* is a traditional mystery reader's dream. In this first of what I hope will be many adventures for Lena and Camilla, Buckley captures the sublime bond between beloved author and ardent fan. *A Dark and Stormy Murder* has it all: plenty of action, a dash of romance, and *lots* of heart."

—Julie Hyzy, *New York Times* bestselling author of the White House Chef Mysteries

"An engaging cozy with a touch of Gothic, *A Dark and Stormy Murder* is a not-to-be-missed page-turner. Bring on book two in this charming series!"

—Terrie Farley Moran, Agatha Award–winning author of the Read 'Em and Eat Mysteries

Berkley Prime Crime titles by Julia Buckley

Writer's Apprentice Mysteries

A DARK AND STORMY MURDER

DEATH IN DARK BLUE

A DARK AND TWISTING PATH

Undercover Dish Mysteries

THE BIG CHILI

CHEDDAR OFF DEAD

PUDDING UP WITH MURDER

A Dark and Stormy Murder

Julia Buckley

BERKLEY PRIME CRIME, NEW YORK

An imprint of Penguin Random House LLC
375 Hudson Street, New York, New York 10014

A DARK AND STORMY MURDER

A Berkley Prime Crime Book / published by arrangement with the author

ISBN: 9780425282601

PUBLISHING HISTORY
Berkley Prime Crime mass-market edition / July 2016

PRINTED IN THE UNITED STATES OF AMERICA

10 9 8 7

Cover illustration © by Bob Kayganich.
Cover design by Alana Colucci.

For Mary Stewart, who was the best.

Acknowledgments

As always, I am grateful to my agent, Kim Lionetti, who shares my love of Gothic romantic suspense, and who helped me dream up the premise for this book.

I am very thankful to Miranda James, Julie Hyzy and Terrie Farley Moran, who said kind things about this book. Thank you also to the Mystery Writers of America and Sisters in Crime for their inspiration and support.

I am indebted to my editor, Michelle Vega, for her grace and kindness, and for her support of my books—this series in particular; indeed, thank you to everyone at Berkley Prime Crime for their admirable professionalism. I am also grateful to the folks at WYCC and their Mystery Marathon crew for letting me talk about the book on the air!

Thank you to my father, Bill, who serves as both editor and fan. I send gratitude as always to all of my teaching colleagues, especially those in the English Department:

Terese Black, Maggie Carey, Rose Crnkovich, Linda Harrington, Kathleen Maloney, and Margaret Metzger, and to librarians Molly Klowden and Sue Tindall.

A heartfelt thank-you to my mother, Katherine, for introducing me to the kind of books that Camilla Graham writes, and for reading and discussing them with me. At one time, we were our own little book club: my mother, my sister, and I.

Thank you to all of my siblings and siblings-in-law for their support of my literary endeavors: Bill and Ann in suburban Illinois, Claudia in Virginia, Chris and Cindy in Indiana, Linda and Kevin in Chicago.

Finally, I am ever grateful to the late Mary Stewart. I entered her literary landscapes decades ago, and I never really left. She remains alive in many books, but especially in fifteen suspense novels that enthralled millions of people.

Bestselling books by Camilla Graham

The Lost Child (1972)
Castle of Disquiet (1973)
Snow in Eden (1974)
Winds of Treachery (1975)
They Came from Calais (1976)
In Spite of Thunder (1978)
Whispers of the Wicked (1979)
Twilight in Daventry (1980)
Stars, Hide Your Fires (1981)
The Torches Burn Bright (1982)
For the Love of Jane (1983)
River of Silence (1985)
A Fine Deceit (1987)
Fall of a Sparrow (1988)
Absent Thee from Felicity (1989)
The Thorny Path (1990)
Betraying Eve (1991)
On London Bridge (1992)
The Silver Birch (1994)
The Tide Rises (1995)
What Dreams May Come (1996)
The Villainous Smile (1998)
Gone by Midnight (1999)
Sapphire Sea (2000)
Beautiful Mankind (2001)
Frost and Fire (2002)
Savage Storm (2003)
The Pen and the Sword (2005)
The Tenth Muse (2006)
Death at Seaside (2008)
Mist of Time (2009)
He Kindly Stopped for Me (2010)

(a four-year hiatus)

Bereft (2015)

1

In her youthful and exuberant heart, she had never contemplated that her secret dream could ever really come true, and when it did, she found herself quite at a loss, as though the time of waiting for her miracle had ultimately been preferable to the daunting acceptance of destiny.

—from *The Salzburg Train*

I WAS IMMERSED in *The Lost Child*, one of my favorite Camilla Graham novels, when an unlikely phone call changed my life.

In my quiet living room, things were placid: I sat on my couch in blue jeans, a sweatshirt, and fuzzy socks, cuddling my sleeping cat, Lestrade, whose large body practically warmed my entire right side. In the book, things were tense: it was dusk, and the Eiffel Tower gleamed gold in the background. The young Englishwoman, Philippa Earl, waited for the Frenchman, Henri, to get any news he might have about her lost charge, Colin, a sensitive nine-year-old who had somehow been taken from underneath Philippa's watchful and loving gaze. She feared for the boy's life, and the handsome Henri had told her, in a stolen conversation in the street, that he had more information for her. Now she waited beneath the tower in the chill of a

Paris spring, hoping against hope that little Colin, whom she loved more than his own parents did, would be returned to her. Lingering beneath her fear was a strange attraction to the mysterious Henri, the man who had murmured in her ear and briefly held her hand, hinting that all would be well . . .

The phone rang, and I jumped. Lestrade jumped, too, but then settled against my leg, glaring briefly at me before descending back into his luxurious slumber. His fluffy white belly was too great a temptation, and I ruffled it with my hand while I swiped the screen on my phone. Lestrade opened one eye, not sure whether to purr or swat my hand—both had been responses in the past, depending on his mood. His face, a pleasing mixture of gray, white, and buff, grew curious as I started speaking.

"Hello?"

"Lena. It's Allison."

"Hey, what's up?" I asked, still sort of looking at my book.

"You're reading. I can tell. Your voice is all soft and cobwebby. Take your nose out of the novel—this is important! I'm making your dreams come true!"

This was a clever ploy; she had my attention. "You mean you got Colin Firth to promise he'd call?"

Allison snorted. "He's too old for you. No, this is much, much better! This is better than chocolate mousse with raspberries on top."

Now I was sitting up straight. Lestrade moaned when I displaced him, then covered his little triangular face with his paws. "This is a trick. Nothing is better than chocolate mousse. What could you possibly have done for me in that little Podunk town in Indiana? Did you find buried gold that will help pay off my student debt?"

"I wish. No, but this is better than gold to you, my little book lover. Or should I say, my little Camilla Graham lover!"

Now I was frightened. I had told Allison many times that I loved the Graham suspense novels, but she never seemed to take note of it; Allison wasn't much of a reader, and she had never totally understood my obsession with books, although she had always supported my habit, buying me bookstore gift cards for every Christmas and birthday. She was thoughtful, my friend Allison.

"How are you even remembering her name?" I asked. She was trodding on very sensitive turf. I had loved Camilla Graham since I was thirteen years old and happened across *The Lost Child* in my school library. Within months I had read every book Camilla Graham had ever written; since then I'd reread them all. I perused them often, the way one might seek the comfort of a dear and special friend. I had needed that comfort today, which was why I was rereading her first, and perhaps best, novel.

"Oh, I guess I remember her name from seeing her every Saturday in my knitting group."

"Ha ha. Hilarious. I now owe you one practical joke."

Allison's voice was firm. "Lena. She lives in Blue Lake. She's *in my knitting group*. I only just realized who she was."

"Get out. She's English. She lives in London or somewhere."

"Right. She did. But her husband was American, and he was from Blue Lake."

My arms felt half-numb. It was true, Graham had married

an American; they had fallen in love on her first book tour, back in 1971, when she had ventured to Chicago in winter and met the love of her life at a Christmas party. "So?"

"So she lives here, in what she calls semiretirement."

"She's not retired! She's working on a novel! I read an article about it in *Publishers Weekly*."

"Yeah, she is writing a book. She told me about it. That's where you come in." A happy giggle escaped her.

"Wait. I think there's been a misunderstanding. Some old lady in your knitting group—and by the way, how weird that you're in a knitting group when you're twenty-seven years old—told you that she's writing a novel. And you have mistaken her for—"

"Oh, geez, I knew you'd do this. For a romantic, you're such an unbeliever."

"I'm just trying to clarify—"

"Okay. I just sent you a picture. Click on it."

I held out the phone and opened the message from Allison. A woman sat there, a skein of yarn in her lap. Her gray hair was gathered in a casual bun, and her long, slender fingers held two green knitting needles. I recognized the hair, the perfect posture, the bright eyes, from the various book jacket covers I had studied over the years. It was her. Camilla Graham—my idol. In tiny Blue Lake, Indiana, where Allison had moved because her husband had gotten a job in the nearby town of Stafford. Blue Lake, Allison had insisted dreamily, was the most beautiful town in the area, and she and John had been quite confident about buying property there.

I clicked out of the photo and put the phone back to my ear. "I can't believe this," I whispered.

"Believe it. And also, we talked about you."

"What? Oh God. What? Did you—embarrass me? Did you tell her I worship her like some fawning idiot?"

Allison giggled. "I did not embarrass you. I told her you're her biggest fan, a great admirer of her work. I told her that you're a writer, and your own efforts were inspired by hers. She asked if you had been published, and I said no, but that your graduate thesis was a full-length novel inspired by her work, and that it was very well-received by people in academia. How's that?"

I cleared my suddenly dry throat. "It's pretty good."

"Then she said she would like to read it, so I sent her the copy I have on my computer—"

"Wait. Camilla Graham said she wanted to read my book?"

"Yes."

"Why?"

"I'm getting to that."

"And you've already given it to her?"

"Yes. And she read it."

"Oh God! This is horrifying. And wonderful. And horrifying! I don't even want to know what she said. Don't tell me. *Do not* tell me what she said, Allison! I don't want to know."

"She said she loved it."

"Oh my gosh!" I fell over sideways on my couch, bound by a complicated series of emotions. "What are you even talking about?"

Allison was giggling again, joyful with her news. "And she said she would like to meet you. That she has a job proposal for you."

"A job." I had been looking for one of those for three months, ever since leaving grad school. My debt was looming, my book was moldering, and my bills were accumulating. "What kind of job?"

"She didn't say in so many words, but I get the sense she might want to hire someone to help her with her current book."

"To help her."

"Quit repeating what I say."

"I'm in shock. I don't even know what to think, let alone what to say."

"Say you'll do it."

"You're telling me that my writing idol, my hero since my tender teen years, is looking for a ghost writer. And somehow I am the *only candidate*? All the professionals she knows, with all the people in New York and London—"

Allison's voice was almost an octave higher in its excitement. "But see, that's why you're perfect, Lee. She seems to want to keep this on the down low. Why would she consult anyone already in the industry? People in the book business? Why would she let them know, in that cutthroat world, that she's slowing down a little? And then here you are: a fan of hers who knows her work intimately. A writer who can capture her own personal style. Someone who loves her genre as much as she does. See what I mean?"

I sat up straight. "When does she want to meet me?"

"She said you can do it over the phone. She claims that will be good enough."

"A phone interview? Oh, God."

"Then, when you get the job, you can move here! You can stay with John and me until you get settled—you haven't seen our new house yet, anyway. And you'll love Blue Lake in fall! It's beautiful, like a storybook town."

"What about Lestrade?"

Allison snorted. She didn't like my loveable feline; she routinely called him "your gross cat," but it was a misnomer. Lestrade was meticulously clean and generally charming; he was just large. I had rescued him as a kitten, so I had no idea of his parentage, but my friends always joked that one of his sires must have been a raccoon. Lestrade did have a remarkably stripy tail and a rather large lower body (which Allison called "your gross cat's big butt"). Needless to say, Allison and Lestrade were not dear friends.

"If you get the job, you'll have to drive up here with your stuff, and your gross—I mean, *Lestrade*, and John and I can help you find a place to live. And you'll be able to get out of your claustrophobic little apartment, and you won't have to risk running into Kurt everywhere."

Kurt. It almost didn't hurt to hear his name these days. Today had been the six-month anniversary of our breakup—hence my reading of *The Lost Child*.

"This is going to be so much fun. I'm so excited!"

And so began a series of events. A call was arranged for that afternoon. I had a pad full of nervously scribbled notes, a box of tissues in case I cried out of sheer terror, and a pile of Graham's books, in the event that I needed to consult a reference. I was literally trembling when the phone rang at four o'clock.

"Hello?" I said.

"Hello, is this Lena London?"

"Yes, this is Lena. Or you can call me Lee."

"All right, Lena Lee. I am flattered to hear that you have read my books." Her voice was soft, gentle, and did indeed have a trace of the British accent that I had always imagined.

"Oh, yes, ma'am. I've read every one. I was reading *The Lost Child* today when my friend Allison called."

"Oh, indeed? And I suppose Allison gave you an idea of what I am looking for? A ghost writer, in a sense—someone who can help me brainstorm, and who can even write for me when I'm in a slump. I'd need you to be a bit of everything, I'm afraid. But I can pay you well, if you suit my needs."

"I would love a chance to try, Mrs. Graham." My voice quavered only slightly. I realized that I was clenching my fists, and I forced myself to relax.

"Oh, call me Camilla, dear."

"Camilla," I said, grinning like a maniac at Lestrade, who sat on my coffee table washing his face.

"I've read your book, Lena, so I know you can write. The question is, would you be willing to write as me, knowing you wouldn't get the credit? Aside from a vague mention of you in the acknowledgments, of course."

"That's a fair question. I certainly want to publish my own books one day. But I would view this as an apprenticeship. Every apprentice has much to learn, and if I had the whole population of Earth from which to choose a mentor, I would choose you."

There was a pause. Then her voice, sounding amused. "Normally I disapprove of flattery. But since your adulation is a quality that will benefit us both, I am relieved to hear it."

"Ah," I said, then glared at Lestrade, angry at myself for the dumb response.

"I can tell in an instant whether you will work out or not," she said. "And I suppose it's not fair to put you on the spot this way. But I must ask you: who is your favorite character in *The Lost Child*?"

"That's an easy question," I said without thinking. "My favorite character is Colin, the boy. He comes alive on the page like no one else. He's real to me in a way that none of your other characters are. I love him," I said.

There was another pause; then her voice, slightly sad, was back: "You're hired," she said.

I DROVE TO Blue Lake one week later. Camilla Graham had informed me that, if in fact we felt we were well-suited to working together, it would be best if I lived in her residence, as our working hours might vary. I had agreed to this, and Allison, while initially disappointed, had warmed to the idea of me living with Camilla. "It will give me a chance to visit you both at once," she said.

Allison had assured me that Blue Lake, Indiana, was not generally a tourist town, although it had all the things that tourists liked: charming little shops on a curving, oak-lined main street; enchanting lakefront cottages, painted in bright, sun-warmed colors; a variety of sailboats floating gracefully in the little harbor; and an assortment of friendly locals and delightful eccentrics who would make a visit memorable. The lake itself dominated the scenery, serenely whispering against the docks and reflecting the sky in its cool depths; but the sandy beaches were generally untouched by outsiders' footprints, aside from the few who had found it and hoarded it for their own vacations. The truth, she said, was that Blue Lake didn't need tourists. Most of the cottages were owned by people who returned each year to spend their summers on the water, and the rest of the year the residents lived their quiet and unassuming lives, enjoying a jewel of a town that was generally hidden from the rest of the world.

I had studied some people's vacation videos on YouTube and gotten quick glimpses of Blue Lake. It seemed perpetually sunny and beautiful, yet quiet and restful, too. I was pleased to think that, assuming my little trial period turned out well, I might be living permanently in this endearing town. Unlike its appearance in the videos, Blue Lake today sat under a sky both ominous and beautiful: dark blue and gray patches swirled with strange striated cloud formations. An increasingly cool breeze slipped through my window, sometimes laced with mist. Clearly a storm was coming.

I contemplated this as Lestrade and I drove down the last leg of Green Glass Highway, waiting for the turnoff onto Sabre Street, which would take us into downtown Blue Lake. I reached over to pat the top of his carrier (a rather old model, passed down from my parents), and somehow it popped open. In a flash Lestrade was out and hanging from the ceiling of the car, his claws making a ripping sound. I veered briefly into the oncoming lane as I tried to swat him down. "Lestrade! Aw, crap. Lestrade, come on!"

He streaked around the car in a sudden panic. I pulled over onto the pebbled shoulder of the road, put on my flashers, and climbed out of the driver's seat to try to retrieve him from the back. The last thing I needed was an unruly animal making a scene when I got to Camilla's. I leaned in, trying to grab my gray and white fur ball, but somehow Lestrade wiggled under one of the seats, just out of my reach. "Gosh darn it, you little pill. Get out here," I ordered, as though I believed that for the first time in history a cat would do what its owner asked.

"Need help?" a voice asked from behind me, floating somewhere above my posterior, which, along with my dangling legs, would have been the only visible part of me from outside the car. I wriggled back out and faced a man in a tan jacket and a pair of blue jeans. He was blond-haired and square-jawed, like a Norwegian clothing model, but not quite as tall as a Viking. His hair was slightly mussed by the cold fall breeze.

"Um. Not exactly. My cat burst out of his carrier and seemed bent on making me crash my car, so I thought I'd try to wrestle him back inside."

He nodded at me, as though this were a common problem and he was experienced at helping people with it. "Sure. I have a cat, so I get it." His eyes were an alluring shade of light brown—or maybe they just seemed that way in the sun. "Where is she?"

"It's a he. His name's Lestrade. And he's under the passenger's seat, the little traitor."

He looked surprised and shot me a smile, which came with a pair of impressive dimples. "You like Sherlock Holmes?"

"Who doesn't?" I was distracted, fearing that I'd be late and Camilla would judge me based on my lack of promptness. "I think I might just leave him where he is. I'm supposed to meet someone—"

"You from Blue Lake?"

"No. I mean, I might be moving there, if this job works out, but my cat is determined to ruin it for me."

He nodded. "We'll have him out in a jiffy. Give me one

sec." He went back to his car, which he had pulled up right behind mine on the gravel. I hadn't even heard it.

"Here we go," he said, back in what seemed like less than a minute. He opened my passenger's door and bent down; thirty seconds later he stood up, holding Lestrade, who looked quite peaceful and was letting the man pet his head. "Cute guy," he said. "But sort of huge. I'm surprised he was able to squeeze under that seat. Maybe in Blue Lake he'll get a little more exercise. You guys from the city?"

"If by the city you mean Chicago, yes, we are. And thank you so much. Let me grab his carrier."

The handsome Norwegian stranger watched me, half smiling, as I retrieved the elderly carrier and held it open. He slid Lestrade inside, and the cat didn't resist one bit.

"How did you do that?"

He grinned; he had a nice mouth. "Catnip. I left a little for him. He's gonna get sort of high in there."

I giggled, then looked at my watch. "Thank you so much, for everything, but I have to run. I have a job interview, and I don't know how much longer it will take me to get to Blue Lake—"

"You're here," he said. "Turn left about two blocks up, on Sabre. I bet you'll be right on time."

"Thanks for your help. I appreciate it," I called over my shoulder, and climbed into the car.

2

The train hissed to a stop in Munchen, where the rooftops glinted in the twilight, and she realized with a jolt of disbelief that she was finally here: no longer could she rely on the family who seemed distant now in space and memory. She was here, alone, and the pale faces on the platform seemed as cold and unfriendly as she had imagined them bright and welcoming.

—from *The Salzburg Train*

CAMILLA GRAHAM'S HOUSE, what she had called "the big gray Gothic monstrosity on the hillside," stood out on a bluff, visible as I entered the town. It was true that the house did resemble the type of building that might grace the cover of one of her suspense novels, especially under this moody sky, but it had a certain battered glamour that I admired on sight.

I followed the directions I had programmed into my phone, turning at the foot of a hill and taking a long, unpaved road that wound upward through the colorful autumn trees, their bright leaves in stark relief against the metallic sky. Then I saw mailbox that read "Graham House" and realized I had reached my destination. I pulled up to the long, wide porch, partially obscured in shadow despite the sporadic sunbeams, and parked near another car, which sat with its nose toward the porch.

Turning off the ignition with a sigh of relief, I looked at Lestrade, who licked at the remaining bits of catnip.

"We're here, buddy. I never thought I would meet Camilla Graham—not in a million lifetimes."

Lestrade looked at me then with narrowed green eyes, clearly not impressed by my enthusiasm.

"Okay, I get it. I'll let you out." I stepped out of the car and went around to retrieve Lestrade's carrier. Then, encumbered by his weight, I started moving toward the entryway. It was a grand affair of a porch with stone balustrades flanking long, wooden steps to a doorway under a gray-marble arch. Despite the weird pre-storm light, the porch was dim, as though Graham House had its own weather system. I lifted a large wolf's head knocker and rapped twice on the mahogany door. Dogs barked within, and I heard claws scrabbling inside the carrier; my cat was smooshing himself into the back of his den in a preemptive move. "I'm sure they're friendly," I murmured.

The door opened and Camilla Graham stood in front of me, flanked by two large German shepherds. One of these canines was baring his teeth at me. I said, "Hello, Camilla."

"Lena. How nice to meet you. Come right in. Ignore Rochester there; he's a show-off. He's harmless as a lamb."

Rochester neither looked nor sounded harmless, and he kept up a low growling as I moved gingerly into a long front hallway, also dim. To the right was a large, shadowy staircase, and to the left was a doorway into what seemed to be a wide sitting room. Dominating this space was a huge stone fireplace, currently lit and crackling away. I could feel its warmth even in the hall.

Camilla looked as I had expected, except smaller and slighter. I had anticipated a tall woman, but she couldn't have been more than about five foot four, which meant that I had a couple of inches on her. Her hair was gathered into her traditional chignon, but some strands had fallen out and lay in wisps around her heart-shaped face, which bore only minimal wrinkles. She was wearing a large pair of glasses that magnified her eyes and made her vaguely frightening.

She pointed at the cat carrier. "That little fellow is probably afraid of the dogs. If you'd like to let him explore your room, it's at the top of that stairway there. Perhaps you can get settled, and then come meet me in the library."

"Yes, that sounds great, thanks." I moved swiftly, wanting to get Lestrade, who was deathly silent, away from the growling Rochester and his companion. I started up the stairway; it was a long journey. Suddenly I felt that I was Jane Eyre coming out to Thornfield Hall for the first time. This house had a similar gloomy grandeur; it was ill-lit and papered in an antique style—a prime place to begin a time travel experiment. I had always admired the Gothic mysteries written by Camilla Graham, and now, I realized with a start, it was as though I was in one.

The room at the top of the stairs was large and airy. I put the carrier on the bed, shut the door to keep out the dogs, and set Lestrade free. At first he did nothing; just stayed frozen inside his safe house. Eventually, though, his curiosity got the better of him, and he stepped out for a tentative examination of the large bed. The quilt was patterned with blue roses and white camellias; in fact, the whole room was decorated with blue and white accents, which gave it a cool feeling. The bed was in the center of the room, right beside a large window that provided an amazing view down the autumnal bluff; Blue Lake itself was visible in the distance, shining like a sapphire belt on the horizon. To my right were a beautiful walk-in closet and a small bathroom.

"Our own bathroom, Lestrade! How nice is that!" Lestrade was making dough on a pillow, which was a good sign. He seemed to be adapting to the move.

On the opposite wall was a gorgeous double-length desk with a multitude of drawers. "Ahhh," I moaned. I had always loved desks, and this one was clearly an antique—a grand cherrywood affair with a built-in light, a wide glossy surface writing area, and a multitude of drawers.

I told Lestrade I would return and ran down the stairs to get the rest of my things. Camilla had disappeared, so I was uninterrupted as I made my trips up and down. I didn't think I had packed much, but it took quite a while to unload the car, and then I spent about fifteen minutes trying to put things into some kind of order—hanging up clothes in the indulgence of a closet, setting up my computer on the big desk, putting out my few knickknacks on the dresser and side tables. Lestrade, free and pleased, had fallen asleep on the bed pillow. I set up his litter box in a far corner of the bathroom and put out his food and water in bowls next to the big desk; then I tiptoed out and shut the door so that he would be undisturbed by Camilla's giant guard dogs.

One of those dogs met me at the bottom of the stairs. I was fairly sure it wasn't Rochester; this one seemed to have a whiter face (and possibly a meaner one). Now it stood growling at me, showing all of its teeth in a most intimidating way. I froze. "Camilla?" I said quietly, not wanting to call too loudly and potentially enrage what already seemed like a man-eating creature.

We faced each other for about five minutes. I spent the time wondering if I remembered how to treat a dog bite, and contemplating just how deep I thought those impressive teeth could sink into my flesh. Distantly I wondered if Camilla had been abducted by aliens or swept away by pirates. Surely she should still be in the vicinity of her office, where I had left her?

A knock on the front door interrupted my panicked thoughts and made me jump. Without waiting, the visitor entered on his own and called out. "Camilla? Oh—hello."

The other German shepherd, Rochester, strolled over to sniff at the newcomer's outstretched hand. The man was tall and thin, with gray hair and wire-rim spectacles. He wore a Harvard sweatshirt and a pair of khaki pants.

"Hello," I said. "Do you happen to know this dog, and might you persuade him to stop trying to murder me?"

The man laughed. "Heathcliff, come here. Come here, boy. Are you baring your scary teeth at the nice young lady? Aren't you ashamed of yourself?" Heathcliff turned away from me and practically bowed in front of the stranger, making little snuffling sounds that were the equivalent of dog humility.

"Liar," I mumbled.

"What's that?"

"Thank you very much for rescuing me. He's quite intimidating when he tries."

The man set down a bottle of wine he'd been carrying and began petting one dog with each hand. Both canines looked pleased about it. "I'm Adam Rayburn," he said.

"I'm Lena London. I just got here today."

"Oh, really! You'll have to come out and visit us at the restaurant—I'm the owner and manager of Wheat Grass, out near Green Glass Highway. I don't know if you've heard of it?"

"Actually, I passed it on my way into town this morning."

"Ah, I see. Are you a relative of Camilla's?" His face was perhaps more curious than was appropriate, but then again, I didn't know how well they knew each other.

"I work for Camilla, as of today. I suppose she'll tell you more about it." And if Camilla didn't choose to, I certainly wouldn't.

"Of course, yes. Is she around?"

"I'm not sure. She didn't come when I called her about the dog, and—"

Just then we heard what sounded like a door closing, and some footsteps coming back into Camilla's sitting room. She appeared in the doorway and peered at us; her hair looked rather windblown, and she was holding a couple of logs in her hands. "Oh, hello, Adam," she said. Her manner was cool, yet friendly; I admired the way she could be detached without being rude. "What brings you by on this nice fall day?"

Adam Rayburn leaned forward, his face eager. "I got that new wine I told you about. I thought I'd bring you a bottle so you can see if you like it." He set it on a sideboard in a shadowy corner.

"Well, that's most generous of you. Thank you so much indeed."

He petted her dogs some more; they now looked almost puppyish in their devotion. Camilla smiled down at them. "Well, Adam, I have some work to do. Lena here has been hired on to be my invaluable assistant, and we must sit down and evaluate the state of things."

"Of course, of course," Rayburn said briskly. "I have to run anyway. Martin Jonas never showed up today, so we're short a server. Well, I hope we'll see you down at the restaurant soon."

"I daresay you will," Camilla said regally, and Rayburn took the hint, saying his good-byes and making a quick exit. I watched him for a moment through a lead-paned window next to the door. He descended the steps in what seemed a dejected manner. Had we somehow disappointed him?

"Are you ready to have our meeting, then?" Camilla asked me.

I turned and nodded. With a strong sense of the surreal, I followed her through the dark hallway and into the sitting room with its crackling fire. At the far end of the room were some tall glass sliding doors, out of which was a view similar to the one from my bedroom window. The sky had grown a tinge darker. The other walls were lined with books, and a huge desk dominated one side of the space. Camilla went to sit behind this, and I sat in a purple armchair facing the desk.

My hostess smiled briefly. "I trust you had a pleasant ride up to Blue Lake?"

"It was quite nice, yes, although cloudy and gray. The last part of the drive was scenic. Leaving Chicago, not so much. Lots of trucks and expressway traffic."

"Ugh. I could never live in a big city for long."

"Did you live in London once? I thought I read that on a book jacket."

"Yes. For a few years, when my husband was living." She was sorting papers as she spoke. She seemed to have piles and piles of paper; I wondered if she printed out all of her books for editing, or if she did some of it on the computer.

"I always thought it would be very glamorous, living there."

"Hmmm."

She had made direct eye contact with me a couple of times when I first arrived, but now she seemed to be receding into deep thoughts and only peripherally aware of me.

"What, uh—what's the name of the book you're working on? I always love your titles."

"I labor over them. The title of the work in progress will probably change many times, but it is currently being called *The Salzburg Train*. I'm struggling with it, though." She frowned down at the paper. "It's not right, somehow. I don't know if the setting is wrong, or the character, or the premise. That's the first thing I'll need from you. I'll want you to read this."

She pushed a thick manuscript toward me.

One of the shepherds—Heathcliff, I decided—came and laid his big jaw on my lap. "Geez!" I yelled, startled.

"What's that? Oh, is he bothering you? He's such a big baby. He'll be sitting in your lap next if you're not careful," Camilla said.

I tried to push him gently away, but suddenly the dog seemed to love me as much as he had hated me earlier. He leaned against my thigh, heavily, and let out a sigh. I tentatively began to scratch his ears. They were very soft.

Camilla suddenly came out of her reverie. "So." She clapped her hands. "Here's a schedule—let's see if you can live with it. I'll need you to start the book today. Or tonight. I assume you'll want to see the town, so arrange things to your satisfaction, but try to finish reading some or all of the book so that we can meet in the morning. At that point I'll need your notes: what works, what doesn't, which characters jump off the page, as you said Colin did in *The Lost Child*." Her face softened when she said it.

I was tempted to ask her why that one question had been important enough to get me hired or fired, but it didn't seem the time to do so. "That sounds fine."

"And then, once I get your diagnosis for the book, we will know how much work needs to be done—by you and by me."

"All right. I can't wait to read the book—and Salzburg! What a wonderful setting. You've never set one there before, although I recall one in Vienna."

"Yes. I visited Austria once, when I was in my twenties, and I never forgot its beauty. It was very—" A phone vibrated on the desk, and Camilla picked it up with a disgusted expression. "Excuse me," she said. "I hate cell phones, but my publishers rather demanded that I have one." She clicked it on and said hello. Her eyebrows rose and she stood up. "Yes, I know that," she said. Her voice was cold. "Kindly do not call me on this phone unless it's absolutely necessary. Yes, of course. Well, you can talk with John Kendall about that. That's what I pay him for. Good—that will be fine. Good-bye." She hung up the phone and wandered away from me, toward the back doors, where she stood looking at the view. Her body, from this distance, seemed old and frail. She wore a pair of black pants with a white blouse and a bright blue sweater; it looked chic, yet comfortable. I had always pictured her wearing silk and attending literary salons. Yet, now that I was here,

I couldn't imagine Camilla Graham anywhere other than in this gloomy antique of a house.

"I have a few things to do," she said, still looking out the window. "So if you'd like to take that manuscript upstairs and then show yourself around, that will be fine. I can have dinner ready for you at around seven, if that's all right? Or were you planning to eat with our friend Allison?" She turned to face me again, suddenly looking more cheerful. The thought of Allison would cheer someone up; Allison is like a ray of sunshine.

"She's busy tonight, but I'm hoping to dine with her later in the week," I said. "So yes, thank you, I'd be happy to have dinner here."

"Of course. I have meals served by Rhonda, a cook from here in town, and I'll be sure she knows to make enough for two from now on."

"Thank you." She had looked away again; perhaps she was distracted or uncomfortable with the newness of my presence. I waited until she made eye contact. "Camilla—I'm very happy to be here. I really appreciate the opportunity."

She smiled. "I think you might be just what this dark old place needs. The light of youth and beauty." She looked sad then; I thanked her for the compliment and took my leave, feeling suddenly like an intruder.

Upstairs I set the manuscript on my big desk, holding it as I would a sleeping child. I wondered suddenly if she had copies; surely she worked on a computer, and not a typewriter? Of course. I had seen the computer on her desk. This wasn't 1975, although I had seen enough pictures of Camilla from that era, posing in a tasteful tailored suit and looking quizzically at the camera. In those shots it had indeed been a typewriter in the photo, and she and her Underwood had seemed like ideal companions.

Lestrade was still asleep; I had a sudden memory of the blond man saying that the catnip would make the cat high, and I giggled. I wondered who the stranger was and realized, with a bit of regret, that I should have introduced myself. How rude he must have thought me to have accepted his help and then simply driven away.

I shut Lestrade in the room and made my way down the dark stairwell. What the house could use, in my initial estimation, was a lot of white paint on the dingy walls—something to bring in the sun (surely there would eventually be sun?) and cast out the gloom.

The two shepherds were waiting for me at the foot of the stairs, but they weren't growling now. Their heads were cocked, as though they wondered what I was up to. I realized that they were rather young, because there was still something puppyish about their energy and their big feet and heads. "Hello," I said. In response, two tails pumped with great energy.

"You guys know I'm going out alone, right?"

Again, the happy tails.

I sighed as I stepped off the last stair and moved past the dogs, back to Camilla's study. She was there, at her desk, but not really doing anything. She seemed to be in deep thought.

"Camilla? I'm sorry to bother you, but I thought I'd check out the town, and the dogs seem to think they're going with me. Would you like me to walk them?"

She brightened so much that for the first time I saw evidence of the beauty that I had always admired on her book covers. "Oh, that would be fine! I used to walk them so much more, but lately I've been—distracted. They'll enjoy it, and they're fun companions. No one will bother you while you're walking those two."

I was sure that was true, but I did wonder about the rain. "Do you think we'll beat the storm?"

She peered out the window. "I don't think it will roll in for another hour or two."

"All right, then." I put on my jacket; Camilla directed me to the wall hook where two red leashes hung, and I clipped them on to my new friends, who were suddenly so cute I couldn't recall why I'd been afraid of them. They were cavorting like lambs as they waited for me to open the giant door so that we could take our leave.

"Good-bye! We'll be back in an hour or two!" I called. I barely managed to close the door behind me before the dogs tore across the wide porch and headed for the steps. I had the weird sensation that I was water-skiing on land, holding my reins with great concentration as I tried to contain the power beneath them.

We ran through Camilla's wide yard and back to the tree-lined, pebbly road whence I had come. For the first time I was truly able to appreciate the splendid Blue Lake scenery, and the town I saw in glimpses between the large trees, lying in wait at the bottom of the bluff. In my mind thoughts bounced around, disjointed. I wasn't sure what emotion I was feeling; certainly there was an odd disappointment that Camilla had not immediately become my best friend and confided all her hopes and dreams in me (as possibly I had daydreamed she would). And yet I could not contain the euphoria that stemmed from the reality that I had met my idol, that I was going to live in her house, that her newest manuscript sat on a beautiful cherrywood desk in my room—my room!—awaiting my notes.

My feet moved to the rhythm of my one coherent thought: I met Camilla Graham. I met Camilla Graham. I met Camilla Graham. I felt a very fine mist against my face, but it was exhilarating rather than off-putting. Something about fall air always speaks to my soul, and I felt alive in a new way, ready to grapple with the world and win.

The dogs, still straining at their leashes as we marched down the slope, led me toward a wide, shady driveway that seemed to slope up toward a more modern-looking house. This, I supposed, was Camilla's closest neighbor.

Without warning, a man emerged from the end of the driveway, lighting a cigarette as he walked, one hand on his lighter and the other cupped around his cigarette to keep away the wind. He saw me just as I saw him; I made a startled noise, and he narrowed his eyes at me in displeasure.

"What are you doing here?" he said.

The dogs began to growl.

3

He scowled at her, his dark hair hanging too low over his forehead to be respectable. He wore the disinterested expression and the easy stance of a hero or a rogue—but surely he could not be both, and she feared he was the latter.

—from *The Salzburg Train*

I WAS MUTE for a moment, shocked by his rudeness. He was scowling in an unattractive way, and yet despite that I could tell he was good-looking, in the way of a rugged journalist or an Indiana Jones sort of adventurer. In fact, he wore a Jones-type leather jacket and a pair of blue jeans. He could have been anywhere between thirty and forty; it was hard to tell when he was scowling.

"I'm taking a walk," I finally said. "I happen to be your neighbor. I'm staying with Camilla Graham, who lives—"

He started, turning more fully toward me and flicking some ash from his cigarette. "You're staying with Camilla?"

"Yes. She just hired me as her assistant. My name is Lena London." I put both leashes into my left hand so that I could offer to shake his hand with my right.

For a moment I thought he wasn't going to shake it. He

finally did, but he remained unsmiling. "You—took me by surprise. I bought this house for its privacy, and yet people find their way up to this path: young lovers, wandering children, people gaping, trying to get a glimpse of—well, in any case, you certainly belong here if you live at Graham House." He finally offered me a smile, but it didn't reach his eyes, which were a rather startling blue.

"Yes—I was going to give myself a little tour of the town. I just arrived a few hours ago, and it's all brand-new. I'd like to familiarize myself with everything." Then, wanting to draw attention to his rudeness, I said, "I didn't catch your name."

He took a drag on his cigarette and then blew some smoke up toward the sky. "My name is Sam West." He watched me out of the corner of his eye, as though expecting some kind of reaction. What did he want me to do, tell him how beautiful his name was? People here were weird.

I forced myself to appear cheerful. "Well, it's nice to meet you. I think I may have been elected as a dog-walker, so you'll probably be seeing me around."

He nodded. "Thanks for introducing yourself. Now I won't have to worry that you're an intruder or an autograph seeker." He said the last two words with particular bitterness.

"Do people want your autograph?" What I meant was, *Think much of yourself?*

He sniffed. "Not if I can help it."

That didn't make sense. He couldn't control what people wanted. As far as I could tell, Sam West was bitter, yet narcissistic, and convinced that everyone was in love with him.

"It seems quiet up here. I'll bet people will leave you alone, for the most part."

He nodded with an almost sarcastic expression. "You would think."

A voice inside me told me to stop arguing and walk away. But there was something about this man I couldn't figure out. "From what I've seen so far, Blue Lake seems to be exactly as quiet as you'd like it to be. I don't hear one sound right now—not even dogs barking."

He nodded and smoked some more, clearly enjoying his cigarette. Finally he said, "You're right, it's a quiet town. But it's not a private town. You can't escape from your neighbors—Lena, is it?"

I nodded.

"Haven't you ever heard that Sartre quote—'Hell is other people'?"

I had, in a college English class. "That seems rather extreme. Even Sartre didn't mean it the way people interpret it, did he? It was more about his belief that we cannot escape the gaze of others, which inevitably shapes the way we see ourselves."

He sniffed. His face was bitter. "Right. We cannot escape the gaze of others. And if that gaze is an unfriendly one, then we are forced into a different kind of self-contemplation."

I decided to leave him with his cigarette and his bad attitude. I was in quest of friendlier people. "Yeah, I guess. Well, I'd better get going. The dogs are eager, as you can see. Calm down, Heathcliff! Nice to meet you, Sam."

He raised a hand, I suppose in a sort of good-bye wave, but it looked like a weird blessing.

I continued walking, tugged along by the dogs. I peered back once to find West looking at me, his face pensive. His brown hair was flecked with a few gray hairs at the temples, and now those glinted like silver threads in the weird light.

Rochester and Heathcliff, glad to be moving again, tore down the rocky road and then turned left onto a smoother thoroughfare—the main road that led downhill and into town. I maneuvered the dogs onto a sidewalk and enjoyed the view, still buzzing from the many encounters of the day.

On the main thoroughfare, called Wentworth, I struggled to hold the dogs and to get my bearings. It was a quaint street, with bright red benches set at intervals for weary travelers, and tubs of yellow and orange marigolds scattered throughout the doorways of shops. "Nice!" I said to my companions. They seemed to agree; they yanked me forward with energy. We passed a little Laundromat and a shop called Blue Lake Coffee; someone opened the door, and I got a delicious whiff of earthy, dark-roasted beans in the grinder. Definitely a must-visit, but not with dogs. I moved on, past the tiny, two-storied Bright's Flowers, which had a brick facade with a little Juliet-style balcony that sported flower boxes bursting with an attractive array of purple fountain grass, florist mums, small white pumpkins, and—something I recognized only because my ex-boyfriend had been a botanist—variegated Japanese sedge. The boxes were a compelling advertisement for the business itself, because I wanted to buy all of those plants and create my own luxurious autumnal boxes. I wondered if Camilla would let me hang one from my window.

Moving along, I passed Glenda's Baked Goods. "No!" I said aloud to the smell of chocolate that lured me. The dogs didn't even acknowledge me, which was not a good sign.

At mid-block I reached Bick's Hardware. Allison had told me about this place, and suggested that I would find "literally anything" I needed within its walls. Curious, I decided to peek in for a moment. I tied the dogs' leashes to a convenient streetlamp pole. To my surprise, they were polite about this; they both sat down and panted at each other, seemingly ready to wait for me. I opened the big wood doors and passed through a little foyer in which there were three gumball machines and a large fake grizzly bear who held a sign in his giant paws assuring me that "Bick's Is Best." I moved into the main, high-ceilinged room and breathed in the smell of cedar.

I did a quick visual scan; my eyes didn't know where to land. Bick's Hardware had shelves that went from the floor to the ceiling, and they all seemed to be packed to capacity. As I watched, a tall, thin man in a blue flannel shirt, jeans, and green suspenders came marching down the first aisle with a big ladder.

A young woman with bright red hair stood at the foot of a shelf filled with pots and pans, holding a cute titian-haired boy. The proprietor set up his ladder and said, "Which one, dear?"

"The Farberware fifteen-piece. It seems kind of high up there, Mr. Bick."

"Oh, I'm old, but I'm spry," said Bick, and proved it by whisking up the ladder, swift as a monkey, and claiming the large box of pots and pans, which he slung on one narrow shoulder before he zipped back down. It was terrifying.

I darted down a different aisle before Mr. Bick offered to risk his life for me.

I actually needed some postage stamps, but I doubted

that a place like this would have them—and yet, as my eyes perused the signs above the aisles, I saw some stenciled lettering on the back white wall that said, "U.S. Mail." It was starting to look as though Bick's housed the town post office. I moved toward the back wall, passing through a giant display of shower curtains and then, inexplicably, stuffed animals.

I got into the little postal queue, centering myself behind a woman in a dark gray Notre Dame sweatshirt and light blue jeans. She had bleached-blonde hair with dark roots. I continued to peruse the store, noting a promising-looking spinning rack full of journals and a large book display that spanned several shelves. In an instant I liked Bick's much better.

I waited until the lady in front of me had been served. Then I scooted up and was greeted by a woman whose nametag said "Marge B."

"What can I do for you, sweetheart?" she asked.

"I'd like a book of stamps."

"Just one?"

"Yes—they're so expensive now, aren't they?"

Marge agreed. "Yeah—the post office just can't seem to get in the black, no matter how many times they raise the darn price. I remember when stamps were five cents, that's how old I am."

I smiled. "You don't look old. Blue Lake must agree with people—you all look youthful."

This pleased Marge. She leaned in and said, "Aren't you from here, hon?"

"No—I'm from Chicago. But I'm staying out here for the time being." I decided to venture into a confidence. "In Graham House."

Now Marge's brown eyes were downright curious. "Really! Is that so! And are you a relative of Mrs. Graham?"

"No—I'm actually going to be her assistant."

"Oh! Well isn't that nice! She could use one, I'll bet! I mean, she's getting up in years, right? But still writing, God bless her. Good for her. And how nice to have a pretty young lady in town. What is your name, dear?"

"It's Lena. Lena London."

I could tell that Marge was stowing away that information. She ran a hand through her curly more-salt-than-pepper hair and adjusted some colorful cheaters on her nose. "London. What a fun last name. Like that writer, when we were kids in school. The one who wrote about being lost in the Yukon, or about wild dogs and wolves."

"Jack London."

"Yeah, he's the one!"

"No relation," I joked. "Although I'm a writer, too."

"Are you now? Well then you have the perfect job, don't you?"

"I think so. I'm very excited to be working with Mrs. Graham."

She handed me my stamps, and I paid her. "Thank you so much, Mrs. Uh . . . B—"

"I'm Marge Bick, hon. My husband and I own the store. Just call me Marge."

"Thank you, Marge. The store is great."

Marge inclined her head, accepting the compliment. "We like to think it's unique. And the locals love us because we have everything they need. Not necessary to go to those big horrible strip malls."

"They are horrible," I agreed. "And you really do seem to

have everything. Well, thanks, Marge. I have Mrs. Graham's dogs outside, so I have to get going."

"Have you tried the Schuler's?"

"What?"

"We sell ice cream up front. It's from Schuler's Creamery, over in Daleville."

"Oh—sounds yummy. I'll check it out."

I did, not because of an insatiable sweet tooth, I assured myself, but because I was a woman of my word. Near the register was a glass window with several flavors of Schuler's ice cream, and I ordered a French Vanilla cone. While I waited, I eavesdropped on two men behind me. One wore a flannel shirt and jeans and looked rather scruffy; the other wore a red ski-lodge type sweater and brown corduroy pants. Both seemed to be in their twenties. "Listen, if you don't want to do it, then just give me back the cash." This was from the guy who looked like the host of a holiday Christmas special.

"I said I'd do it. Just stop pressuring me and give me time to do it right, man." This was the flannel shirt guy.

"Fine. I'll call you tonight, and it better be done." Ski sweater huffed out of the store. I sent a sympathetic glance to flannel shirt, which he ignored. He left the shop a moment later.

"Here's your cone." This from my server, a young man who looked to be about nineteen or twenty and sported a sad little mustache with about seven hairs in it.

"Oh, thanks! It looks delicious!" I beamed a smile at him, but he remained stone-faced. He wore a salmon-colored turtleneck and a pair of jeans. None of the guys here seemed particular about fashion.

I marched out to the waiting dogs, licking at my cone. My assessment of Blue Lake so far:

Women = friendly and nice.
Men = rude and dismissive.

I said as much to the dogs as I un-looped their leashes. It was very difficult to hold the pups and eat my cone, and I was passionately interested in doing the latter, so I sat on a bench to eat more carefully. The dogs sat in front of me, not bothering to pretend that they weren't equally interested in my food.

"Fine—you can split the very last part, but until then it's mine. You hear me?"

They clearly did; their ears were huge.

Schuler's ice cream was delicious; I knew that I would be back at Bick's if only for this particular treat. I wolfed down the cone with embarrassing speed, breaking the last part in half for the shepherds, who ate their pieces with what seemed like gratitude, although I might have been projecting that emotion onto their long-nosed faces.

Finally we made our way down the rest of the street, encountering two restaurants (Chinese and Italian), a tiny diner called Willoughby's (whose window sported a sign alerting me, in faded blue lettering, that they were open for breakfast and lunch only), a bookstore, and a little second-run theater before we crossed over and came up the other side of Wentworth, back in the direction of the bluff and Camilla's place. Here we passed a hair salon, a jewelry shop, a secondhand clothing store, a tiny food market, a Mexican restaurant, and a computer store. At the mouth to one little cobbled alley was a sign that said "This Way to the Lakeshore!"

I paused, then turned to a woman walking past. "Excuse me—if I go down here, I'll get to Blue Lake?"

She smiled. "Oh, yes. You'll be right by the dock, and if you go around that you'll get to the shore at the bottom of the bluff. You can climb up any number of stairways to get up to the houses. It's a fun route to take."

"Thanks." I watched her walk away and dart into the jewelry store.

While I stood there, another woman appeared next to me. She was the woman I had seen talking to Mr. Bick, asking for the Farberware. She was youngish, with red hair and a dusting of freckles across her attractive face. She held the same little boy in her arms, and a slightly older little girl stood next to her, clutching the hem of her shirt. "Hello," the woman said, her face earnest.

"Hello." Chalk another one up for friendly Blue Lake women.

"I overheard you in Bick's just now—saying you were living at Graham House."

"Oh? Yes, I'm staying there. I'm Lena," I said, holding out a hand and shaking the tiny fingers of the shy boy who looked at me under his lashes. "Didn't you buy some pots?"

The woman laughed. "Yeah. They have to deliver them later, because I can't hold them and these little stinkers. He's Tommy, and I'm Lane. And this is Penny." She hugged the little girl against her with her free arm.

"Well, hi, everyone. Did you get some of that delicious ice cream?"

"No, just the cookware and some diapers. Although someone talked me into a candy bar."

Penny held up small chocolate-covered hands and smiled proudly at me. Unlike her mother's, her hair was more of a caramel color, and it shone in the gray light.

"I like chocolate, too," I said. "This seems to be a town for chocolate lovers."

Lane snorted. "Sugar lovers, you mean. Every other shop is selling fat on a stick."

"Well, you look great, so I guess you haven't succumbed to the temptations of Blue Lake."

She smiled uncertainly. "You talk like a writer. Are you a writer, like Camilla Graham?"

This surprised me. "Yes, that was my major. Right now I'm just working as Camilla's assistant."

"Ah. I worked at the bakery over there until Tommy came along; then my husband and me figured I should stay home with the kids."

"That's nice. I'm sure your children are glad to have you with them."

"I wish I'd known Mrs. Graham needed an assistant. Tommy's getting older now. Maybe I would have applied—mostly for a way to get to see inside that awesome house!"

This was surprising, not because Graham House wasn't an interesting structure, but because it certainly wasn't the most beautiful dwelling in Blue Lake.

"It's very nice," I said. "But it could use some updating."

"Couldn't they all," she said with a laugh. Her face was open and friendly. Penny ventured forward to pet one of the dogs, and he licked her entire face with one slurp of his tongue.

"Gah," she said in a tiny voice, and it made us all laugh.

I stole a glance at my watch then. "It was nice meeting your whole family, Lane—what was your last name?"

"It's Waldrop. Lane Waldrop. I'm in the phone book. Maybe we could have coffee sometime. There aren't a whole lot of young people in this town, so it's nice to meet someone my own age. We could go to Willoughby's over there, or to Blue Lake Coffee. They roast their own beans, and the coffee is amazing."

"That sounds nice! And I'm sure I'll see you around. I plan to be in town often."

"Okay, then. Say bye-bye, Tommy." The little boy waved, and then he buried his head in his mother's shoulder. Penny waved, too, but she was looking at Heathcliff and Rochester, who were sniffing at the chocolate on her hands.

"Leave her alone and be gentlemen. That's not good for you," I told the dogs, and pulled them away. I walked on after one final wave to the Waldrops. I hadn't yet seen the lake up close, and I really wanted to. When Camilla had come in from outside, I glimpsed a stairway in her backyard that probably led down to the water. The rails, if I recalled correctly, had been red; surely I would recognize them if I walked down the beach and studied all of the stairways? And, I assumed, I'd see glimpses of her house, and Sam West's, between the trees.

Satisfied, I walked down the little cobbled alley and across a parking lot; I crossed a street called Lakeview and found myself on a small wooden dock that looked out onto the inlet that widened into Blue Lake. To my right, I could see the town curving around the shoreline. To my left was a sandy shore and the colorful bluff. And in front of me, the water undulated and gleamed. The multicolored sailboats

I had seen on YouTube dotted the harbor. The air smelled like rain, and Blue Lake glistened in cerulean splendor beneath gray clouds.

"This is gorgeous, boys," I said to the dogs. "How do you not walk here all the time?"

We strolled to the end of the dock and found ourselves on the cool sand; on this we began our trek back to Graham House. We passed several stairways that did not look familiar. I kept my eyes on the lake, which, as it grew wider and more eternal, made me feel that my journey would never end. Walking in the sand was much harder work than walking on the wooden dock had been, and even the dogs were beginning to slow down. I thought I spotted Camilla's red stairway in the distance, so the dogs and I picked up our pace. A man emerged from one of the stairways and appeared a few yards in front of me. It was the flannel shirt guy from Bick's Hardware. He marched up to the lakeshore and a small wooden dock, where a white boat was moored. Sailboats dotted the shore as far as the eye could see, their sails a variety of colors, bright against the afternoon sun. He climbed aboard the white boat and went belowdecks, and he didn't come out again.

Then, in an instant, the rain came—not with hesitation or an introductory drizzle, but with a full-out, body drenching cloudburst. "Ahhhh!" I screamed, but it was drowned out by a clap of thunder so loud that my startle reflex knocked me right onto the sand. I got up again and pulled the now-willing dogs toward the stairs. They walked with their heads down, shrugging their bodies against the rain and trying to shake off the moisture as they moved. Every minute or so I got an extra blast of wet-dog-scented water.

"No!" I yelled as we clambered up the stairs, but I was

laughing, too, because what else could I do when nature had so effectively humiliated me? The dogs and I were making all sorts of crazy noises as we tried to keep the rain out of our eyes and noses. It was most uncomfortable, but also hilarious and weirdly invigorating.

By the time we got to the top the dogs were tired and thirsty. I had to knock at the glass doors; luckily Camilla was right there.

"Oh, you poor dear. I've been watching for you. Here—the nice towel is for you. These old ones are for the dogs. I'll get to work on them." She began to massage Rochester and Heathcliff, those big babies, who leaned on her and snuffled and closed their eyes under her ministrations.

I dried as well as I could and left my wet shoes at her doorway. "I don't think I'm dripping any sand," I told her. "Let me run upstairs and get cleaned up."

"Did you have a nice visit, Lena? Before the storm?"

"Yes," I said. "It was actually quite enjoyable."

I RETURNED TO my room, where Lestrade had not only awakened, but had polished off the food in his bowl and was now taking a bath on the windowsill.

"Hey, buddy," I said. "I need a shower and some clean clothes." I went into the bathroom and disrobed, then hung my wet clothes on a towel bar above a heating vent. I'd have to ask Camilla how to do laundry. Outside more thunder clapped—two large and scary ones, then a smaller, more distant one. I tried not to jump every time I heard the noise.

I treated myself to my first shower in Graham House. The water pipes made odd noises, but the water was warm and rejuvenating, and there was a delicious-smelling body wash in the bathtub that seemed to have a French name. "Classy," I said to no one.

I emerged ten minutes later feeling great. "Lestrade, I am experiencing a certain euphoria." He gave me a sleepy glance. He didn't seem angry or agitated. Perhaps Lestrade was one of those cats who just went with the flow of things. I strode across the room and spent a moment petting his silky ears, enjoying his soft fur. Lestrade turned on the outboard motor that was his purr, and I laughed. "I guess you forgive me, huh? You seemed pretty nervous in the car."

He turned away from me and looked out the window, where the raindrops on the pane were providing him with quite a show. The rain had lessened a bit, but it was still coming down. I looked out and realized that my room offered not just a view of the lake, but of Camilla's backyard and red staircase, all the way to the sand below, where I saw something familiar and yet jarringly out of place.

"What the heck . . . ?" I asked Lestrade, leaning closer and squinting down at the beach. My eyes were probably deceiving me. Still, it wouldn't hurt to check.

I left Lestrade to contemplate the raindrops, and I jogged down the stairs.

I walked into Camilla's lounge and looked around. She wasn't there. I turned to scan her wall of books, then heard something behind me. I twirled to find Camilla there, holding two canning jars. She had a disconcerting habit of appearing without making a sound.

"Camilla," I said. "Do you have pair of binoculars?"

She didn't look surprised that I had asked. "Oh, I'm sure I do. I know once I lent them to Bob Dawkins and his horrible son, and they might still be out on the porch near the woodpile. Bob and his son deliver my wood and do odd jobs for me."

"And what makes the son so horrible?" I asked, smiling.

She did look surprised at that. "Hm? Oh, I don't know, really. That's just what everyone calls him—Bob's horrible son. It suits him."

"Okay—uh, I guess I'll check by the woodpile."

I went out onto her porch, and there was in fact a giant pair of binoculars sitting on the outer window ledge; I paused to wonder what Bob and his son needed them for. Then I grabbed them, protected from the rain by a large awning, and jogged down the hallway. I went to the back patio doors and out onto the grass behind Camilla's house. I aimed the binoculars down the bluff and turned the focus wheel until I had centered in on the sand below us. I scanned, looking for a sign of what I had seen farther up. There it was—the purple, red, and blue plaid that I had seen twice that day. The flannel shirt. It was still on the man, but he was lying prone on the sand . . . and he wasn't moving.

"Camilla?" I called in a voice that didn't sound like my own.

I turned and ran back to the house, calling through the patio doors. "Camilla? Can you come here?"

She appeared a moment later, her face a question.

"There's something on the beach. On the sand. Can you look?"

She took the binoculars and walked past me to the edge of the bluff. I waited while she searched and focused. "Oh, my," she said.

"Do you see him?"

"That looks like Martin Jonas. Do you remember that Adam said he didn't show up for work today? He's not moving at all."

"No, he's not. I'm going down there. Maybe he's unconscious."

"Do that; I'm going to call the police."

I ran down the stairs, barely noting that I was being soaked anew, and moved across the empty expanse of sand to the prone form of the man in the flannel shirt. "Sir?" I said. Then, "Martin?"

There was no response, so I moved closer. He was facedown, and I touched his neck. It felt cold. His hair and clothing were drenched and sticking to his skin. I took him by the shoulders and shook him a bit. "Martin, are you all right?"

Still no response. I lifted his hand to feel for a pulse, and that was when I noticed blood on the sand; it had not washed away because it had been pooling beneath him, under his chest and arm. "Oh, no," I said. "What happened?" I was speaking more to myself than to him, but in any case he did not seem to hear me. There was no discernible pulse in his wrist.

I stood up and took a step back, suddenly horrified to be touching him. I could already hear the sirens blaring; Camilla's call had gotten a quick response. My eyes felt wet beyond the wetness, and I brushed at them with the back of my hand.

Despite my fascination with hypothetical murder and suspense novels, I was seeing death for the very first time. I stood over the dead man like a sentry until the first police officer moved toward us, creating a dark shadow on the sand.

SOON THE QUIET beach was filled with official-looking people, one of whom was a nervous young officer who kept telling Camilla and me to move farther away; every few minutes he pushed us back a few more inches, perhaps with the intention of having us off the beach by evening. Camilla had provided two black umbrellas, and we stood under them like women in an Edward Gorey drawing, watching the ghastly proceedings.

The emergency personnel all wore yellow slickers and rain hats, but they had also quickly erected a canvas lean-to over their crime scene; the people underneath it were relatively dry.

The person on the sand was indeed dead, and thanks to the excellent eavesdropping skills I'd honed as a teenager (when I was always convinced my parents were talking about me, and in fact they rarely were), I learned that he had been shot twice, and that Camilla was right, it was Martin Jonas, the waiter that had never showed up for work at Wheat Grass—the one who had left Adam Rayburn in the lurch, and the one I had seen in Bick's Hardware. I assumed Rayburn would forgive him now, since he had sacrificed far more than a paycheck and found himself facing Blue Lake and eternity.

"Such a shame," said Camilla, who had retained her equanimity throughout the proceedings, but who wore a sad expression nonetheless. "And such a mystery. We'll ask Doug what happened."

"Doug? Is he that trembly officer who keeps watching us like a nervous Chihuahua?"

"Oh, no. Doug is the detective in charge. He's the pride of Blue Lake—they drafted him right out of college, but word was he was also being courted by the FBI. Still, he chose this place because his father was sick at the time. Doug wanted to be nearby. I daresay he made the right decision."

"Why? Did his father die?"

"He's quite alive, I'm happy to report. And now Doug likes his job; people rarely leave Blue Lake. But why would they?" she asked, looking almost mournfully at the horizon, which shimmered with midday light filtered through filmy clouds. "It's so unrelentingly beautiful."

She had her arm tucked into mine. For a time I had told myself I was offering her support, but I soon realized that it was the other way around. "Are there places like this in England? Places you'd want to visit again?"

"Oh, of course. There are always the dreams of 'someday.' Those lovely images one has of spectral landscapes, decorating the imagination and glittering like gold."

I stared at her, my mouth open. She had said that without really thinking, distracted as she was by the people milling around like worker ants tending to a dead body. That was the sort of sentence Camilla Graham tossed off as a matter of course. That was why her books were all bestsellers.

"Lena, you're making that worshipful face again. Be careful, or I shall become addicted to it, the way some people crave money."

"Did you have a Camilla Graham, when you were a young woman?"

She nodded. "Charlotte Brontë, I suppose. I must have read *Jane Eyre* more than any other book. And I'm sure I borrowed from her again and again. Oh, here's Doug now."

A man in a green rain poncho walked toward us, holding an iPhone with its own little umbrella attachment. He gave us a strange look—both solemn and slightly wry. "Good morning, Milla."

"Hello, Doug. Oh, I suppose I should say—Detective Douglas Heller, this is my new assistant, Lena London."

He and I exchanged a glance. "Is that so?" he asked, glancing down at his phone, then up again. His eyes were twinkling, but his face remained solemn. "Miss London and I have actually met."

"Oh, really? Why didn't you say so, Lena?"

I shook my head. "We didn't exchange names. It was just a quick interaction on the side of the road." For some reason that sounded obscene, and my face grew hot. I studied my shoes and listened to the rain pattering on my umbrella.

"Yeah. But now I know your name is Lena," said Doug Heller. His voice was gentle but firm when he said, "I need to ask you both some questions."

"Of course," Camilla said.

"How did you happen to notice the body?" Heller asked, focusing on me. His eyes looked gold, even in the gray light.

"I had seen him earlier. I was walking the dogs in town, and I stopped at Bick's Hardware for some stamps. He was in there, talking to another man."

"What time?"

"Oh—about three?"

"And who was this other man?"

"I have no idea. I got to town *today*," I said. "I can tell you he had sandy-colored hair and looked like he worked at a ski resort."

Doug Heller paused for a moment, his eyebrows raised. "Okay. And did you see the dead man at any other point before finding him on the beach?"

"Yes. When I was coming home on the shore, I saw him again, by Camilla's stairs, but near the dock. He walked right past me, moved down the dock, and got in the white boat there." I pointed at the boat.

Heller nodded, his eyes on the floating craft. "How much later was this?"

"Maybe half an hour. And half an hour before I saw him out here."

"And did you speak to him?"

"No. We barely even looked at each other. The storm was about to come. And he wasn't—very friendly. I had already determined—well, anyway."

"Determined what?" His gaze lasered in on me.

"Just—none of the men in Blue Lake seemed very friendly. Not him, not the man in the ski sweater, and certainly not—" I was regretting starting the sentence at all.

"Yes? Who else?"

"Sam West, one of our neighbors."

He stiffened, but made no comment about West. "And what about gunshots? Did you hear anything like that?"

I shrugged and looked at Camilla. We both shook our heads. Camilla said, "It's so loud here, Doug, with the sounds of the waves, and that darn thunder booming every two minutes."

The thunder. "I did notice that one of the thunder

claps—it seemed different from the other. Smaller and less—thundery," I offered.

"What time?"

I hesitated. "Camilla, do you know what time I returned? Because I went upstairs to change, and then I was going to take a shower, and I heard it just before I got in. So maybe—"

"About four thirty, then," Camilla said.

He typed her response, using his thumbs as though he were writing a text message. "Okay," he said again, his digits working. "And when was the last time you spoke with Martin Jonas, Camilla?"

"I suppose it was last week, when I dined at Wheat Grass. Martin waited on me."

"Did he seem preoccupied?"

"Not at all. He was polite."

"Do you know of anyone who had a grudge against Martin?"

Camilla shook her head. "I can't think of anyone, no."

"And you, Lena?" He switched his gaze to me, and I was surprised again by the attractiveness of his face: square-jawed, almond-eyed, capped by that thatch of blond hair, now smooshed under his rain hat. He didn't look tough and weathered like Sam West; his features bore a fair amount of sensitivity, though I had the sense he could handle the ne'er-do-wells of Blue Lake. "Did the conversation with Jonas and the other man seem heated?"

"Not exactly. But it was sort of an argument. The ski sweater man said that Jonas had to do something, and he better do it soon. He was going to check in by tonight, he said."

He frowned. "Is that so?" He looked up at me, assessing, and then back down at his phone.

"Anyway, I looked out my window at the storm and happened to recognize the man's shirt. Then we called the police. You."

"Okay." He looked thoughtfully at his phone, then out at the tossing lake. I could see what Camilla meant about him being the pride of Blue Lake. He had a star quality about him, as though he were playing a cop in a movie. Perhaps that was how he saw himself. A mixture of admiration and annoyance jolted through me.

"Why is that officer so nervous?" I asked, pointing at the man who kept moving us back. "He's like a cross between Barney Fife and a hunted rabbit."

A smile flitted across Detective Doug Heller's face and disappeared. "Chip? He just has a high metabolism."

"What? That doesn't even make—"

Camilla said, "Doug, how much longer will this take? Lena and I both have work to do."

"We're done. For now." That smile again, like a quick fish, and then he met my eyes with his solemn gold ones and said, "It was nice to see you again, Lena. I'm sorry it had to be under these circumstances. We'll be in touch if we have any more questions." He turned to Camilla. "Same for you, Milla."

She nodded, and he sauntered away.

"Let's get off this beach. It feels dreadful now, with violence lingering over it," Camilla said.

We walked toward the bluff; at the foot of the red staircase we met Sam West, still looking like an adventurer in his leather jacket and jeans, his acorn-colored hair tousled by the lake breeze and dampened by the now-dwindling rain. He nodded to Camilla, his face solemn, and then turned to me. "What's going on? I heard the sirens. . . ." His eyes went past me then, to the place where the attendants were lifting the stretcher that bore the unfortunate Martin Jonas. "What happened? Are you all right?"

Camilla put a gentle hand on his arm. "Thank you, Sam. We're all right, but Lena had the misfortune of seeing a dead man on the beach. It's Martin Jonas, a waiter from Wheat Grass. He was shot to death—a terrible thing."

West's face looked pale in the late-day sun. "Shot? Have they caught whoever did it?"

"No," Camilla said. "Doug Heller is investigating."

West looked about as happy to hear Heller's name as Heller had looked to hear West's. It seemed as though he was about to say something regarding the policeman, but then he bit it back. Instead, he said, "It's a shame. I'm sorry to hear it." He directed a look at me that seemed to have special significance, but I couldn't imagine why.

"In any case, we're hoping to put this terrible thing behind us. Have a good evening, Sam."

"You, too." West lifted a hand in a brief wave as Camilla and I made our way to the red staircase. I looked back to see that he had wandered closer to the scene and was watching the crime scene team do their rapid work before they lost the light of the sun.

Camilla led the way up, and I was surprised by her agility; I wondered how many times a day she walked up or down the bluff.

Reaching the top of the stairs for the second time that day, I felt as though my legs had turned to wet noodles. "How do you make this climb every day?" I panted as we moved inside and shut the door. "Adaptation," she said.

"Wonderful exercise for a senior citizen." She was gazing out the window with a rather melancholy expression. I followed her gaze and saw a little figure on the sand, wearing a brown jacket. It was Sam West, standing alone in the rain.

"That poor man," she said. "There's something about him you should know, Lena, before the town gossips try to bend your ear."

"Oh?"

She turned to me and sighed. "Apparently, about a year ago, Sam's wife went missing. The police are presuming foul play and perhaps murder. Sam, for the longest time, was their prime suspect, but they had no body and no evidence. So they let him go. He was in New York then, but he left soon after, and came here."

"Oh my gosh. And his wife was never found?"

"No. Neither alive nor dead. The more obnoxious people in Blue Lake have taken to calling him 'the murderer.' I don't believe it for a second."

"No, of course not." But I was remembering the way Sam West had looked at me when he thought I was an intruder—how he had scowled and seemed ready to strike at me.

I had been vaguely afraid of him, and perhaps for good reason. If Sam West were indeed a murderer, could he have killed Martin Jonas? This thought troubled me until it was replaced with a more sinister one.

If Sam West had killed his wife but had not killed Jonas, then there were two murderers in Blue Lake.

4

She was introduced to Frau Albrecht when she arrived at the inn; the older woman was not particularly warm, and yet Johanna longed for her affection as one yearns for sunshine, and when the Frau indulged in a brief smile, Johanna's spirit lightened and flew of its own accord around the high-ceilinged room.

—from *The Salzburg Train*

INSIDE THE HOUSE Camilla murmured that she had some correspondence to see to, and she blended quickly into the gloom of Graham House. I ascended the stairs alone and took another quick, hot shower, then changed into some sweats. I really would have to ask Camilla about how to do laundry for myself, I mused as I hung my second wet outfit over the shower rail.

I found Lestrade sitting in the same large window, watching the leaves fall from a big elm in the backyard. I sat on the bed and felt a burst of exhaustion. Lestrade jumped off the ledge and onto my pillow. He meowed at me, clearly annoyed by my absence, but he allowed me to pet him, and, after I provided a good massage, he settled down.

My predominant thought, even after discovering a murder in the backyard, was that I was sitting in Camilla Graham's house. A memory came back to me in a sudden, random flash. I was thirteen again and had finished my first Graham novel. I was in that state of detachment where a part of me was still inside the book and another part of me was returning—reluctantly—to reality. I walked into my kitchen, where my mother was preparing dinner. I often think of her there, at the stove or the sink, cooking or cleaning and never receiving a word of thanks from me. "Mom," I said, almost accusingly. "Have you ever read a book by Camilla Graham?"

My mother turned, surprised, and said, "Oh, yes. Isn't she great? I read a lot of her stuff back in the seventies and eighties. I didn't know you liked romantic suspense, or I would have told you about her long ago."

After that we were like a club, my mother and me. She reread all the books with me, and we would exchange them and talk about the characters. Nothing bonds two people so well as loving the same books. I smiled at the memory—that special time of discovering the wonderful Graham novels and spending precious moments with my mother. I couldn't have known that we had few years left together.

Now new thoughts forced their way into my mind, and my head began spinning with what felt like millions of details about the day—just one day!—that I had spent in Blue Lake. Despite the demise of poor Martin Jonas, I felt that my best bet was to put everything out of my mind. I looked out of my large window and saw that the dark clouds had lifted and a trace of pink stretched across the sky just above the lake. What I needed was a distraction, and I had a wonderful one sitting across the room.

I went over to the desk and sat in the wooden chair. There was a pencil holder sitting in one corner; it held a variety of writing utensils. I grabbed a soft-lead green pencil and sat down, pulling *The Salzburg Train* toward me. Later, I was sure, I would look back at this as one of the most triumphant moments of my life.

I pushed aside the title page and found myself looking at Chapter One. The first sentence said, "When Johanna Garamond boarded the Salzburg train in the autumn of her twenty-eighth year, she bade farewell to her lovely mountain town and its splendid, rushing river, and rode through the night to face murder on the other side."

"Oh, boy. Lestrade, this is going to be one heck of a ride," I said. Lestrade said nothing; I peered over my shoulder to see that he had dozed off on the pillow.

I went back to the book and smiled down at the page.

I got through five wonderful chapters before outside thoughts began to intrude into Camilla Graham's plot. I thought of Allison telling me that Camilla Graham was in her knitting group—and yet I had seen no knitting needles in her sitting room, nor any sort of bag with yarn in it. Interrupting that thought was an image of Sam West, smoking his cigarettes and looking angry at the foot of his long driveway. Why did Douglas Heller dislike him, and vice versa? And why was West convinced that people were spying on him? Was he paranoid after his wife's disappearance? Meanwhile, there was a dead man on the sand, shot by an unknown assailant. A dead body that I had found on my very first day in town.

I shook my head. I would not let the terrible event ruin my experience. It had happened, and I felt bad for the family of Martin Jonas, but I would have to put that aside and concentrate on my job.

I looked at my watch and saw that it was seven o'clock. Camilla had said dinner would be ready then, and I was hungry.

I left my green pencil sitting on the beginning of Chapter Six and went down the creaking stairs to the shadowy landing.

AT A GRAND oak table in Camilla Graham's dining room, we dined on fresh spinach salad with chunks of feta cheese, chopped walnuts, and an herb vinaigrette dressing. After that came a delicious casserole that Camilla's chef had left for us to bake and serve, filled with chicken, fresh vegetables, and a hint of sherry. Camilla looked tired, but she proved to be a gracious conversationalist. While I polished off the last of my salad (I found that I was famished after the day's events), she asked me about Allison—how we had met, how long we had been friends.

I took a sip of water. "Allison and I were in the same homeroom in high school. She was one of those theater kids who was always in a show, always full of energy and outrageously happy and dramatic."

Camilla smiled. "She's still that way."

"The first day I met her, she said, 'I'm Allison! How about if you take your nose out of that book and we can talk?' I had been hiding, really, because I was afraid to be in a big new school. And just like that, Allison walked up and demanded to be my friend."

"How perfect."

"Yes. She's so unlike me, because I've always been a quiet person. In school I walked around with my blank journal and doodled ideas in it when I had free moments. When we got together, Allison would jump around, learning some new dance for whatever inevitable play she was in and talking about every boy in school. But she made me laugh and brought me out of my moodiness. And she said I was the person who could always calm her down when she got too manic."

"I can see that—what a fine pairing. But you seem like the sort who should be in a play, as well. A name like Lena London, and that pretty face."

"Thank you." I felt myself blush at her compliment. "I've always been more of an introvert." I forked up some food and then, embarrassed, said, "I hope you don't think I'm eating too much."

Camilla laughed. "Of course not. You probably haven't eaten all day, and Rhonda always makes too much—she seems to be laboring under the delusion that I am a lumberjack."

Now it was my turn to laugh.

"Besides," Camilla said, turning her fork tines down to signal that she was finished, "I despise leftovers. One never knows what to do with them."

"Well, if my appetite stays this hearty, you won't have to worry about leftover food. And I'm guessing the canine companions who are currently warming our feet would help you out with them."

"They often do," she said. Then she leaned back and sighed. "Have you started reading the book?"

"Oh, yes. What a pleasure! I've only read five chapters,

but I'll get back to it when I go upstairs. It's wonderful, Camilla. I feel so honored to read it before the rest of the world."

"Good. But of course I'll need your suggestions."

"It definitely has that Graham magic that your fans love. So far I just have two main notes."

She looked amused, but interested. "Good—go on."

"Well, the heroine—Johanna—leaves Salzburg in the first line, and it's implied in the first chapter that she leaves out of necessity. Later, though, she tells the man she meets in the café that she left on a whim. So either she's lying to the man in the café, or this is a contradiction of what the narrator tells us earlier."

Camilla leaned forward, her eyes bright. "That's an excellent note. You might find that the issue resolves itself by chapter ten."

"Ah," I said. "Okay, then there's this issue: on Johanna's passport, her middle name is listed as Alina. But later, when she signs the form at the embassy, she writes 'Johanna T. Garamond."

Camilla clapped her hands. "This is what I need you for more than anything else, Lena! These small errors are the bane of my writing life, and the older I get the less I can keep track of them. Do please note these things down for me."

"Of course! Would you prefer a typed sheet?"

"Perhaps that would be best. You have your laptop, correct? So if need be you can e-mail the comments to me, and I can send them to the printer in my office."

"And should I wait until I'm finished, or just send notes section by section?"

"The latter will be best. Then your mind is fresh on the chapters you've just read."

For the first time since I had arrived, I thought I was seeing the real Camilla Graham. Her face was flushed with excitement as we talked about the process of feedback and revision, and I realized that she truly loved writing her books—it wasn't just a job to her. But then again, one could guess that from reading her novels. Each one was a special journey for the reader, and perhaps for Camilla herself.

Camilla sat back in her chair and stifled a yawn. I stood up and began to clear our dishes away.

"Oh, don't bother with that," she said, but without much energy.

"It's the least I can do after you've fed me such a delicious meal."

"You can just set them in the sink, then. Rhonda does the washing up when she comes in to cook."

"I look forward to meeting her," I said. I moved into the kitchen, illuminated only by a light over the stove, and scraped a few uneaten scraps into the big dog bowls by the sliding doors. Rochester and Heathcliff loped over to them and snuffled for a while. They were surprisingly slow eaters. When I was a teen, I'd spent a lot of time with Allison's golden retriever, who inhaled food so quickly she was often confused about where it had gone. These two shepherds were more delicate about their eating, their long snouts buried in the bowl as they processed the food piece by piece.

"Enjoy," I said. I took the plates to the sink and set them down with care. Then I looked out at the dark night and the twinkling lights nestled into the bluffs of the town, and it struck me: I was looking at Blue Lake from inside *Camilla Graham's kitchen*. I did a silent little dance, and the dogs watched me with interest, their ears up straight.

I walked to them and patted their heads with new affection.

"Good night, boys," I said.

I made my way back out to the dining room, where Camilla had tidied the table. "I think I'll head on up for the night," I said. "It's been a surprisingly long day."

"Yes. Thank you for making the journey; I think our partnership will work out quite well, don't you?" she asked.

"I do." I smiled at her, and she smiled back briefly. Then her face grew troubled.

"I'm sorry for all that you had to witness today. It was most unfortunate. Martin was a nice young man, when all was said and done."

"Hopefully they'll find the perpetrator quickly."

"I have the utmost faith in Doug," she said, but her face was still solemn. I wondered if she was thinking about Sam West.

We wished each other good night, and I went up the creaking stairs to Lestrade and *The Salzburg Train*. I knew that I could count on a Camilla Graham novel to make me forget all of my problems—even the unhappy reality that I had seen murder.

I went to the beautiful desk and flicked on the green lamp. Lestrade jumped onto one corner and began to take an elaborate bath, but soon I had lost track of what he was doing, because Johanna Garamond was leaving the café and realizing that the man who had given her information was now following her . . .

When I stopped reading I was on chapter fifteen and

nearly gasping with suspense. "Camilla, you are amazing," I murmured. I pulled my laptop toward me to type my notes while they were fresh.

It was clear that Camilla had not lost her gift for writing, and this made me happy. She had long been my idol, but for a very powerful reason: opening a Camilla Graham novel was like stepping into a wonderland.

5

She had been in town less than a week when she realized that something evil lurked beneath the gingerbread facades and cobbled lanes.

—from *The Salzburg Train*

I WAS DOWNSTAIRS early the next morning; Allison had texted me the night before and asked if I wanted to meet her for breakfast before she went to work. She was a nurse, and she worked at the emergency room of St. Francis Hospital. I explained my plans to Camilla, who sat drinking coffee at her desk. "I sent you some notes last night," I said. "And I will finish the book when I return."

She waved a hand. "That's fine, dear. The schedule can be fluid as long as we find time to work each day. Meanwhile, tell Allison I said hello."

"I will—thank you."

I donned my warm jacket and scratched the heads of the disappointed dogs, who had clearly been hoping for a walk. "Later, guys, I promise," I said, and I slipped out the door. I almost tripped over a bald man in a fleece jacket who was kneeling on Camilla's porch, bisecting a two-by-four with a handsaw as the board sat propped on a small sawhorse. A younger man with dark hair and a long, thin nose held one end of the wood, keeping it steady.

"Oh, hello," I said. "Doing some porch repairs?"

The older man spared me a quick glance. "Who are you? The niece?" he said.

"Um—no. I'm Lena London—I'm Camilla's new assistant. Does she have a niece? I didn't—"

The younger man assessed me with widely spaced gray eyes. "What are you assisting her with? She doesn't do anything. Just sits in her big house."

I disliked him instantly, and then it hit me: I was meeting the legendary Bob Dawkins and his horrible son. Camilla was right about the latter—the name suited him. "Camilla is one of the most famous suspense novelists living today. Writers all over the world wish they could do what she does."

Bob's horrible son snorted and wiped at his long nose with a gloved hand. "Yeah. Drinking tea and writing about people drinking tea." He slapped his father's arm and got a laugh out of the older man.

"You are utterly underestimating the woman for whom you work," I said coldly. "But I realize that not everyone can find the mental stimulation that you do, cutting your boards in half."

My sarcasm was lost on them; in fact, they seemed to puff up slightly, their faces smirking, as though I had given them a compliment. Bob Dawkins became a fraction more human. "Watch your step on those stairs. The bottom two are rotten, and they won't be fixed for another hour or so."

I wondered if they were charging Camilla more than was necessary; yet she didn't strike me as the sort of woman who would suffer fools gladly. "Thanks," I said, my tone still cold. I moved quickly down the stairs and onto the path. I could still hear the two of them reminiscing about the terrible joke Bob's son had made.

"Books about people drinking tea," Bob said, and they both laughed.

I made a mental note to ask Camilla to consider firing them, and then purposely put them out of my mind so that I could enjoy the day. The sun had returned to Blue Lake, and I was getting my first glimpse of fall as the light shone through the multicolored leaves rustling above me. The forested bluffs and the town below them glittered like gold.

Inspired by the beauty, I made rapid time down the path and onto the main street, where I quickly located the diner Allison had recommended—the one called Willoughby's. I reached it, recognizing the sign I had seen in the window the previous day, which read "Attention: we have delicious food, and we hope you'll visit us for breakfast or lunch. Willoughby's is not open for dinner!"

I opened the wooden door, and a tiny bell jangled at my entrance. I was in a small room with delightful décor that made it seem I was being given intimate access to someone's private dining room. Polished wood tables sat at regular intervals, each sporting a bud vase with a yellow rose. Family pictures and wooden plaques with famous sayings filled the walls. A young woman in a red gingham apron approached me. "Are you dining alone today?"

"Uh, no—I'm meeting a friend. Can I have a table for two?"

"Sure! How about there by the window?" She pointed out a narrow table with a view of the street, where the yellow rose and its crystal vase shone in a bright sunbeam.

"Perfect, thank you."

"Can I get you something to drink while you wait, hon?"

"Some tea, if you have it."

"Sure."

I sat down and looked around me. The restaurant wasn't full, but there were ten or fifteen people scattered around the room in various-sized groupings, and based on their relaxed body language, they all seemed to be regulars. The waitress, whose nametag said "Carly," was quick and efficient; she was back with a pot of tea in less than a minute, and then she swept through the tables—dropping off creamers here, ketchup there, and a bill somewhere else.

The doorbell jangled and I looked up to see not Allison, but Sam West, looking a bit disheveled but somehow even more handsome because of it. Carly was at the door in a moment, and he murmured something to her; she led him to a table near mine, also by a window.

He saw me when he was halfway to his chair and lifted a hand. "Hello, Lena. How are you this morning?"

It was surprisingly pleasant, coming from the man who had been so rude the day before. "I'm fine, thanks. Meeting a friend for some breakfast."

"Enjoy," he said, and then he disappeared behind a large red menu that bore a giant, gold-embossed "W" on the front.

I took a deep breath and relaxed into my chair, taking pleasure in the preparation of my tea. I took it with a bit of cream and two sugars, and I enjoyed the ritual of making it almost as much as the act of drinking it. I was stirring in the sugar when I noticed a sort of rustling in the room; I looked up to see that a great deal of attention was being focused on Sam West. The diners were observing him while trying not to appear to be doing so. Suddenly a variety of people were pretending to look at art on the wall, or searching for something outside the window where West was sitting, or, in the most brazen cases, merely staring directly at West.

If he knew it was happening he pretended he did not, but continued to peruse his menu, which lay on the table now, with a relatively serene expression. I realized that I, too, was staring. I looked down at my tea, my face red with indignation on his behalf. What must it feel like to be West in a town this small? Why would he stay in a place where the populace believed the worst of him? Camilla had expressed nothing but sympathy for West, and had sniffed indignantly at the thought that he could be a murderer. And after all, West's wife was only missing—why would everyone assume that she was dead?

The waitress appeared at West's table, and he gave her his order in a low tone.

My phone buzzed on my table; I had received a text. Sighing, I realized this meant that Allison was probably running late, but when I clicked open the message I saw that it was worse:

"Lena, so sorry—there was a car accident and I've been called in early to help the emergency staff. Can we reschedule?"

"Oh crap," I said, apparently more loudly than I'd thought, because I glanced up to see Sam West grinning at me.

"Problem?" he said.

I sighed and texted back, assuring Allison that we could meet later. How stressful to have a job like that, when one had to be called in to witness terrible things. But in addition to that, I had a very selfish response. I'd had so much to tell her . . .

"It can't be that bad," West persisted, his eyes bright. Clearly I was providing his morning entertainment.

I shrugged. "My friend can't make it for breakfast. No big deal."

He was up in an instant and moving toward my table; then he was sitting across from me. I realized my mouth was hanging open, and I clamped it shut.

"I can't let you eat alone," he said. "That wouldn't be hospitable—seeing as you just got to town." He smiled again, and with a rush of admiration I realized that a smiling Sam West was far, far preferable to a scowling one.

"Well, thanks. I'm not big on solo dining." I stole a glance at the faces in the room: they weren't hiding their interest now. I was aware of many sets of eyes, some shining with interest, some narrowed with hostility.

"You always make this big an impression?" I said lightly.

"You get used to it." He looked out the window as he said it. "I suppose Camilla has filled you in on the reason for my celebrity status?"

"Only minimally. She told me of an unfortunate label you've earned in town, and she scoffed at it."

Carly the waitress was back with Sam West's coffee. She didn't bat an eye at his change of location. She set it down in front of him, and I ordered a waffle with extra butter. She jotted it down and said, "Your breakfasts will be out in a jiff."

We thanked her, and she whisked off again to make her rounds. I wondered if she had sore feet by the end of the noon rush.

Sam West opened a creamer packet and poured it into his coffee; he stirred it in with a thoughtful expression. "Camilla is a good woman. I respect her."

"That seems to be mutual."

He nodded. "Has Camilla hired you, then? Is this a permanent position?"

"It seems to be a good fit."

"Good, good." He took a sip of his coffee and ran a belated hand over his disheveled hair.

"I'm very excited about her latest book. It's spectacular, as they always are."

His eyes met mine for a moment. "How did she happen to find you?"

"It's a strange story," I said.

"I'd love to hear it," said Sam West, leaning back in his chair with his coffee cup.

So I told him: of my lifetime devotion to Camilla's books, of my friendship with Allison, of Allison's marriage and relocation, and then of Allison's life-changing phone call and my own unexpected move. "So, in the end, it can't be called anything short of serendipity," I concluded.

"Indeed. As though you were destined to meet this woman you idolized."

I felt the hugeness of my own smile. "I still can't believe it, to be honest. That I'm living in her house, and reading her work in progress, and dining with her at mealtime."

"Except today."

"Today I was supposed to meet Allison and fill her in on everything."

"And here I thought it would be a young man meeting you here."

"I don't know a soul in this town, aside from Camilla, you, and Doug Heller."

West's face grew shuttered. "Ah, yes, Detective Heller."

"You two don't seem to like each other."

"We don't."

Carly appeared with a plate of eggs, sausage, and hash browns for West and a preposterously large waffle for me. I was torn between greed and embarrassment. West saw my expression and laughed—a surprisingly youthful sound.

I rolled my eyes and then grabbed the syrup, which I slathered over the divine-smelling waffle. "Why are you at odds? Does he suspect you of something?"

West speared some eggs with his fork and ate them. Then he said, "Let's just say he'd prefer that a man with my reputation not sully his idyllic little town."

"It's not his job to make assumptions."

"No, but he has to save the populace from me. He stakes out my place sometimes."

I had been about to consume my first bite, but I paused. "That's an invasion of your civil rights."

He smirked. "I should hire you as *my* personal assistant. You're very persuasive."

I ate a piece of my waffle, then a few more pieces. "God, this is good."

"You make eating look like a very pleasurable experience."

"I refuse to be self-conscious. I'm going to eat this whole giant waffle in front of you. However, I will offer you one bite."

"And I'll take it," West said, surprising me. He sliced off a corner of my breakfast with his fork and shoved it into his mouth. "Mmm. You're right."

He smiled at me, and I realized that his eyes were a truly beautiful shade of blue. Something twisted in my stomach—a familiar feeling that had me panicking and seeking a conversational topic.

"Anyway, back to Allison. I had a million things to tell her, and now I don't know when I'll get to do it."

"A million things, including your splendid move—and then a murder in your backyard."

"Yes—that's right at the top of the list of things we were going to discuss. Did you know him—the dead man?"

West nodded and squirted some ketchup on his hash browns. "I went to that restaurant now and again—Wheat Grass. He worked there. He was a good waiter, too, but kind of a zero as a person."

"Meaning what?"

"Not much personality. At least not that I noticed."

"Did he have any enemies that you knew of?"

West's face was wry. "For obvious reasons, I don't involve myself with the lives of people in this town. I came here to be exactly what I am—a recluse who enjoys his silence."

"Yet you eat at places like this, and Wheat Grass, where you know everyone will stare at you."

"True. But a man has to eat. This place has good food, as does Wheat Grass. You should go sometime. Preferably with me."

I felt a blush rising on my face and wished that I could control that sort of thing. "Why with you?"

His eyes were wide and innocent. "Because I'm tired of eating alone." He shifted in his chair, and I caught a whiff of smoke, probably lingering from his morning cigarette.

"You should stop smoking," I said. It was utterly inappropriate, but again West seemed amused. He gazed at me for a moment with his azure eyes.

"I have," he said finally. "For the most part. I have one in the morning and one in the evening. And oh, how I look forward to them both."

"Still unhealthy," I said.

He pointed at my waffle, on which I had spread a ridiculous amount of butter, and I laughed. "Okay, okay. Point taken. Lung disease, heart disease—potato, potahto."

"You're a nice person, Lena," he said suddenly.

"Uh—"

"And you're so polite you would never ask, so I'm going to tell you something." He leaned forward, clearly on the verge of an admission.

"You don't have to—"

"I don't know what happened to my wife," he said in a low voice. "I've hired my own investigator to try to find her. I maintain a residence in New York City, and I go back from time to time to see if there are any new developments, and to check in with the neighbors who still speak to me. But for reasons that are probably obvious, I don't like being there. In the meantime I am attempting to do my work in a quiet place that is extremely distant from New York. Despite my unpopular reputation, I find Blue Lake is working out quite well for me in that respect."

"What is your work?"

"I'm an investor. I started out in banking and now I work with private clients. All I need is a phone and a computer to do my job well."

"Well, that's convenient—I mean, that you wanted to relocate and didn't have to leave your job behind."

"Yes, I suppose."

"And how did you happen to choose Blue Lake?"

The doorbell jangled, and I looked up to see Douglas Heller entering and flashing a smile to Carly and saying something about wanting his usual. He was halfway to a table before he noticed me and West. He stopped in his tracks, his face unreadable, and then he walked toward us. "Hello, Lena." Then he turned his face slightly to the right and said, "West."

"Detective Heller," said Sam with painful politeness.

"How are you and Camilla doing today?" Heller asked, his eyes back on me.

"Quite well, considering. Have you found out who shot that poor man?"

Heller shook his head. "We're working on it. Meanwhile, since we can't explain why there was a gunman on the beach, you might wish to refrain from going there, or from walking around unaccompanied. Did you walk here this morning?"

"I did. And I was unaccompanied."

Sam West showed his teeth in what was meant to be a smile. "I was also *unaccompanied*. Perhaps Lena and I should walk back up the hill together."

Heller did not look amused. "I suppose that, under the circumstances, it would be a good idea." He looked tired today, and his gold-brown eyes were red-rimmed. I wondered what sort of hours one had to keep when investigating a crime. He focused back on me. "I thought you said that you found the men in Blue Lake rude and off-putting."

I paused, surprised. Did he somehow resent the fact that I was sitting with Sam West? I sent him a pacifying smile. "I found you very friendly, and you were the first person I met." I pointed at Sam with my fork. "I found him rude and *unfriendly*, but he has made up for it this morning, I can only assume because he realized how unacceptable his behavior was. Would you like to join us for breakfast?"

West rustled in his seat but said nothing. Doug Heller's eyebrows rose. "That's kind of you, but I'm going to eat at the counter and then be on my way. Carly probably has my order ready as we speak."

"Have a good day, then," I said. "Good luck with finding—the perpetrator."

"Thanks," Heller said. He turned to West briefly. "West."

Sam grunted out an acknowledgment, and Heller moved back to the counter after one last inscrutable glance at me.

"Wow," I whispered when he was far enough away. "Why don't you guys just challenge each other to a duel?"

West grinned at me, then put his palms down on the table. "I'm getting tired of this place. Finish your waffle and I'll walk you home. Or did you have errands to run?"

"Not this morning. And I should probably walk the dogs. They were bummed out when I left without them."

"So thoughtful," West murmured. He signaled for the bill, which Carly brought in her quick and efficient manner. West insisted upon paying for us both, despite my protestations.

"I owe you this and more, for brightening my morning the way you did."

I let him pay after all, which seemed to agitate the people in the diner even more. Once the door of the place was shut behind us, I could only imagine how rapidly the wheels of gossip were turning.

West read my mind and said, "I'm afraid you've committed yourself to the local rumor mill. By the end of the day everyone will know your name, or at least that you were the dark-haired beauty who had breakfast with the murderer."

I felt a sudden chill, and it wasn't just the October air, but the way West said that word with a smile, as though it didn't have a terrible rhetorical power. "People should mind their own busincss."

"Yes." His smile disappeared. We walked back up the bluff in relative silence, but it was a comfortable quiet. As we neared his driveway, he said, "I'll stop off here, but I'll watch until you get to your place. Make sure no boogeymen jump out of the bushes."

"Thanks. And thanks for breakfast, Sam." I waved at him. For an instant, there was a strange expression on his face, one that I couldn't decipher, but he quickly masked it with a polite expression. He returned my wave, and I made my way back to Camilla's place unmolested.

Bob Dawkins and his horrible son were gone, but there were two new stair treads that smelled like fresh-cut wood.

6

His name was Gerhard, and though he had done nothing but scowl at her from the time of her arrival, she found she couldn't stop thinking about him.

—from *The Salzburg Train*

I DID TAKE the dogs for a walk, but Doug Heller had made me just paranoid enough that I stayed close to the house. Then I returned to Graham House and saw, to my great consternation, that Lestrade had escaped and was pawing tentatively down the grand staircase. "Uh-oh," I said, and then, in a cacophony of barking, the two dogs went leaping up the stairs, and Lestrade yowled once before scrabbling back the way he had come, the fur on his back standing comically straight and his tail puffed to twice its normal size.

Camilla peered out of her office. "Is everything all right?"

"My cat got out, and the dogs are chasing him."

I must have looked upset, because she moved forward and patted my arm. "He can't get out of the house, so there's no danger of him running down the hill and getting lost. Once the dogs lose interest, he'll come out from wherever he's hiding. They had to meet at some point, didn't they?"

"Yes, I guess so." Still, I was worried about Lestrade. What if he found some obscure cubbyhole and got trapped in there? What if he found his way into the attic or the basement and simply never reappeared?

I frowned up the staircase. Camilla called the dogs and they came loping back down, but Lestrade did not. "I guess I'll go up and look around. And then I'll return to the book."

"Excellent. I'm just working on your last notes. They're so very helpful," Camilla said. "Oh, before you go—let me introduce you to Rhonda. She's the one making that delicious aroma that will eventually be our lunch."

"I just had a huge breakfast," I confessed. "But my appetite seems to be constant here. I don't know if the air is fresher, or—"

"A good appetite is a sign of good health," Camilla said. "Come into the kitchen for a moment."

Rhonda was a plump woman with caramel-colored hair that she had pulled up into a sort of waterfall with a couple of side combs. She wore a white Fawlty Towers sweatshirt and a pair of blue jeans, as well as an apron that bore signs of her having wiped her hands on it while she cooked. "Hello, nice to meet you," Rhonda said, tossing the remark over her shoulder as she strained some noodles at the sink.

"The dinner you made last night was just delicious," I said.

She shrugged and dumped the noodles into a pot. "Oh, that was just some backup food."

"It was divine. Rhonda is an artist, but she downplays

her skill. Her cooking is innate," Camilla said. "I was lucky to find her."

Rhonda blushed slightly with the compliment. "And I was lucky to find you," she said. "I used to work at a public school, doing those horrible mass-produced lunches. Didn't pay as well, and it was soulless work. Graham House—well, it's like cooking for the people in Downton Abbey."

Camilla laughed. "Hardly."

"No, I just mean—it's classy. Not that you're snobby, or anything."

Camilla patted Rhonda's arm and said, "Well, this 'grande dame' is going back to work." She left the room, shaking her head at the very idea.

"She's a great boss," Rhonda said to me. She lifted the strainer full of noodles and poured them into a pot on the stove. Some sort of sauce was already simmering there, and it smelled wonderful.

"She's an amazing person," I said. "My idol. I still can't believe I'm here. I was just saying that to Sam West at breakfast."

Rhonda turned and faced me, surprised. "You had breakfast with Sam West?"

"I was supposed to have breakfast with my friend, but she had to cancel. He was there, too, so we just sort of sat together."

"I wonder about that guy," she said. "He has such a bad reputation in this town."

"I don't think it's deserved." I wasn't about to tell her what West had confided in me about his wife.

"I hope not," she said. "I don't like to think some murderer is walking around town."

"There *is* a murderer walking around—whoever killed Martin Jonas. Camilla and I saw his body, and the police say he was murdered. Sam West had nothing to do with that, because he looked really surprised when he found out."

Rhonda shrugged. "It's a strange world. We don't know who the hell we can trust. But I'll tell you this. I've got two kids, and I thought Blue Lake was a great place to raise them. Now I'm not so sure."

"Every town has bad people in it. It seems to me that, in general, Blue Lake is just what you think it is." I seemed to have said that a lot since I got here—assuring people that the town they lived in was not an illusion.

"I hope so."

"It was nice meeting you, Rhonda. I have to go check on my cat. The dogs chased him upstairs."

"Oh, poor thing." She was back to her pot now, mixing the noodles and sauce and sprinkling in some salt. "I hope you find him. Lunch is at noon."

I thanked her again and went toward the stairs; I peeked into Camilla's study and saw that Rochester was resting at her feet with his eyes closed. Clearly he had tired of stalking Lestrade. Heathcliff was not in the room.

I moved up the stairs with some trepidation, half fearing that I'd find the shepherd with my poor cat in his mouth. The door of my room was slightly open—had Lestrade picked at the door? Had I not shut it all the way? But of course—Lestrade had somehow pried it open and escaped. I pushed on the door, peering around the edge. Then I almost laughed right out loud.

Lestrade was lounging in a large sun spot on the carpet to the left of my bed, his head pillowed on the belly of Heathcliff, who lay like a dead thing behind him. I knew the dog was fine, because I could hear him snoring, and in between those rather loud sleep sounds I could hear Lestrade purring.

"Hilarious," I murmured. I went to the desk, retrieved the manuscript, and sat down to read some more before lunch. My laptop distracted me, though, and on an impulse I pulled it toward me, opened an Internet browser, and Googled "missing wife of Sam West New York." Articles related to Sam West sprang up instantly, and with them the pictures.

I clicked on a picture labeled "Victoria West," and there was her face, filling the screen. She was attractive, with a long graceful neck and reddish hair that was swept up into a gold clasp. Her face was not quite perfect—her eyes were a bit too far apart and her mouth was narrow and made her look disapproving—and yet she was a stunning woman. I stared at the picture for a long time, then clicked back to the story, which had been reported the previous year. It was an objective piece, a rarity these days on news blogs, and it said merely that Victoria West, a New York designer married to investor Samuel West, had been missing for two weeks, and police had no leads as to her whereabouts. The last line suggested that Sam West was "a person of interest" in the disappearance, but that he had not been arrested.

Assuming Sam West was telling the truth and he really didn't know where his wife was, this must have been terrible for him—he must have been worried for his wife and disturbed about the implications. Had this affected his job? His friendships? His family life? How did one recover from something like this, especially when there had been no resolution? And where in the world was Victoria West?

I looked back at the list of headlines and scrolled to one

that had appeared two months later: "Police say Victoria West had filed for divorce from her husband."

"Oh, my," I said. I clicked on the story. According to an AP reporter named Wallace Brent, Victoria West had indeed filed for divorce a month before she disappeared, and Sam West had not contested it. The paperwork had been supplied by both parties, and the lawyers had been processing the file when Mrs. West disappeared.

This seemed to be a good sign for Sam West. If he and his wife had amicably agreed to a divorce, then surely he had no motive for killing her? Assuming, as the world seemed to do, that she had been killed.

Most of the headlines that popped up seemed to have an implied judgment of West and his guilt, despite their supposed objectivity. I did find one article, written by a Jeremiah Tolson, which suggested that West was being railroaded by the press. The part that interested me said "It seems odd that West, 35, and his missing wife Victoria, 33, had already split before her disappearance, and there is not a sizeable insurance policy, investigators say, for either party, yet the press is content to push West into the role of murderer rather than to investigate what might actually have happened to his wife. Perhaps the media is jumping too quickly into tawdry assumptions because of the elements of the story they already have: the beautiful woman, the reportedly distant man, and the wealthy set of New York. In this respect the press is forgetting its function of telling the truth at all costs, to the detriment of the much-maligned Mr. West."

I clicked out of the story and drummed my fingers on the desk. Why was this the only person who had defended West? Perhaps he was right in his contention that people wanted to jump to the most evil conclusions because it made for readable news.

I needed to get to work, but my curiosity was still working. I Googled "Douglas Heller, Blue Lake Police." Up popped all sorts of articles related to Detective Doug Heller, including one about him taking the job in Blue Lake and another about him solving a cold case in 2011 and receiving a commendation. Some further investigation allowed me to pull up his college graduation program; Douglas Heller had been salutatorian of his class at Indiana University.

"Overachiever," I said, and Lestrade mewed in apparent agreement. Seemingly tired of Heathcliff, he wandered to the desk and jumped on it and began to play with a pencil that was lying there. He deliberately knocked it on the floor, then looked at me.

I scratched his ears. "Google is our friend, Lestrade. What do you want to know?"

He squinted at me, perhaps surprised that I wasn't going to get upset about the whole pencil thing. Sometimes Lestrade just wanted a reaction. In that way I supposed he was just like any person. I had a sudden inspiration and Googled "Martin Jonas." This brought only a few results: one was a crime report from five years earlier, when Martin Jonas had been a senior in high school. Jonas and two other boys were arrested after "significant vandalism" of their school. They had been caught in the act by a passing patrol car. All three of them had spent some time in jail.

I found an older article about Jonas winning an art award; apparently he had been a promising painter. So why had he stopped going to school and gotten a job as a waiter? Surely his jail record hadn't kept him from pursuing more education? Or maybe Jonas was just one of those kids who couldn't wait to get out of high school and had no intention of going any further. I sighed. One day in Blue Lake, and I was surrounded by mysteries—and not just Camilla Graham's, which I had been avoiding in order to follow my curiosity about the locals.

I had accomplished very little on Camilla's manuscript by the time I wandered down for lunch. I amused Camilla and Rhonda with the tale of Heathcliff and Lestrade. Rhonda stood in the doorway, holding a dish towel, and chatted with us a bit while we ate another delicious salad.

"Where do you get such fresh greens?" I said. "Salads in the city are nothing like this."

She grew pink with pleasure. "Sometimes they're from my own garden. But we have a little farm stand here in Blue Lake called Dooley's. It's on Green Glass Highway—you probably passed it when you drove into town."

I had seen it—it was visible when I pulled over to get Lestrade off the ceiling of my car. That's when I had met Doug Heller without knowing who he was . . .

"It's delicious as always, Rhonda," Camilla said in her quiet way.

Rhonda shrugged. "I'll get started on the main dish." She moved back into the kitchen, and I turned back to Camilla.

"I was doing a little research upstairs. I happened to see that Sam West and his wife were in the process of divorcing when she disappeared."

Camilla's eyebrows rose as she speared some greens with her salad fork. What seemed like a smile flitted across her lips and was gone. "That's true. It was over for all intents and purposes."

"Which means he would have no motive to, uh—eliminate her. So why is Doug Heller staking out Sam West's house?"

"Is he doing that?" She looked surprised.

"Yes, Sam says so."

"And when did you speak with Sam?"

"This morning Allison couldn't make breakfast after all. I was sitting in the restaurant alone, and Sam was there, so he joined me at my table. He was actually really nice, and sort of funny. So much different from the first time I met him."

"Perhaps he was just wary of you. You would be horrified, Lena, to know what perfect strangers have said to him, written to him. People who have decided that he is evil when the police themselves don't even know if a crime has been committed. It's *those* people out there, Lena—the ones who would be judge and jury and executioner if they could—they are the ones to be afraid of. Not people like poor Sam West."

I opened my mouth to ask another question, but the doorbell rang, which set off a cacophony of barking. Heathcliff and Rochester came bounding into the hall and put on their scary dog impressions. Rhonda whisked past and said, "I'll get it." Soon enough she was ushering in Adam Rayburn, the man who had saved me when Heathcliff had trapped me on the stairs. "Hello, ladies," he said. He held a huge sheaf of roses in his hand—a rainbow of pastels—and set them down next to Camilla. "We got a new flower delivery for the vases at Wheat Grass, but they sent too many. I thought I'd brighten your day with a sampling."

Camilla pursed her lips at him. "Those are absolutely

beautiful, and they are not just leftovers. That bouquet looks expensive, Adam!"

He held up his hands. "I swear. I just took the extras and put them in some paper."

"They're divine," I said. "You have a knack for presentation."

"Sit down, Adam," Camilla said with a wave of her hand. "Would you like some lunch?"

He shook his head. "I can't stay. I have some interviews to do this afternoon. And I'm on the way to speak to the mother of Martin Jonas." His face grew grim.

"Oh, my. How is she holding up?" Camilla asked.

"Not well, although thankfully she has a big family that is providing a great deal of support. Martin was always a challenge, I understand. But he was the youngest, and much loved."

"Why are you going to see her?" I asked.

"Just to send my sympathy, and to give her Martin's last check and some money that we collected at Wheat Grass for the family."

Camilla pushed her salad plate away and pulled one of the roses out of the paper. It was a creamy yellow, just out of bud and beautifully fragrant. She held it to her nose and closed her eyes for a moment. For an instant she looked twenty years younger and quite lovely. "It is so sad about Martin. He was just a boy, really."

"Yes."

"Do the police have any leads?" I asked.

"Not that I've heard. I hope to speak with Doug Heller today, as well." He looked at Camilla for a moment, then stood up. "Well, I must get going. Thank you for the offer of lunch. Perhaps I might join you on another day."

Camilla stood up and offered her left hand; in her right she still clutched the yellow rose. "Of course, Adam. Rhonda will make something special when you come by. Let us know when you have a day off."

"I will. Good-bye—Lena, is it?"

"Yes. Good to see you again, Adam."

He left the room, and soon after we heard the front door open and close. Rhonda walked in with a hearty casserole, and I found that I was in fact hungry again.

I didn't bring up Sam West again, and Camilla seemed slightly distant for the rest of our lunch, as though something were on her mind. Perhaps she was thinking about revisions for her book. It was time, I realized, to stop letting Blue Lake and all of its inhabitants distract me. I needed to go upstairs and finish *The Salzburg Train*, and then Camilla and I could begin our work in earnest.

FIVE HOURS LATER I did finish the book. I had made seven pages of notes, but that hadn't kept me from fully enjoying the novel, which in many ways was the best she had ever written. I sighed and stroked my hand across the manuscript. "Beautiful," I said. My mind was already fashioning potential covers for this eventual bestseller, and all of them were fascinating, filled with mysterious blues and lavenders and greens as the train rushed through an Austrian forest at twilight.

Lestrade clawed at my door from the hallway; Camilla and I had agreed that, since the dogs seemed to have accepted him now, he could have the house to explore. He seemed to understand, though, that my room was his home base, so he had made a few trips in and out since I had started reading. I got up, stretched, and let in my fluffy feline friend. "Had a nice walk?"

He leaped up on the bed and began his bathing ritual. My phone rang shrilly, making us both jump. "Sorry, Lestrade," I said, grabbing it and clicking it on. It was Allison, her voice comforting and familiar.

"Hey, Lee," she said.

"Hey, pal. How were the accident victims? I hope no one died."

"No, thank God. We had a couple of broken limbs, though. Sorry to leave you in the lurch."

I sighed in her ear. "Well, I can't really begrudge your services to sick people, but I was bummed out that I couldn't talk to you."

"That's why I called—to invite you over for dinner tomorrow. I want you to see our house, and we're inviting a fourth person, too. A guy John wants you to meet. That way you can get married and we can all raise our kids in Blue Lake."

"Wow. No pressure or anything."

"You sound weird. Are you under stress?"

"Do you have time now? Or does John need you to rub his feet or something?"

She giggled in my ear. "You crack me up when you're crabby. I have all evening for you if you need it, my dearest friend."

"Fine. Then get comfortable. There's stuff I have to tell you."

So I did: about Camilla and her house, and her dream of a manuscript, and the dead man on the beach.

"Oh, God, I heard about that on the news. Martin, of all people. We knew him from the restaurant, and sometimes when we had Wheat Grass cater our events, he would be the one to show up with the food—"

"Wait, there's more. I went to meet you for breakfast and you didn't show up, so I thought, fine, I'll eat alone, and then Sam West came and sat at my table, and—"

"What?"

"Sam West. I don't know if you've heard of him—"

"Oh, I've heard of him."

"He was being nice. He saw that I was alone and he didn't want me to look like a loser."

"Lena, stay away from him. There's something you should know . . ."

"I already do. The people in this town have already decided that he's some evil murderer when his wife hasn't even been found. Sam has no idea—"

"Sam? You've been here a day and you're calling him Sam?"

"It's his name. Anyway, he has no idea what happened to his wife."

"And how do you know that?"

"He told me."

There was silence at the other end. I envisioned Allison desperately pantomiming to John across the room, probably suggesting that I would soon be murdered.

"Allison?"

"Yeah, I'm here. Listen, we need to talk about this in person. Can you come tomorrow night? I'm making a lasagna."

"Yes, I'll be there. Text me the address and the time."

"Don't be mad at me, Lee-lee. This is just—a lot has happened to you in one day."

"Tell me about it. You said this was a quiet little town."

"It is. This stuff—this is an anomaly. Normally the most exciting news is that someone stole a bicycle or knocked over a mailbox."

"So far I have found Blue Lake to be full of conflict—from the storm that ushered me into this place to the evil looks I got at the restaurant yesterday. Not to mention the dead man that I saw up close and personal."

"That must have been scary. I'm sorry you saw that, Lee."

"Have you seen them at the hospital? Dead people?"

"Yes—a couple of times. It's easier to process there because it's not always unexpected. Your experience was shocking. I hope you'll be able to put it out of your mind."

"I can, sometimes. But then it floats back in."

"Poor Lena. You need good friends, some good wine, and a good home-cooked meal."

"Yes." I looked at Lestrade, who had cuddled into a ball, and felt inexplicably sad. "You know what? I'm suddenly really tired. Just text me that info and I'll see you tomorrow, okay? Looking forward to it."

"Okay—bye, Lee." She sounded a little uncertain. Allison had always been an uncanny barometer of my moods, and she knew something was going on with me—perhaps better than I did, since I wasn't quite sure of the source of my melancholy.

I said good-bye and clicked off.

For the rest of the day I fought the bad mood that hung like a cloud over my head, just like the clouds that had hung over Blue Lake on the day of my arrival.

7

Gerhard took her one day on a jaunt in the Black Forest, where the giant trees stood like sentries over the curving, rutted path, and leaves littered the ground like two-toned confetti, silencing their footfalls so that the only sound was the "twee twee" of the red crossbill who sheltered in the branches far above them. She had the sense that she had entered another world, and that the silent man she followed was leading her into oblivion.

—from *The Salzburg Train*

THE NEXT MORNING I walked down the hill, heading toward the main street and Bick's Hardware. I needed to tap my sadly depleted savings account in order to get some cash for my expenses. I had not signed any official contract with Camilla, and now, as my hero worship receded enough for me to be practical, I wondered if I should ask about it. Even if this were a standard job, I wouldn't be paid for a couple of weeks, I realized, so Camilla was within her rights to test me out, as it were. Still, I felt a bit precarious in the financial sense.

My father, far away in Florida with his new wife, Tabitha, texted me occasionally to ask about my money situation. It was his largesse that had allowed me to finish graduate school, but I hated relying on him for money at the age of twenty-six. This morning's text said:

Hi hon. How's the new job? Living the dream. Need money?

This was my father in a nutshell. Always fond, always providing. My mother had been the same, before her untimely death, and I felt the prick of unexpected tears as I neared my destination. Our life together—father, mother, daughter—had been wonderful, but seemed distant now.

I paused at the door to Bick's and breathed in some cold Blue Lake air. This calmed and refreshed me. I marched through the crowded store with its odd arrangement of items and went to the back counter, where an unlikely ATM sat beside an antique cigarette machine. With a surreptitious glance around the room to make sure I was not being observed, I punched in my information and retrieved my cash, which I stowed in the little purse with a long strap that I wore slung over one shoulder and tucked underneath the other arm. In Chicago, it had taken one pickpocket and one purse thief before I had finally gotten wise about security and conscious of the way I carried my possessions. Now, in this little town that sometimes looked to have only about one hundred residents, I was as cautious as a cat.

I gathered a few items, then went to the window of the little post office. It was my stepmother's birthday in a few days, and I had written her a silly card. For some reason, Tabitha thought I was hilarious, so I always tried to live up to that reputation, but with her alone.

"Hello, hon," said Marge Bick, leaning toward me over

the counter. "You're Lena, right? I remember that name. Sort of old-fashioned, somehow."

"I suppose. How are you, Marge?"

"Oh, hanging in. Do you need stamps again?"

"No. Just to mail this."

She took my envelope and read it with inappropriate curiosity. "Florida, huh? What, do you have a boyfriend out there?"

I felt my friendliness diminishing with her invasion of my privacy. "No—just some family."

"Oh, that's nice. Although you probably don't get to see them much."

"They come up now and then. And I always have an excuse to vacation in Florida, so that's good."

"Horace and I went to Daytona Beach in spring once. So pleasant, and the weather was so nice. A big gang of bikers there, too, though." She looked at my letter again. "But I see your folks live in Jupiter."

"Yes."

She looked at my face, shrugged, and tossed the letter into what was apparently an outgoing mail bin. "Anything else today, hon?"

"Just these." I pushed forward a bag of cat food, some toiletries, and a local newspaper.

Marge pointed at the headline—"Local Man Slain"—and frowned. "This happened up by you, didn't it? Right by Mrs. Graham's house."

"Yes. It's a terrible thing."

Marge sighed as she rang up my items in the slowest way possible. "That boy, though. You sort of knew he would end up in trouble."

"Why?"

"I saw him in here all the time with unsavory types. I always told my own kids, pick your friends wisely. The peer group." She nodded with a sage expression and pushed her cheaters up on her nose. "They are the biggest influence, for good or bad. Isn't that true? Think of your own pals, when you were a teenager. But you're just a youngster. That wasn't long ago, was it?"

"Fairly long. Who were the people he hung around with?"

"I don't know all their names. Some of them were regulars from the bowling alley down there. That place is unsavory." She clearly liked this word. "They hang around and drink beer, and when they're not bowling, they're playing darts."

I pretended I was yawning to conceal my laughter. When I managed to reclaim a blank face, I said, "That doesn't sound so bad."

"You'd have to go in there to know what I mean. And I do NOT recommend that you go in there. You're too nice a young woman. For one thing, the place smells awful, like old beer and body odor and onions. And maybe something else, if you know what I mean."

"Do you mean drugs?"

Marge darted a glance around, as though we might be under surveillance. "Yes, I think so. I don't claim to know what they all smell like—all the drugs—but I know a weird smell when I smell it."

"So you weren't a fan of Martin Jonas?"

"Oh, he was okay. A nice enough boy at heart. But it's like I said—he picked the wrong crowd. And now I'm proved right, because they killed him, didn't they? They killed that poor boy."

A woman got in line behind me; I darted a quick glance back and saw that it was a very sleepy-looking Lane Waldrop, holding a package of diapers. "Hello," I said.

"Hey!" Her face brightened slightly. "Lena, right?"

"Yes. And you're Lane."

"Right. Our names are kind of similar." She grinned at me, and I realized she was very pretty when she smiled.

"Looks like you ran out," I said, pointing at the diapers. I've never claimed to be a great conversationalist.

"Yeah—Tommy had a little accident in bed last night and I had to clean him up and calm him down at three this morning, and then when I woke up, I saw we had only one left. That kid can go through them, I swear." She brushed some of her red hair off her shoulder, and I realized it was a beautiful shade—the kind you couldn't buy in a box.

Marge leaned in with her curious face. "Where's Clayton? Can't he help when you're half exhausted?"

She shrugged. "Clay's got a new client who wants all these shrubs dug up and then a whole new landscaping thing done in his front yard. He had to get up at five and drive to Frontsville to pick up the sod and wood chips. He offered to take Tommy with him, but I just asked Selby from next door to come over."

Marge sighed. "Ah, parenthood. I remember those days oh so well. And I had four of them under six at one point."

Lane offered a thin smile, and I got the impression she had heard this story before. "Anyway, I've got to pay for these and get home before Tommy decides to fill the one he's got on." She looked pointedly at her watch.

Marge didn't see it as a brush-off. "Oh, right you are. Those little ones keep you on your toes, don't they?" She rang up the diapers and put them in a bag.

"I'd better get going, too," I said. "It was nice seeing you again, Lane. Bye, Marge."

Lane held up a finger as she took her change. "Hang on, I'll walk you out."

We made small talk as we moved back through Bick's Hardware, and then on the sidewalk Lane said, "Hey, we were supposed to make a lunch date, remember? I'd have you over to my place, but it's a disaster. I bet I can get Selby to watch the kids and I could come up to your manor house." She said the last two words with an ironic twist of her lips.

She certainly seemed fascinated with Graham House. And yet who was I to judge? I had a near-obsession with the woman inside Graham House. "I would love that, but I don't feel comfortable inviting anyone unless I ask Camilla first. Maybe I can text you and let you know?"

"Sure! Hand me your phone." She set her bag down and took my proffered cell, tapping it expertly with quick fingers. "There. I put myself into your contacts. Now call me, so you'll be in mine."

I took the phone back, found Lane's number, and pressed it. She took out her own phone, clicked it on, and said, "Hello?" holding it comically up to her ear. We laughed, and I realized that I liked her. She was whimsical and fun—I wondered if Allison knew her. They seemed to have a great deal in common.

I tucked my phone in my pocket. "I'd better get back—but I'll text you today or tomorrow, okay?"

"You got it. Meanwhile, parenthood calls."

"Your children are very cute."

Her face softened. "I know. They drive me nuts, but I know." She sent me a last wave and went loping over to a red Ford station wagon. She climbed into the driver's seat and fiddled with the radio; moments later she was driving past me and I was being treated to a bar of Taylor Swift asking why someone had to be so mean.

I made my way back up the bluff, enjoying the serenity of isolation and trying to dream up a plot for a mystery that could be set in Blue Lake, Indiana. The fact that it already contained many mysteries made me wonder, briefly, if I might consider writing true crime.

I hesitated at the bottom of Sam West's long driveway and wondered if he considered me a friendly neighbor at this point. Should I wander up and say good morning? And yet he had made it clear he valued his privacy. I stood there, uncertain, staring at the little stones on the curving driveway and half expecting West to wander out with one of his cigarettes, holding a hand up to keep the flame alive. Would he appreciate a friendly face? A non-judgmental voice? Or would he just want to be alone, focused on his investments and his investigation into his wife's disappearance? After a moment's hesitation, I turned and continued up the hill toward Camilla's house.

Bob Dawkins and his horrible son were on the porch again, this time installing some marigolds and mums in the window boxes on either side of the front door. It was a surprisingly bright and attractive addition generated by two opposingly dark and dingy human beings. I pretended I didn't see them as I walked up the stairs, but the older man pointed at me with a dirty finger. "You been to town?"

I help up my Bick's Hardware bag. "Yup. Running some errands."

"You should be careful walking all alone," he said. He made eye contact for a millisecond before he stared back at the dirt and his flowers. The scent of soil permeated the air.

I hesitated. Was that a threat or a warning? Either way it felt rather sinister, especially because, while Bob Dawkins' face was expressionless, his son's wore a smirk that was, as Marge Bick would put it, "unsavory."

"Why do you say that?" I said.

He shrugged. "A man's been killed. Never know what kind of loonies are running around. Plus there's him down the road." He beckoned with his head toward the end of the driveway while his hands continued to knead the soil, plunging the roots deep into their new home.

A burst of defensiveness filled me. "I have nothing to fear from Sam West—or probably anyone else. It seems to me that Martin Jonas was killed because of some sort of personal issue. I certainly hope no one else is going to be harmed."

"Yeah, let's hope," said Bob Dawkins to his flowers.

His son said nothing. I wondered if he were socially impaired in some way.

I moved into the house and glimpsed Camilla sitting at her desk near the fireplace. "Good morning," I said.

"Oh, Lena—good. Did you go out for some breakfast?"

"No. I just had to pick up some items at Bick's."

"Rhonda left breakfast in the kitchen. Do help yourself. What would be a convenient meeting time?"

"I can meet in half an hour, or any time after that. I just want to feed Lestrade and have a bite to eat."

"Fine. Half an hour." She waved and went back to her work. I moved upstairs with my bag and looked for

Lestrade in my room, but he had wandered out. I poured him some food anyway, figuring that he would search for it sooner or later. I stowed the toiletries in my bathroom and sat near the window with my newspaper, where I read the story about Martin Jonas. He had been twenty-four years old, the article said, and helping to support his war veteran father and cancer-ridden mother. Someone had started an online fund for the family, and it had already raised eighteen thousand dollars—an example of one of the more positive things that the Internet could do.

There was a picture of Jonas, apparently taken when he was much younger, and his face bore a certain vulnerability that I had not noticed in person. Perhaps Marge Bick had been right, and Jonas had changed due to his ill-chosen companions.

Doug Heller was pictured, too, squinting in the sun as he stood on the beach. The caption read "Detective Douglas Heller of the BLPD says that the case is still under investigation, and as of yet the police have no suspects."

What must it be like, I wondered, to have to face a puzzle so daunting, with no guarantee that the answer would eventually emerge from the mist of clues? Doug Heller faced such a puzzle, but so did Sam West. Did he sit in his house at night, trying to work out what might have happened to his estranged wife? Did Doug Heller fear that his job would be on the line if he did not come through with answers?

Suddenly glad about my own job and my confidence that I could do it well, I grabbed my annotated manuscript, went down to the kitchen, and ate a quick plate of scrambled eggs with toast and a little fruit salad, which Rhonda had displayed attractively in individual blue ceramic bowls.

I put my dishes in the sink, feeling decadent, and went in to Camilla and her warm, cozy study.

"Is now an okay time?" I asked, holding the sheaf of papers awkwardly in my arms.

"Of course. Here—pull up that purple chair. Then we can both use the desk."

I set the book down and dragged over the stuffed chair she had indicated. It was firm, yet comfortable.

She smiled at me, then pointed at the manuscript. "This has annotations, as well? Wonderful. I'll take that, too. I've been going through your notes. They are splendid, Lena."

"Thank you. Your book was an inspiration."

"Mmm." I needed to remember that, as a rule, Camilla was immune to compliments.

"Where should we start?"

"I am concerned at this point about the scene in the Black Forest. You made some fine notes there, and clearly there is a problem. What do you think is lacking?"

I settled into my chair while I thought about it. "The thing is—the location alone is thrilling. She's left Austria and has become embroiled in the mystery in Altensteig. And then there's that amazing scene where she's being chased through the Black Forest by the man whose criminal enterprise she has stumbled upon. It's compelling. But—it's not as suspenseful as it should be."

"Yes. You're right, of course. I reread it last night, through your eyes, and I can see that it needs to be much more intense. I need them on the edges of their seats, not just appreciating the scenery."

"Which I did," I said.

She laughed. "Lena, you are irrepressible."

"I sense that you've seen it firsthand—the Black Forest. Have you been there?"

Her expression grew soft. "On my honeymoon. Many, many years ago. Beautiful places tend to stay with you, especially if they are the settings for beautiful experiences."

"Camilla—I know we're just getting acquainted, but someday—I'd love to hear how you met. You and your husband."

She nodded, her expression brisk again. "And someday I would like to tell you. Now—here is what I propose. We will both rewrite the scene in the forest. We will share, and decide on the best parts of each for the most suspenseful experience. Is that all right with you?"

I'm sure my face was bright red. "I—it—I would love to. I—if you think—"

"Good. In the meantime I'll finish the other notes and work on addressing them, point by point. How long will you need to write the scene? It's approximately, what? Fifteen pages."

"Uh—let's say two days. That way I can write and rewrite and bring you what I think is best."

"Excellent." She held out her hand like a business executive, but she was laughing. I shook it, and then I was laughing, too.

I wanted to say something about how honored I was to have the chance to write with her, but it was clear she already knew that. I stood to go, but she held up a hand.

"Wait one more moment, Lena. I realized that we haven't really addressed the issue of your pay. I took it up with my accountant yesterday, and she put you on the payroll. If it's all right with you, you'll receive compensation on the first and the fifteenth of the month. Since today is the fifteenth, I had her generate a check and bring it to me this morning."

She handed me an envelope, which I took, feeling awkward. Did I open it in front of her? Did I wait to open it in my room? What was the etiquette?

Camilla seemed to read my mind. "You'll probably want to open it later; when you do, I want you to know that this is the going rate in New York and London for people doing exactly what you are doing."

"Okay. Thank you," I said. Was she warning me that it was a low amount? Or suggesting that I might find it too high? I feared it was the former.

"In addition, I've had my lawyer write up a contract." She slid a packet over to me. "You'll want to have your people look it over."

"Oh—uh, yes."

"Is something wrong?"

"I don't really have any . . . people."

Camilla's mouth twitched. "There are several worthwhile attorneys here in town who work on a sliding scale. And now that I think of it—your friend Sam West used to be an investment banker. I think he'd be quite good at this."

"Oh! Okay, yes. Thank you. Thank you, Camilla." I had stood up and was backing away as I spoke, clutching my contract and my envelope, which I was dying to open. Then I stopped. "Oh—I meant to tell you that I'm having dinner with Allison tonight. So Rhonda only needs to feed you."

She nodded. "She always makes too much. I hate to have all that food just sitting around—who might . . . perhaps I'll have Adam over—as a thank-you for the roses. What do you think?"

"That sounds great. I hope he can make it. Also, I ran into Lane Waldrop in town this morning."

"Yes, I know Lane."

"She spoke about us having lunch together. I had the feeling she was hinting that she'd like to be invited here. I think your house has a certain mystique for the locals—"

Camilla shrugged. "God knows why. But you're welcome to have her here for lunch. Just let me know the day and I will tell Rhonda. Actually, I'll be out of town for half the day on Thursday. I have a doctor appointment in Daleville. I love my doctor, and she moved farther away, so I followed her."

"I see. All right, Thursday then. I will tell Lane to come at—noon?"

"Make it twelve thirty. Rhonda will want to have everything just so. She's very particular about visitors. As though I were the queen and this were the castle."

I laughed. "Well, thank you, Camilla. For everything."

"The gratitude is mutual, dear."

Out in the hall I increased my pace, practically running up the stairs and diving on my bed to tear open the envelope. I stared at the amount in the box with my mouth hanging open. After taxes, my pay came to twenty-five hundred dollars. AFTER taxes. Which meant I was being paid five thousand dollars a month. I was getting free room and board and a ridiculously high salary for work that was easy and did not confine me to a rigorous eight-hour schedule. Lestrade flew up onto the bed, breathing his cat food breath on me.

"Lestrade, I am rich. I'm rich and lucky and happy. I can pay off my debts and buy gifts for my father and new tires for my car. I am an *employed woman*." I said this to him earnestly, but he yawned as though he'd heard it all before. I scratched his fluffy head and got up to set the check and the contract carefully on my desk. I would have to decide on a bank in the area. Meanwhile, I needed someone to look at the agreement.

I opened my laptop and searched the local white pages for Blue Lake. Then I googled Sam West. I figured his number would be unlisted, given the extent of the harassment he had received, but to my surprise, his name and number were right there on the page. I felt nervous about approaching him for a favor, but I grabbed my cell phone and dialed before I could talk myself out of the decision.

He answered on the third ring. "Sam West. Is this Lena?"

"Uh—yes. Hi, Sam. You have caller ID?"

"I do. Nice to hear from you."

"Yes. You might not think so when you hear that I'm calling to ask for a favor."

"I have no problem doing a favor for you. You granted me one the other day by dining with me." His voice was deeper than I remembered, rumbling into my ear.

"That's nice of you. Okay, here goes: Camilla gave me a contract, and said I should have someone look it over. Except I don't know a soul in this town, and I know zero about contracts and money and things."

"I know everything about them. We are the yin and yang of contracts." He sounded amused, and my tension eased.

"I wonder if you would look at it and advise me? I would owe you another favor in return."

"That is the best part of all. Knowing I have a favor coming from Lena London."

I said nothing, and he laughed.

"Of course I'll do it, Lena."

"Oh, thank you so much!"

"When would you like to meet?"

"Um—I'm basically free, except I'm having dinner with my friend Allison tonight. She's the one who stood me up for breakfast the other day."

"I am in her debt."

"What?"

"Tomorrow, then?"

"Yes, I guess so. Would you like to meet for breakfast again?"

"Sounds good. But this time you come here and I'll feed you. I've had enough evil stares for one week."

"Um—okay."

His voice became businesslike. "Meanwhile, why don't you drop the contract off on your way to dinner, and I'll look it over tonight."

"Thank you! That would be great. I'll do that. Probably around six."

"I'll meet you in the driveway. As you know, I like to contemplate the evening while smoking a cigarette."

"And as you know, I disapprove on principle."

He sniffed his amusement into the phone. "And what is your friend serving tonight? No giant waffles to endanger your own health?"

"She's making lasagna with an unfortunate side of a male companion for the evening. She seems to think she should fix me up as a part of welcoming me to town."

"Hmm. Avoid the interference of matchmaking friends, that's my advice. They are often trying to kill two birds with one stone rather than giving great consideration to what sort of man would make you happy."

"Exactly! I agree, Sam."

There was a sound in the background, a pinging that could have been a text message or a computer. I could sense that his attention had shifted. He said, "I'll see you tonight, then."

"Thank you again. Bye, Sam." I hung up and sat still for a while. I needed to rewrite the forest scene, but my head was swarming with thoughts.

I got up to search for my green pencil, which I had set down somewhere. In the midst of my quest I stopped and remembered that Camilla had called Sam West "your friend." Not "our friend," but "your friend."

Why would Camilla, who had introduced me to West and his reputation in town, suddenly refer to him as my friend alone? It was a curious distinction for someone whose business was words.

Troubled by this, I located my pencil on the carpet (I suspected Lestrade had been batting it around again) and went to the desk.

It was time to return to the Black Forest.

8

Gerhard did not return, and they began to worry about his whereabouts; Johanna experienced a general dread, not just about the consequences of involving Gerhard in her suspicions, but of life itself, with all its hidden pitfalls, and the existence that the giant trees had made her call into question. What, really, did she know of the world, or herself, or her future? Why, really, did it matter?

—from *The Salzburg Train*

I HAD FINISHED a draft by late afternoon; it was not one I would show Camilla, but it was a start. I dressed with a sense of satisfaction; I knew that writing was a layered process, and one had to find little joys as one went along. A finished novel was a culmination, but Camilla had once said, in a 1981 interview, that "the real joy is in going down the path, pen in hand, and meeting your story as it comes. You never know what adventures await you, and it's the start of the journey that is the most thrilling. At the end, when the book is done, you all say good-bye. I far prefer the start: my characters as my friends, and a whole adventure awaiting us."

In Camilla's formula, this was the beginning of the adventure, in so many ways, and I intended to relish every moment of it. Perusing the outfits in my closet, I said as much to Lestrade, who was stropping against my leg in an attempt to get me to open the door. He had a new world, too, and he longed to explore it. I smiled down at him. "Okay! Just tell me what to wear first." I scooped him up and edged toward my hanging clothes. Lestrade, who had actually done this before, stuck out a paw, which happened to land on a blue sweater.

"Fine. I was leaning toward that one anyway. Here you go. Say hi to your new pals." I walked him to the door and let him out, and he made his fluffy way down the stairs.

I returned and donned a bit of perfume before I slipped the blue sweater over my head. It was a midnight blue, a gift from my parents when I turned twenty-one. My mother had grown ill soon afterward, and I had always valued this sweater because it was a beautiful memory of a time when we were all together.

I pulled on my "dress jeans"—the nicer, newer black pair that looked well enough with a sweater and a pair of black boots—and viewed the result in the full-length mirror on the bathroom wall. "Yeah, that works," I said. Allison knew that I wasn't a frilly person, and never had been. But I also felt that casual clothes suited me, and that I could still project a certain elegance with them, especially when I donned some matching jewelry. I slipped on a long, blue-stoned necklace that my ex-boyfriend Kurt had given me one Christmas, along with the matching earrings, which I now fastened into my ears.

"Blue is your color," he had said to me once. The sad reality was that it was probably the most romantic thing he had ever said. Kurt wasn't frilly, either, and it had turned out he also wasn't thoughtful or kind.

With a sigh, I grabbed my purse and made my way downstairs, where Rhonda was making dinner and Camilla was nowhere to be seen. I leaned into the kitchen and said, "Rhonda, if you see Camilla, could you tell her—"

Rhonda turned, surprised. "Isn't she in her little study there? I just saw her stoking the fire."

"Uh—I'll look again." I walked back to the study, and sure enough, Camilla was sitting on the edge of her desk, flipping through a book.

"Hello, dear. All ready to go? Did Allison give you good directions?"

"Yes, thank you. I was looking for you earlier, and I didn't see you in here. It seems like a couple of times I've had that happen . . ."

"Hmm? Oh, I'm sorry. I was hunting for this book. It has a reference that I needed for my German character, my Gerhard."

"Oh, I love him!" I said.

"Did you find time to work on the scene?"

"I did. I finished a draft, but it's not ready for your eyes yet."

"Wonderful. I'll look forward to us comparing notes." She snapped the book shut. "Seeing you going out reminds me—I should probably wear something other than this old sweater, since I have a dinner companion."

"You look stylish—it seems effortless with you."

Camilla gave me her shrewd, assessing look. I had forgotten that she didn't like flattery; then she softened. "Oh, Lena. I could have used your kind support in the last few years." Her face, though lined, looked oddly young and vulnerable for a moment. Then she stood up and regained her traditional composure. "Do tell Allison that I said hello."

"All right. Should I tell her that you're working on your knitting?" I asked, looking pointedly around the room.

Camilla laughed. "Observant girl. I'm trying to learn, but I've been terrible about practicing. I'm not very good at it. Allison is much better. She's making a blanket."

"I'll tell her that you said hello. Have a nice dinner with Adam. Make sure you put those beautiful roses in the center of the table."

Camilla waved as I made my way out to my car, which I hadn't driven since arriving at Graham House. I climbed in, started the engine, and then pulled Allison's directions from my big purse so I could study them one more time. I also retrieved Camilla's contract. Then I pulled out of the driveway and drove halfway down the hill; I parked in front of Sam West's place and got out of the car, contract in hand. He was there, leaning on a tree and stubbing out a cigarette with the toe of his boot. He squinted up at me, his hair slightly mussed by the wind.

"Hello," I said.

"Hello. We look like spies, passing a mysterious document in the shelter of the woods."

I laughed and handed him the contract. His hands were ungloved and large, with long fingers. For an instant I imagined him caressing Victoria West's face and was jolted by unexpected jealousy. I shook my head and pretended to be brushing something off—a leaf, an insect? Perhaps West wouldn't notice that there was nothing there.

"Hopefully it won't be too mysterious. I'm truly appreciative of this favor," I said.

"No problem, Lena. Have a nice dinner with your friend."

"Thanks." I started to move back to my car, then turned

around and saw, to my surprise, that he wasn't going in, but just standing there, watching me. Even in the shadow of the tree, in the autumn evening light, his eyes looked very blue. "What time should I be here in the morning?"

He shrugged. "I'm not that early a riser. How about nine?"

"Perfect. Thank you again."

He waved, and this time he did turn and walk away. I remembered that the news article had said he was thirty-five, which meant that now at most he was thirty-six. In some ways he seemed ancient—especially in the defeated expression he sometimes wore—but when he smiled he looked young.

The wind had picked up, even since I'd left the house, it seemed, and I was glad to tuck back into my car and turn on the heater. I needed to get back on Green Glass Highway and drive south for about a mile, then turn left into a subdivision called Forest Glen. I would take this to a street called Winterbourne, where Allison's house sat on the corner lot.

This was easy to remember, and I set the directions aside and enjoyed the scenery of autumn in Blue Lake. We had not yet turned back the clocks, so I was treated to a glorious sunset over the water. This was the sort of place one could get used to as a permanent home. I recalled what Camilla had said when we stood on the shore and watched the technicians work on the body of poor Martin Jonas. She had said that Blue Lake was "unrelentingly beautiful." Her voice had been resigned. Had she wanted to leave at one point? At many points? But perhaps she had fallen into a comfortable existence here, or perhaps she had even come to rely on those profound sunsets and the horizon that seemed to go on forever.

At the edge of town, about to turn onto the highway, I saw the young man I had first seen in Bick's Hardware on the day of the storm—the ski-sweater man who had been talking to Martin Jonas. In the evening light I could see that his hair was actually red, a detail I had not noticed when distracted by his weird sweater. Now he was wearing a Windbreaker and jeans and walking rapidly toward the restaurant called Wheat Grass—Adam Rayburn's place. It was a charming restaurant with beige stucco walls, large windows, and a water view. Now that I had money I could dine there . . .

The man in the Windbreaker looked once over his shoulder, almost directly at me, and I accelerated past him and the restaurant and turned left onto Green Glass. He and Martin Jonas had been arguing. And hadn't he sort of threatened Martin Jonas, this man with the red hair? It seemed perfectly obvious to me that he was the prime suspect for killing poor Martin—so why was he still walking free? Was it because my description of him had been lacking? If so, now I had more information to give the police. The man had red hair, and at nearly six in the evening on October 15, he had walked into Wheat Grass wearing a blue Windbreaker. Surely they could find security footage of him and arrest him right afterward?

What would Adam Rayburn think if he learned he had a murderer in his restaurant? Rayburn's name made me think of something entirely different: had Camilla seemed nervous about having Rayburn over? If so, why would she invite him? And what, I wondered, was Rhonda making for dinner?

Once again the people of Blue Lake were dominating my thoughts. I tried to think of nothing but the topaz sky as I drove to Allison's house for my first dinner away from Graham House.

ALLISON'S MARRIED NAME was Branch. and she had told me to look for a house on the corner. I knew I had the right place immediately, not only because it sprawled on a corner lot with a leaf-strewn yard, but because there was a stone placard that read "Branch House" sitting in the center of the lawn. It was stately and expensive-looking; I wondered if it had been a wedding present.

I pulled into the driveway and gathered my purse and a little housewarming gift that I had purchased back in Chicago: a huge caramel-colored candle in a driftwood stand, scented with some alluring spice that I couldn't name. Allison was mad for candles, so I felt confident it would be a hit.

I got out and marched to their front door, which flew open. Allison stood there, blonde and good-looking as always, her hair gathered in a casual ponytail that should have looked scruffy but looked fashionable instead. She wore a cream-colored sweater and a pair of black knit pants with high-heeled black shoes. "I'm so glad to see you!" she cried, hugging me against her.

"I come with gifts," I said when she released me, handing her the package the clerk had wrapped for me. "Although I just realized I should have brought wine or something."

"We have plenty—and our other guest brought a bottle." She turned and pointed to the men who had just entered the room. "You know John, of course. And this is Doug Heller, our good friend and neighbor."

Douglas Heller stood there, looking different and out

of context. He wore jeans and a green sweatshirt that said "IU." He held a beer in his right hand, but he lifted his left to wave at me. "Hey," he said, grinning.

"Hey. I did not expect to see you here. I thought you were busy solving murders."

He nodded. "The Blue Lake PD never sleeps. But I took a break because my friend Allison said there was someone I should meet." His voice was slightly hoarse, as though he had a cold.

Allison barged between us. "What do you mean you didn't expect to see him? Do you guys know each other? How could you possibly know each other?" John was smirking. It cracked him up when Allison got all hyper.

"First of all," I said, "Detective Heller was the one who came to the beach when Camilla and I found—Martin Jonas."

"Oh, my gosh, of course. How did I not put two and two together?" Allison looked disappointed. Clearly she had wanted to spring Doug Heller on me as the ultimate surprise—which he would have been, considering his good looks and Viking-like demeanor.

Doug Heller spoke in his new, scratchy voice. "But even if I hadn't met her then, I had already met her on the day she came to town. I saw her legs dangling out of her car on the side of the road, and figured I might have a motorist in distress."

He sent me a twinkly look, and Allison didn't miss it. She moved even closer. "What happened? What's the story? I feel totally out of the loop here."

John held up a hand. "Allie, let them sit down. Why don't you offer Lena some of these nice appetizers you made?"

"Hang on, hang on," Allison said, pouting slightly. "Spill it, Lena. Or Doug. Whoever."

John was holding a tray of cheese and crackers. I helped myself to one of each and moved to a large oak table that sat in the middle of the room. "Okay, I'll tell you. It's actually very funny in retrospect, and I'm sure it was funny to, uh—Detective Heller."

"Doug," Heller supplied.

"Yes. I'm sure Doug found it funny even at the time." I paused to take a bite of Swiss cheese, dainty as a mouse, and Allison looked as though she might explode.

I laughed, as did the two men, who sat down at the table with me. "Okay, okay," I said. I told them the story, with occasional ironic interruptions by Doug Heller. I explained about the faulty cat carrier and Lestrade not being a great passenger. About the ominous storm, and my potential lateness while meeting my one and only idol. About Lestrade leaping around the car and hanging from the ceiling like a fat, furry chandelier. About Doug Heller magically having catnip and saving the day. "But I never even got his name," I said. "It was sort of a Lone Ranger situation."

"Who was that masked man?" asked John, laughing and pointing at Doug.

I looked at Heller. "You really did save the day. I got there on time—almost—and eventually made a good impression on Camilla. And now—thanks to my best friend, Allison—I am living a dream I didn't even know I had."

Allison moved to the back of my chair and hugged me around the neck. "Everything is going so well!! I mean—aside from the murder."

"Yes. That was not an auspicious start to my stay in Graham House," I said.

"You talk like a writer," Doug Heller noted.

"Thank you for the compliment, which I will assume it was," I said, taking more cheese and crackers. John slid a little plate under my food after wiping up the crumbs I had already made. Allison poured a glass of wine and set it before me with a flourish.

Doug Heller leaned forward, looking defensive. "Of course it was a compliment. I don't know how anyone could be a writer, especially of a whole book. I can barely get through one paragraph of a police report before I'm wishing I could be finished. To write hundreds of pages—and to have to be profound on all of those pages—that seems like it would take a miracle. I don't know how Camilla does it."

Allison sat down with us, her Pinot Noir clutched in one hand. "Lena has written a book, too. She's going to be a big-deal writer someday, like Camilla. That's why this job is so wonderful."

Doug Heller studied me. "Well, that is impressive. Again, I don't know how you do it."

I shrugged. "Just a certain way of thinking, I guess. I don't know how anyone could solve a crime. I was pondering that yesterday. It's this big puzzle that you can't give up on because justice itself is at stake. It must create so much pressure."

Heller nodded. "But murder is an unusual thing in Blue Lake. Usually I just have to solve such complicated crimes as who vandalized the statue by writing his own name on it—true story," he added as I laughed in disbelief, "or who stole the lawn ornaments from his neighbor's house and set them up on his own grass. Also true."

I giggled and looked at John and Allison to see if they

shared my incredulity. They seemed to have heard these stories before, because their faces were placid and only mildly amused. "But you're a cop," I said. "You see the dark side of humanity. You must have witnessed terrible things."

"I have," Heller admitted, his eyes flicking downward. "But those don't make for good party conversation."

"Yeah, this is becoming a downer," Allison said, smacking the table with her hands. "Let's change the subject."

"Just one more thing," I said. "I saw the guy again—the one who was with Martin Jonas in Bick's on the day of the murder. He has red hair. He was walking toward Green Glass Highway, and he went into Wheat Grass. He was wearing a blue Windbreaker and jeans. I wanted to tell you, because initially I said he had sandy-colored hair, but it was red."

Doug Heller nodded. "I'm relatively sure that's Dave Brill you're describing. He's well known to us down at the station. We did interview him, along with all of Jonas' other friends and acquaintances."

I stared at him, trying to read his face. "But, I mean—can't you hold him? He was fighting with Jonas in the store, and sort of threatening him."

"Not exactly," Heller said. "What you told us on that day was that he wanted Martin Jonas to do something and had given him a one-day deadline. We asked Mr. Brill about that, and he said that he and Jonas buy and sell rare comic books. He had a buyer for some, and he needed Jonas to go out of town and make the sale. He had even given Jonas gas money up front."

"Which was why he said 'If you don't want to do it, then just give me back the cash,'" I said. I thought about it. "Did you believe him?"

His expression was inscrutable. "At this point we have no reason to disbelieve him. We have no evidence—or witnesses—placing him at the scene."

"Well, anyway," Allison said, her tone breezy. "Let's talk about something else."

"Whose boat was it?" I asked.

"What?" Doug Heller said, looking slightly annoyed.

"The boat that I saw Martin Jonas board. Was it his? Maybe the owner of the boat knew something—"

"Believe it or not, we thought to check out the boat. It is registered to a Mr. Darren Zinn, who does not, in fact, exist."

"Oh." I realized that Doug Heller did not appreciate being told how to do his job, and that I was possibly being rude. And yet I was curious about the case, and about that other case that I didn't dare question him about . . .

John rose and peered into the oven in their big brown stove. "Dinner's just about ready. Allison, if you want to give Lena the tour, Doug and I can set the table."

Doug sprang up. "Sure thing."

I stood and began to follow Allison, who was already chattering about some décor they had recently changed. I paused when I reached Doug Heller's side of the table.

"What happened to your voice?"

He shrugged. "Some kind of throat cold. Probably from standing on the beach in the rain for about four hours."

"Oh, man. We should have brought you all hot coffee. I can't believe we didn't think of that."

His expression was benevolent. "You had other things on your mind. You sure had a lot happen on your first day in town, didn't you?"

"I really did!" I said with feeling. He smiled and reached out a casual hand to touch my arm. It wasn't a "there, there" pat, though. It was almost . . . proprietary. But then he took his hand away, and I was sure that I must have been mistaken, especially because neither Allison nor John seemed to have noticed anything.

I followed Allison into her living room, with its tall windows that looked out onto a wooded backyard, and then upstairs to view three large bedrooms and a luxurious bathroom. I struggled with a twinge of envy before I gave myself a stern, internal lecture. I was exactly where I wanted to be. "This is beautiful, Allison."

"Thanks. We're so happy we chose Blue Lake. It's close enough to Indianapolis that we can still have the big-city experience if we want to go away for the weekend, but it's rural enough that we can hike in the woods and see the lake without competing with masses of humanity."

"I've noticed that. It's a far cry from the Chicago lakefront."

"And now we get to be neighbors!" Allison said happily as she treated me to one of her crushing yet enjoyable Allison hugs.

"It's kind of unbelievable. A week ago I was still living in the city with no prospects."

"Life changes rapidly, doesn't it?" Her expression lost some of its sprightliness, and I touched her hand.

"Hey, how is your job going? Is it stressing you out?"

She shook her head. "Not every day. Some days, yes. Like the car accident day. But overall—I love it. You know me."

I did know her. "Come and open your present," I said.

* * *

ALLISON LOVED HER gift, and after we ate her salad and homemade chicken lasagna, she lit the candle and put it on the center of the table, though we had to push it to the side when we chose teams for Trivial Pursuit. No one was allowed to visit Allison without playing this game—it was her favorite, and she was very competitive.

"We're going to do girls against boys, because Lena always gets the arts and literature questions, and I know sports and history. So you guys are doomed," Allison said, making me high-five her.

Doug and John exchanged a secret glance. "Yes, she's always like this," John said. "She got the competitive gene."

Allison grinned at her husband. "John is more of a pacifist. He's Switzerland. He actually tries to help other players when they don't know the answer."

"It's fun that way, too," said John, running a hand through his chestnut-colored hair. I noted with surprise that his hairline was receding slightly. I doubted it mattered to Allison, who had once assured me that John had good bones and would look very sexy as a bald man.

"Okay, enough stalling. We rolled, and we're on blue. Geography. How's your geography, John?"

"Great."

The two men faced us with steely expressions. Allison handed me a card and I read, "Helsinki is the capital of what country?"

Allison groaned, and the men said "Finland" in unison.

"Correct," I said. "Not very difficult, but correct."

"Sore loser," said Doug Heller, smiling at me.

I smiled back and tossed my head. "Roll again."

They got two more questions right and earned an orange chip. Then it was our turn. As Allison rolled the die, I said, "What do you guys know about Adam Rayburn?"

Allison paused in moving our piece and said, "Adam? Why?"

"I don't know. He comes to Graham House a lot, and Camilla's invited him for dinner tonight. I just get—sort of a weird vibe from him."

"He's a nice man," Allison said. "He helped me change my tire once when I was late for work and it blew outside his restaurant. He gave me a muffin, too."

John laughed. "You are Allie's lifelong friend if you give her food."

"It's true," Allison said, batting her eyes. "But the best gifts I ever got were that gorgeous candle and Doug's delicious wine."

"You were born to be a hostess," I said dryly.

Doug Heller had been studying his game piece. "Why does Rayburn give you a weird vibe?"

"Um—I don't know. There's just a certain—urgency about him. Like he wants something. I don't know what he could possibly want at Graham House. It's not like it's built on a gold mine or anything."

Heller's eyes widened, but then he lowered his gaze back to his game piece. "Right," he said. "Does she get a lot of visitors?"

"Well . . . yeah. I mean, she's got workmen who always seem to be on her porch, Rayburn and her chef, phone calls coming from her agency, and her accountant, who was there this morning. Oh, and I met someone at Bick's who asked if she could come over."

"What?" Allison cried, shocked.

"No, I mean—we were chatting and we said we should do lunch sometime, and she said her house was a mess and could she come up to Graham House. It's weirdly popular. Even Marge Bick was asking questions about it."

"Huh," Doug Heller said.

"But I guess when you're famous, you get a certain amount of—traffic."

"Remind me never to become famous," John quipped. "I like my quiet life with my beautiful wife."

Allison blushed and sent him a secret glance that we all saw.

A phone buzzed, and Doug Heller took a cell from his pocket. "Sorry," he said. "This is the work number."

"Heller," he said, standing up and moving away from the table.

"That guy is never really off duty," John said, shaking his head. "I'm glad I'm in a nine-to-five job."

"It's not nine-to-five at tax time," Allison said proudly; John was an accountant. It occurred to me then that I could have asked John to look at my contract; somehow, though, I was still glad I had gone to Sam West. It would have been rude to bring the contract to the dinner, asking John to do work when he was busy hosting.

I found myself wondering what Sam West was doing now in his lonely hilltop house. Was he drinking wine, too, and going over the pages of my agreement? Or was he working with his clients from his distant location? Perhaps he spent a lot of time on the computer, investing in things. I had no idea, I realized, what that really entailed.

"Are they sure it's blood?" asked Doug Heller from the other side of the room. "And when will we know the DNA—okay. And then they need to issue a warrant. I'm not going to act on this unless—all right. Fine. Keep me updated." He clicked off the phone, but he didn't immediately return to the table; he just stood at the window and looked into Allison's now-dark yard.

"Doug? Everything okay?" Allison asked brightly.

He turned and strode back toward us. "Yeah. Sorry. Some work stuff that—came up suddenly."

"Do you need to leave?" asked John, who clearly loved the cop stuff.

"No. Not unless they call back. I don't think this particular—event—will be cleared up for a day or two."

"That's mysterious," I said. I was playing with the brown chip—the one I wanted to win if I ever got any darn literature questions.

"Yeah. I'm not at liberty to discuss this one."

"So it's not someone writing his own name on a statue?" I asked.

His lips twitched. "No."

Allison made a huffing sound. "Well, I hope they don't call you back. I'm serving coffee and dessert soon, and it's going to take a while for us to beat you guys."

Heller clapped John on the back. "A very long while, right John?"

"Perhaps an eternity," agreed John.

"Ha! I landed on the green chip. Read us the question," demanded Allison.

THE GAME WENT on and on, through Allison's coffee and apple pie and beyond. I started stealing glances at my watch, and one time Doug Heller saw me do it. He lifted his arms in a stretch and said, "You guys—we might need to call it a draw. I've got to be in super early tomorrow, and I bet Camilla has Lena up early, too."

Ah—he was offering me a way out—a conspiracy of departure.

Allison moaned and made disappointed noises, but John was up in an instant. "Let me get you guys some leftovers."

"Oh no, I couldn't," I said. "Camilla's chef keeps me stuffed as it is. If I'm not careful I'm going to gain a million pounds."

For just an instant I saw Doug Heller's gaze flick over my body, as though he were assessing any potential weight gain. "I doubt that very much. I've noticed that you walk about four times as fast as the average human."

"What?"

"Oh yes, she always has," Allison agreed. "Kids used to joke about it in school."

I turned to her in surprise. "They did?"

"Rob Stallman called you Lena the Lively."

Doug laughed. "Yeah, I think you'll safely burn up all your extra calories."

I lifted my chin. "In that case I shall take home a piece of pie."

They all laughed at me, but I was already dreaming of my sinfulness: I would eat it in my bed as a midnight snack and let Lestrade lick the plate of crumbs at the end.

TWENTY MINUTES LATER we were calling our good-byes, and Doug Heller said he would walk me to my car.

"Are you afraid I'll be accosted?" I asked lightly.

"See, there you go, talking like a writer. Does that mean mugged?"

"Yes, sort of."

"No, I don't think you'll be *accosted*, but I'm a gentleman, and I like to walk ladies to their cars."

"Lots of ladies, I'm sure."

"Not so many. And none so pretty as you."

We had reached my door, and I fumbled for my keys in the dark. "That was quite a line, Doug Heller."

"Yeah. But it was true," he said in his hoarse cold voice.

I dared a glance up at him and saw that I had not been imagining things; Doug Heller wanted something to happen between us. Had he known, somehow, that Allison would be inviting me? "Well, thanks. That was sweet."

I was grasping the door handle when he stopped me with a hand on my arm. "Lena, one thing. I know this will make you mad, but I have to say it."

"What?" I peered at him in the dark driveway; he looked handsome and mysterious under Allison's back porch light.

"I know you've made friends with Sam West. No, don't say anything yet. The thing is—I know things that you don't. And I'm telling you, as a friend, that you should keep your distance from him. I'm asking you to."

I took a deep breath. "I appreciate that, but I have to tell you that Sam West has been nothing but kind and helpful to me. And at no point did he try to murder me."

"It's not a joke, Lena."

"I know. But I also know that man has been through a lot, and no one has proven that anything happened to his wife, *and* I'm not going to contribute to the general cruelty to which this town has subjected him."

"No, of course you aren't. Because you're Lena London, and you do your own thing."

"Damn right."

"That's why I like you," he said.

"Stop turning everything into a compliment. I'm trying to be indignant here."

"Sorry." He leaned in, blocking out the light, and treated me to a moonlit glimpse of his brown eyes. "I'll say good night then, Lena."

"Good night." He walked away, and I watched him recede into the darkness.

I climbed into my car, relieved to be out of the cold air, and let it warm up for a few moments. I switched on the radio; I hadn't grown familiar with the Indiana stations yet, so I never knew exactly what I was going to hear when I spun the dial. Tonight I heard A Great Big World singing "Say Something." There in the cold dark the song seemed especially melancholy.

I pulled out, singing along, because that's what I did when the radio was on, and wondering if it were just the song making me feel sad. Or perhaps I sensed even then that something was terribly wrong.

9

On nights such as this, in darkness like this, one could lose her way.

—from *The Salzburg Train*

BACK AT CAMILLA'S I crunched over the pebbles of the driveway and parked my car; it felt weird and unfamiliar in the windy dark. I wondered what I had done on nights like this in past Octobers, which now seemed as distant in time and space as the stars that glimmered above Blue Lake. Those stars were much brighter and more plentiful here, and I had a stronger sense of the universe as the context for my existence, making me feel large by association and miniscule in contrast. Disjointed philosophies floated in my head, but in my weary state I could not process them all. I climbed the stairs and opened the door with the spare key Camilla had given me.

There was a small light on in the hallway; it seemed to be on a timer. Other than that, the house was black. Camilla was an early riser, so it didn't surprise me that she had retired at—I consulted my watch—just after midnight.

I started climbing the stairs. They creaked eerily in the tomb-like space, and my imagination began to tell ghostly stories. Something brushed against me, feather-light and horrifying, and I almost screamed until I saw that Lestrade was climbing the stairs with me, his weird eyes switched to night vision and glowing like green stones.

"You scared me," I hissed in the dark, and he started to purr.

We made it to my room unscathed, and I switched on the bedside lamp. Lestrade jumped onto the bed, mewing now and then to tell me about his evening. "That's interesting, but I have to get ready for bed. You can relax out here."

He did, stretching out full-length and displaying his fluffy white belly. I went into the bathroom; despite Camilla's wonderful heater, the room felt cold, as did the tile walls and—I found to my great displeasure—the toilet seat.

I dressed quickly in my flannel pajamas. These had been a Christmas gift from my father, and I loved them. They were cocoa brown and covered with books of all sizes and colors. They also happened to be toasty warm. I donned some fuzzy socks to complete the ensemble, brushed my teeth, washed my face, and flicked off the bathroom light.

Lestrade was already in a light doze, but he got up to let me pull back the covers and turn off the light; then he rearranged himself along my side. Lestrade was good at gauging the spots that would bring him optimal warmth.

"You're a silly boy," I said, stroking one of his soft ears. "But I'm glad you're here. Do you like this big old house? Do you feel at home here with your scary dog friends?"

He purred and rubbed his head against me, then relaxed

into slumber. Cats do that so easily. Human beings, on the other hand, often find themselves staring at the cracked white ceiling, unable to sleep no matter how many sheep they count. Some of those sheep morphed into the various residents of Blue Lake, whose faces were surprisingly clear in my memory . . .

I must have slept eventually, because when I woke up it said three A.M. on the bedside clock, and it was clear that something had changed.

Lestrade was at the door, for one thing, listening with his ears twitching. I heard another sound, soft and menacing, which I realized was the growling of the dogs. Something was wrong; I felt that reality in the dark like a physical presence. I was out of bed in an instant and looking for a weapon. A cast-iron doorstop in the shape of a cow sat to the side of my door near the heating vent. I picked this up and opened the door slowly, peering into the hallway.

A shadowy form loomed before me, and my breath caught in my throat until I realized that it was Camilla, bearing no doorstop but touching the heads of two very attentive German shepherds, the best weapons in the house.

"What's happening?" I asked, my voice hushed.

"I don't know. The dogs woke me. They normally sleep through the night," she said. "I think I might need to investigate."

"Not by yourself, you're not," I said. "Should we turn on a light?"

"Yes, yes. Let's illuminate the situation."

I felt the wall for a switch and filled the hall with a speckled gold light. Camilla was wearing a long flannel nightgown with a cream-colored, fluffy robe. Her glasses were gone, and her hair shimmered silver as she moved toward me.

The dogs suddenly lunged away from us and rushed through the hall and down the stairs. Camilla hesitated. "I guess we need to go down." She didn't seem particularly eager to do so.

I realized that she felt intimidated, and that I was the younger and stronger person here. "I'll go first," I said, moving down the shadowy hall with a sense of the surreal. I flipped on another light at the stair landing; this made part of the main hallway visible, along with the door to Camilla's study. The dogs were not in view.

Down the stairs I went, Camilla close behind me, and I paused at the bottom to get my bearings. The house was dark and quiet; I didn't have the sense that evildoers lurked in the corners. "Maybe the dogs just heard a car backfiring or something," I said, my voice hopeful. I was still clutching my cow doorstop.

"They've never done something like this before—at least not recently. And at this ungodly hour! It's strange," she said.

I walked to the door of her study and peered in. Both dogs stood in front of her desk, their faces vigilant, their bodies as still as lawn ornaments. "They're reacting to something," I said. "Camilla, I think we should call the police."

"At this hour? I would feel terrible bothering them . . . but perhaps you're right. Just to have them check the place out." She hesitated, then walked to her desk, where an old-fashioned rotary-dial phone sat on top. It was her preferred method of calling; her cell phone was something she used as little as possible. "Lena, would you run and turn on some more lights? Be sure to turn on the outer porch, too. Thank you, dear."

I did as she asked, feeling slightly nervous, but less so with each corner I illuminated. When I returned to her study, she was in the center of the room, her expression distracted.

"Everything all right?" I asked, setting the cow down on her desk.

"Hmm? Oh, yes—yes, I think so. They're sending someone out. Just a few minutes, the dispatcher said."

"Wonderful. How was your dinner with Adam?"

"Oh, quite nice. He appreciated the invitation. I realized I had never invited him for a meal before—quite remiss of me, since I've known him for years. I'm sure he enjoyed the change of scenery; most nights he eats dinner in the kitchen at Wheat Grass."

"Ah."

"You're right about this house fascinating people. Adam insisted on the full tour."

"Is that so?" I thought about this for a moment, frowning.

"And how was your evening with Allison?"

"Oh—a bit complicated. She insisted on bringing a man for me to meet, and it ended up being Doug Heller."

Camilla clapped her hands, smiling. "Oh, how funny. But he was a good choice, really. He's probably the most sought-after bachelor in this town."

"Yes, well. I'm not seeking any bachelors at this point. I need to concentrate on your book, and here I am swanning around making all these social plans. In fact, I have to dart out again in the morning; Sam West was kind enough to look at the contract for me, so I'm going to pick it up at his house. And then, as you recall, I invited Lane Waldrop for lunch."

Camilla shrugged. "Sometimes you have to pay your social dues. And I'll be gone at the doctor anyway, remember? We can work on the book when I return."

"Yes, all right. Oh—someone's at the door!"

It was not Doug Heller—I wasn't sure whether I felt relief or disappointment about that fact—but the nervous, Chihuahua-like man who had wanted to push Camilla and me off the beach on the day of the murder. At his side was a younger officer in uniform, a sandy-haired man with a baby face. I wondered if there were any women on the Blue Lake Police Force.

"You say you heard sounds?" said the nervous officer that Doug Heller had called Chip, and whose nametag said "Officer Johnson."

Camilla yawned, then nodded. "Thanks to the dogs, we were alerted to something—I'm not sure what. The dogs never get up in the night, but they are both trained to ward off intruders."

I had not known this; I looked at Rochester and Heathcliff, who sat nearby, posing and panting, and sent them a look of respect. They seemed to acknowledge the attention with a slight raising of their chins.

Chip Johnson and the younger policeman spoke to each other in low tones; then the younger one went outside, murmuring into his radio.

"May I look around the house?" Chip asked.

"Feel free," Camilla told him. "It has a great many nooks and crannies, but we've tried to turn on enough lights."

He moved importantly past us and marched up the stairs to the second floor.

I made a face at Camilla, my impression of Chip Johnson's officious expression, and she giggled. "Oh, Lena, you make me laugh. You've brought new life into this house." She reached out and patted my hand. "You must promise never to leave."

She said this last sentence lightly, ironically, and I chuckled. "If you promise to never stop writing."

The outside man returned, holding something small in his hand. "Where's Chip?" he asked.

"He's checking the place out—currently upstairs," Camilla said.

The young officer went bounding up the stairs after Chip, and we moved to a small couch in the corner of the study, to rest our bones, as Camilla rather mordantly put it. After about twenty minutes, Chip came in with his companion and cleared his throat, ready to make a report.

We remained sitting, but Camilla sat a bit straighter. "Did you find anyone?"

"No people, no, ma'am, but I am concerned that someone might have been here. No footprints to speak of, but the ground's pretty dry right now."

"But?"

"But we found this scarf." He held up a gray knitted thing. "It's not wet or dirty, which makes it seem it may have been dropped quite recently. And we found this fluttering against your trellis."

He held up a fifty-dollar bill. "Have you lost money recently, Ms. Graham?" he drawled.

Camilla snorted. "I am not in the habit of carrying large

sums of cash, and I don't deal in big bills like an American gangster. For the most part I write checks."

"This money ain't been affected by the weather, either," said the young officer, looking pleased.

"It *hasn't* been affected," Chip corrected ostentatiously, looking at Camilla out of the corner of his eye; he seemed to be standing on his tiptoes. I almost laughed; apparently I wasn't the only one in this town who felt the need to impress Camilla Graham.

Camilla sighed. "I confess I am at a loss to imagine what might have occurred out there, or what visitor might be lurking in the shadows with pockets full of money. It does sound intriguing, though."

I could see that if she had ever been frightened, that feeling had passed. Now she looked tired.

"Thank you so much for coming out," I told the two officers, both of whom seemed rather curious about the house and its pajama-clad occupants. The baby-faced officer pointed at my flannel night attire.

"Are those flying books?" he asked.

I assured him that it was merely a pattern on the material, and that the books were simply open and ready to be read. This made me want to be in my bed, reading a book.

"You give us a call if you have any other visitors," Chip said. "Right now I'm guessing it was just someone taking a shortcut, or some kids on a lark."

We thanked them again and ushered them out the door, which Camilla locked with a firm click.

I turned to her. "A shortcut?"

"To what, I wonder?" she asked. "We're at the top of the bluff."

We thought about this for a moment.

"Lena?"

"Yes?"

"Do you like cupcakes?" Camilla Graham asked me with a mischievous expression.

"Who doesn't?"

"Rhonda made us some delightful ones for our dinner, but goodness. As if two old people are going to eat six large cupcakes after a full meal!"

I shrugged.

"Come on," she said. "Let's have a midnight snack at three in the morning."

We went to the kitchen, where, through the dark window, I could see a glimmer of Blue Lake on the horizon. Camilla flipped on the light over the sink and rummaged in the refrigerator. She took out a little cake plate, removed the cover, and revealed that Rhonda was a genius at desserts. Each cupcake was uniquely decorated and piled high with a different color of frosting.

I sat down and Camilla set the plate before me. She saw my face and said, "Yes. I am trying to encourage her to write a cookbook. She has a gift and doesn't fully realize it." She pointed at a cake piled high with a froth of cream-colored frosting. "That one is a carrot cake. This one?" She pointed at another, frosted blue with a little sailboat on top. "Has jam inside. Surprisingly delicious."

I moaned softly. "And that coffee-colored one?"

"Chocolate cake with hazelnut frosting."

"Sinful. Yes, Rhonda needs to be recognized by the world."

Camilla poured us each a glass of milk and returned to the table. She sat across from me and took a pink cupcake covered in red glitter and a red frosted heart.

"A romantic choice," I said.

She shrugged. "You've read my books. You know I'm a romantic at heart." She took a bite and pointed at the cupcakes. I selected the chocolate one and bit into it. It was a perfect moment of blissful flavor that exceeded expectations.

"Mmmm!"

"Yes. I've thought about a way to hook a publisher. What if she called it *The Blue Lake Cookbook*? Is that too vague? They could market the small-town appeal."

"I think it's great. I would buy it, and I know Allison would. All the Martha Stewart types would. It's all about the visuals. If you put these cupcakes on the cover, it would sell like crazy. But even one of her salads or casseroles would make people buy. She has a visual flair."

"Here we are planning Rhonda's success; perhaps we should also focus on our own," Camilla said with an almost conspiratorial tone.

"Yes." I took another bite and closed my eyes to enjoy it. When I opened them, I was surprised by the look on Camilla's face. For the first time since I had met her, she looked happy; not just quietly amused or laughing at me, but happy. I wondered why.

"How is the chocolate?"

"As good as you'd imagine."

We grinned at each other, and the dogs snuffled at our feet, half asleep now that their job was over.

"Camilla?"

"Yes."

"I really love *The Salzburg Train*. I love all your books so much."

"Thank you, dear."

"Can I ask you something?"

"Of course."

"When I interviewed with you, over the phone—it seemed that you decided to hire me after that one answer—when I said my favorite character in *The Lost Child* was Colin, the boy. I wondered—I'm not sure how to put this—if Colin was important to you because he was perhaps based on a boy you knew?"

Camilla licked some frosting from her finger and smiled down at her plate. It was a sad smile. "You really do understand me, so much better than even my editors do. They wanted me to make changes to Colin, to his character and the overall plot, and I had to refuse."

I sat up straight in my chair. The thought that someone had wanted to tamper with the perfect plot of that book was shocking. "Of course you did."

"Colin is not exactly a boy I knew. None of my characters are anything but amalgams of other people. But—when my husband and I had been married for two years—long, long ago—I became pregnant. We were quite excited, and made plans to raise the baby in England with summer visits here, to Blue Lake, where his (or her) father would teach him to fish and sail. We had many happy times, imagining it."

I couldn't look at her. I had read every biography of Camilla ever written, and I knew that she had no children.

"In the fifth month, I developed complications. I ended up in the hospital, and we were eventually told that our child was not meant to be—that no child was meant to be."

"I'm so sorry," I said.

She picked up a crumb with one finger, then brushed it back off again. "It was a boy—my lost child."

"Oh, Camilla."

"He stayed with me—the boy who might have been. He is my child, in many ways, and he appears in a variety of books, at different ages. In *The Lost Child*, he is Colin, aged nine. In *Twilight in Daventry*, he is Maximillian, aged sixteen."

"And in *Stars, Hide Your Fires*, he is Ian, aged six," I said.

"Yes. He is my boy in all his possible incarnations. In my books, I can give him life—the best life I can imagine for him."

"That's beautiful. Thank you for telling me, Camilla."

"I've never told anyone, as a matter of fact."

She must have seen my surprise, because she gave a Gallic shrug and said, "No one ever asked."

I nodded, suddenly speechless. I tried to picture Camilla when she was twenty-something and awaiting a child with her husband. She had been quite young when she published her first book—only twenty-four. How old had she been when she became pregnant?

Camilla yawned. "I've enjoyed our culinary tryst, but I must get back to bed. Please eat all that you want, and then just pop the plate back in the refrigerator. We can let Rhonda snack on her own creations tomorrow."

"Of course."

I watched her walk out of the room and heard her slow tread on the stairs. I stared at the brightly colored cupcakes on the plate and wondered about Camilla's lost child. If he had been born, would she ever have written all those wonderful books?

Her life, to me, had been a study in glamour—from London editorial offices to European book tours to speeches before screaming fans—and yet I was sure she would give it up in a second for a chance to go back, to somehow save her boy.

For a moment, the idea of loss overwhelmed me: Camilla and her lost child; Sam West and his lost spouse; Martin Jonas and his lost life.

With a sigh I wrapped up the remaining food and put it back in the fridge. I looked back out at the glimmering lake, so mysterious and cruel in its relationship to nature and fate.

Lestrade wandered into the kitchen, his night eyes glowing. He blinked at me in the dark, clearly surprised to see a human up at this hour.

"You're the one who woke me up, remember?"

He licked his paw. I scooped him up and walked up the staircase. "Sometimes life is funny, Lestrade. And sometimes it is terribly unfair," I whispered in his ear.

By the time I climbed back into bed, Lestrade was purring and half asleep. No cat had ever lain awake worrying over some external drama. I vowed to live my life in a more catlike manner.

It worked; I was asleep in minutes, and the next morning I woke refreshed.

10

How quickly the sweet can turn bitter, Johanna mused as she read the note Frau Albrecht had given her with a pitying expression. Perhaps she had always known that disappointment awaited her, from the moment she stepped off the train and into her new life.

—from *The Salzburg Train*

I GOT TO Sam West's place at nine o'clock and was surprised to find he was not smoking at the end of his property. I walked farther, realizing that I had never even seen the entrance to his house. The driveway curved, and around the bend I beheld a grand brick and stone structure—not a Gothic-looking home, but a modern, Wright-inspired building that seemed at one with the bluff. The landscaping was minimal but meticulous; I wondered if West had done it himself. That was one way to fritter away the hours while one avoided humanity. I remembered him quoting Sartre to me on the day I met him: "Hell is other people."

I reached the large wooden entrance door and rang the bell embedded in the brick on the right-hand side. West's voice came over an invisible intercom: "Come on in, Lena—it's open."

It was. I stepped into a hall with rust-colored tiles and

sandstone walls. It was refined and masculine; I'm not sure what I had expected to see in Sam West's house—perhaps an empty building with an open suitcase and minimal furniture?—but what I found was a well-appointed home with sophisticated décor. The painting above his hallway table looked expensive, and if I knew anything about art (which I didn't, really), I would have guessed it was an original Remington—a Native American with an elaborate tribal headdress sitting proudly on a beautiful palomino.

"Hello?" Sam called.

"Hello. Where are you?"

"End of the hall. Turn right. That's the kitchen."

I followed these directions and turned into a big, bright space dominated by floor-to-ceiling windows that looked out onto the forested bluff. "Wow," I said.

"Great view, right? I do a lot of philosophizing in here. Look what I have for you."

I turned to his kitchen—surprisingly cozy, considering its size—and saw that he had set a plate of waffles on his antique wood dining table, and that he was making more with a homemade waffle press.

"You made me waffles," I said in disbelief.

"You clearly loved them. I also ordered a vat of butter," he joked with a crooked smile. In the bright light of his kitchen, his eyes were impossibly blue.

"I am overwhelmed. This is lovely. Are those fresh flowers?"

"I confess, they are from the florist on Main Street. I picked them up the other day for a little color."

"This place is stunning. I had no idea. And yet you don't entertain—?"

"Not to speak of. Camilla has been over for the occasional lunch, as have a couple of other select people I do not despise. Sit down. Take off your coat," he said, pulling out a chair for me. "Coffee?"

"Yes, please." I looked around me, feeling dazed, at the scrubbed white walls, the gleaming silver appliances, and the custom-made backsplash of blue tile, on which was painted something that looked familiar.

"Is that—da Vinci?" I asked.

"Good eye. It's a reproduction of one of his drawings—he sketched it for ten years, honing the image until he was finally ready to sculpt it. This one is called *The Rearing Horse and Mounted Warrior.* I've always admired it."

"So naturally you had an artist re-create it as a backsplash in your kitchen," I joked.

"Naturally." He grinned. "Listen, I'm afraid these first few waffles came out sort of—crispy. I'm sure there's a secret to it, but I'm still getting the hang of it. I'll do it until I succeed, if I have to pile waffles to the ceiling."

"It smells amazing in here. This is so nice of you, Sam."

He walked toward me, holding a serving plate; his natural gait looked deceptively lazy, just as his jeans and V-neck sweater could almost fool someone into thinking that they weren't expensive. My eyes lingered for a moment on his jeans, his sweater, and the curling brown chest hair visible at the edges of his collar. He reached the table and leaned over me, setting down a plate. His scent was clean and masculine and inexplicably erotic. "There you go. Give them a try."

"I should be all polite and wait until you sit down," I said. I was already putting two waffles on my plate and reaching for the butter. He had a bowl of pecans sitting there, too—something else to sprinkle on an already indulgent feast. I thought with guilt of my cupcake snack with Camilla. Would this town make me fat in a matter of weeks?

"I would be disappointed if you didn't eat them while they were hot."

He stood for a moment, watching me. I glanced at him briefly and noted that his hair was still slightly damp where it curled against his ear. Then I returned my attention to my food. I forked off a huge bite and shoved it into my mouth. "Mmmm," I said, smiling at him with syrup-coated lips.

He grinned. "Let me get your coffee."

"You didn't smoke today, did you?"

His expression was both surprised and distracted. "Uh—no. I was busy."

He brought coffee for me and for him, then another plate of waffles. "It's delicious, Sam. Thank you again."

"You're very welcome. It's only fun to cook for people who enjoy eating."

"I'd be embarrassed by that if there were any point in it." I was still savoring the flavor of the food in my mouth. There was something special about these waffles—they had a vanilla aftertaste and some other flavor I couldn't name—and they had been specially made just for me. "I might have to eat an unusually large number of waffles just to be polite."

He laughed, sipped his coffee, and put some food on his own plate. Then he pointed to his windowsill, where I saw the manila envelope that contained my contract. "I looked that over," he said. "I suppose you know that Camilla has been very generous."

"I had that idea. But she suggested that I have someone look it over for me, because she wanted me to be sure."

"You can be. She's even put in some extra codicils for your protection. First, you can back out at any time if you feel that the arrangement is not beneficial to your career. She defines that more clearly in the part I marked with a yellow tab. Second, you have opportunities for salary raises every six months, assuming you meet certain criteria. Those are marked with the red tab. She's put a lot of thought into this. The pay seems fair—"

"It's more than fair."

"And she allows a great deal of latitude regarding your hours and your workload."

"She's amazing. And so is this waffle. This is like a fantasy town where all my dreams come true. It's like Brigadoon."

His face closed for a moment, and I set down my fork. "I'm sorry. I know it hasn't been that for you. I've been thinking about it a lot—how horrible it must have been to have them turn on you that way, when they clearly don't know what they're talking about. They don't know a thing about you!" I said indignantly.

He studied his fork, smiling slightly. "Neither do you. Why would you defend me?"

"Because you're a nice man. You told me you have no idea what happened to your wife, and I believe you. I have good instincts about people."

He poked at his food without actually taking a bite. "I assume you've been warned away from me."

"Don't be silly," I said.

"You're a bad liar. Lena, it means a lot to me that you would take my side."

I picked up my fork again, stealing a glance at him, focusing on his eyes, then lowering my gaze to his sweater.

It was a cerulean color and seemed to be cashmere; it would be outrageously soft to the touch . . . "Can I ask you a question?"

"Of course." He sipped his coffee.

"Your wife—I don't see how she could just disappear without them being able to trace her. I mean, are you thinking she ran away?"

He shrugged. "I suppose I hope so. I hate to think she was the victim of foul play. We were—estranged at the time she disappeared, which of course makes me look fishy to the police—but I didn't wish any harm to Victoria." He sighed and stared into his coffee cup. "Still, after a year, it's hard to imagine a scenario in which she runs away, yet doesn't use her credit cards, or call friends or family."

"What about her phone? Can't they trace that?"

"The police have the phone. She left it behind. She hadn't used it for quite some time."

"Oh. Wow. But—I mean—you hear stories about people who get new identities and things. I don't want to sound foolish, but is there any chance that she—planned to run away?"

He leaned back, his face solemn. There were deep laugh lines next to his mouth and tiny creases next to his eyes, so deep that one could touch them with a gentle finger and sense the struggles of the man beneath the skin. "She was the kind who ran away—from problems, from fights, from confrontations. She would tell me, when we were at odds, that someday she was just going to sail away. Or fly away. Or run away. She had a variety of metaphors, but they were all graceful images of retreat. She wasn't much of a stay-and-deal-with-it type of woman."

This made me sad for Sam, but also for Victoria, who sounded troubled. "She was unhappy?"

Sam sighed. "Not exactly. But she was selfish, and that can lead to discontent. There's no doubt Vic was self-centered. It's one of many reasons we were splitting up. She was all about herself. She had ruined her company—she had her own fashion line—and had declared bankruptcy a few months before she disappeared. And she was dabbling in drugs. Pot, at first, but I thought she was getting into harder stuff. We were so different, with opposing stances on almost everything, and one day we looked at each other and couldn't even imagine why we were together—God, I'm talking too much. And I don't think I even answered your question."

On the contrary, he was supplying me with information I'd been craving since I'd met him. "Could there have been another man?"

He sighed. "It's funny you would say that. I tried to argue that a year ago. I told them that she had been texting constantly a week or two before she disappeared, on a phone I had never seen before—a red phone. When I asked where she got it she just shrugged, said a friend had lent it to her so she could decide if she wanted to buy one for herself. That seemed plausible enough."

"Sure. Did the police try to trace this phone?"

"They can't—we don't know who gave it to her. And frankly, I'm not sure if they believed me. Remember Harrison Ford in *The Fugitive*, telling everyone about the one-armed man? No one thought there was really a one-armed man. He had to prove it to them." His jaw tightened, and he looked out at the beautiful bluff.

"Wow."

He sighed. "Anyway, I asked her what her latest obsession was—she had an obsessive personality, and she would go through things, hobbies, people—in waves. She'd be fascinated for a certain time, and then eventually she was done. That was the pattern of our marriage, as well. We fascinated each other, at the beginning."

I leaned forward. "So it was probably a *man*, Sam! Who else would give her a phone when she already had one? He wanted her to have something private, something you couldn't check, because she was having an affair!"

He shrugged. "Why would she bother? We were all but divorced. She could have started a relationship with anyone she wanted. We were only still living together so that we could sort through our possessions. How pathetic does that sound?"

"It doesn't. You're not the first person to get divorced. Were there—any children?"

"No. I'm glad of that now."

I swirled a bite of waffle in some syrup; I had lost interest in eating, though. "It still sounds like there was a man."

"Maybe. But even if she ran away with someone—I can't believe that Vic, despite her selfishness, would let me take the rap for all this. She wasn't an evil person. There—you hear that? I'm talking about her in the past tense. The cops picked up on that, too, and then they made their decisions about me."

"Oh, Sam."

He said nothing. He ate his food and looked out the grand windows.

I thought about what he had told me. "If she had the red phone with her, she would have been able to call or text you, right?"

"Yes. But there's nothing. The phone is either off or

destroyed. It's never registered once since she left, so we can't trace the account. It's a dead end. It drives me crazy thinking about it, since that phone probably has all the information we need. As does Vic, if she's still out there."

His face looked briefly tormented before he resumed his normal closed expression. I realized suddenly why he had probably spent so much time renovating this house. He kept busy so that his thoughts wouldn't consume him.

"What about the friends you spoke of? Did you talk to them?"

He nodded tersely. "She had lots of acquaintances, and one best friend named Taylor Brand. She's in fashion, too, and has some annoying blog that I never read. Vic and Taylor spent lots of time together, so I tried to get information out of Taylor after Vic vanished. Taylor blamed me; she said that I was cold, and that Vic had met someone who was good for her, someone passionate and devoted. I tried to get a name out of her, and she admitted she didn't have one. She said Vic had told her it was brand-new, and she was keeping it to herself for a while, but that she loved how jealous this new man was."

"Jealous?"

He nodded, his face regretful. "Vic was one of those women who needed a lot of validation. She would try to make me jealous a lot, early in our marriage, and I just—didn't respond to it. It disappointed her, but I didn't want to live out some reality-TV-type drama in my own life."

"But this new man was jealous! There's a motive right there."

"I told the police. They spoke with Taylor and said they were satisfied that she knew nothing concrete."

"There has to be something," I said. "What about the man you hired?"

"He's working hard. I give him credit for that. There's just nothing to go on. All I could give him was one thing—one word I had seen on her new phone: 'Nikon.'"

"Nikon? Did she have a camera or something?"

He shook his head. "No. She took all her pictures on her phone. And it wasn't so much the word as the way she reacted when I saw it. Like I had stumbled on some big secret."

"What did she say about it at the time?"

"It's just a word I saw over her shoulder when she was texting. She turned off the phone and said it was nothing, that I should mind my own business."

"So she was protecting some kind of information. Could someone have taken—I don't know—incriminating pictures or something?"

"God only knows. I didn't want to keep asking her about it; I figured if she wanted to keep secrets, that was her business. To be brutally honest, Lena, at that point I just didn't care what she did. I had no idea how important it would be. The things we know in retrospect . . ."

We sat for a moment in the bright and fragrant kitchen, thinking our thoughts.

Finally I said, "She was very beautiful, wasn't she? Your wife. Could someone—predatory—have lured her into a relationship? That sort of thing happens every day, and not just to unsuspecting teens."

He nodded. "I tried to get the police to explore that idea. They seemed to think that I was trying to create a red herring. And without her phone, there was nothing for them to pursue. I think it's just easier to suspect that I killed her. It explains her disappearance and gives everyone a scapegoat."

"It's a terrible situation. I'm sorry you've had to go through this alone. Don't you have family, friends who have stood by you?"

He cleared his throat and looked at his watch. "We should stop talking about this. You came by for a little advice, and I burdened you with my problems."

"You didn't burden me; I asked. And they are significant problems. I want to help you."

He studied me for a moment with his compelling eyes. "Lena," he said softly, leaning in to touch my hand. His doorbell rang. He got up and went to his refrigerator; from this angle I could see a small box to the left of the fridge that seemed to be a security camera. "Oh, shit," he said. Then he pressed a button. "Come on in—it's open."

Seeing the question on my face, he said, "It's the cops. Maybe they don't like the fact that you're in here. Maybe they fear for your life."

"Don't be ridiculous," I said.

A moment later Doug Heller and a woman in a brown pantsuit were standing in the kitchen. Doug Heller's face was about as friendly as a wood plank. His voice was almost as hoarse as it had been the evening before. "Mr. West."

Sam nodded. "What can I do for you, Detective Heller?"

Doug sighed. "The fact is, I'm doing something for *you*. I don't have to be here, I want you to know that." He shot a look at me that said he was surprised and a bit wounded to find me at West's table. "I'm here to suggest that you might want to get on the horn with your lawyer. Let him know that I'm waiting on a warrant for your arrest, at which point I will be fielding an extradition request from New York. I don't know exactly when this is going to happen, but it will be soon. I am telling you because I know you won't run, and because I thought you might want time to—get your affairs in order."

I felt Sam's tension from across the table. "What's happened? Did you find Victoria? Is she dead?"

Doug Heller's gaze flicked to me, then to West. "Police have located a significant amount of blood at your New York apartment."

"Blood?" Sam asked.

"This is ridiculous!" I shouted. "He hasn't been there, he's been here! If there's blood, it must be new, right? Didn't she disappear more than a year ago?"

Doug Heller looked at the tips of his boots. The woman with him said, "Mr. West has recently visited New York."

I looked at Sam, who nodded. "On business. About three weeks ago."

"Come on, Doug!" I said. "Have you ever really listened to the details? She's not dead! This blood has appeared very conveniently, hasn't it? Can't you see what's happening here? Someone is framing him!"

No one said a word, but Sam West looked at me as though he had never seen me before.

Heller said, "Mr. West? What do you want to do? Officer Dillon here is ready to accompany you to New York if you'd like to go before the warrant comes down."

"This is crazy! He's had just about enough of this!" I yelled, and grabbed some pecans from the bowl, which I hurled at Doug Heller and his partner. The nuts bounced off their jackets and landed on West's polished wood floor. Both cops stared down at them, their eyebrows raised.

"Call your lawyer, Sam," I said bitterly. "See what he advises. See if this is even legal."

West pulled out a phone. "That does seem to be the next step. Excuse me for a moment," he said, and went into the hallway.

"What are you doing here, Lena?" Doug Heller rasped, his face grim.

I shook my head. "I had some business with *Mr. West*. Don't give me that disappointed look. I'm disappointed in *you*, Doug. You're a cop. You should care about the truth. And so should you!" I said to the woman, who was still studying me with her mouth open.

"Lena, I told you—you haven't got the whole story," Heller said under his breath. He ran some fingers through his hair and then settled both hands on his hips.

"Neither have you. What have you found out about all the texting Mrs. West was doing on the red phone before she went missing? What have you found out about the word 'Nikon' that Sam saw on her phone when she was texting some mysterious person?"

Heller looked on the verge of saying something, then sighed. He exchanged a glance with his partner, which, from my point of view, seemed to say, "Don't acknowledge her—she's insane. She threw nuts at us."

Sam West walked back into the room. I couldn't look at him; I stared at the table, with its bright flowers and the breakfast that had been ruined.

"Give me a moment to pack a bag, and I'll meet you at the door," West said. "My lawyer will be waiting at the airport. I appreciate the heads-up. It will be better to go there on my own steam than to be hauled in like a criminal, so thanks. And thank you for being my advocate, Lena."

He moved toward me and pressed a key into my hand. "Would you look after the place for me? I just have a few plants by the window there that need watering, and if you could take in the mail, I'd appreciate it." He turned and left the room; we heard him jogging up the stairs.

I had no idea what was going through his mind. What was this fresh blood, this sudden evidence? Why would there be blood now, almost a year after his wife's disappearance, and why would they assume he had anything to do with it when he had made a new home in Blue Lake?

He had been back to New York, they said—but why did that matter? He was a businessman. He had to do his business, didn't he?

I was still bristling, clutching West's key. "How can they dare to demand that he go all the way to New York when this blood could belong to any person or animal? How can they possibly arrest him on such limited evidence?" I asked. I could feel the belligerence of my own face and my weirdly thrusting jaw. I felt a terrible urge to cry.

Heller spoke to me in a gentle voice, as one would to a child. "Lena, it's his wife's blood. They've had it tested. And it was in his apartment—the one he still owns in New York and stays in when he goes back there. The one they once shared."

I felt this news viscerally, with a sudden pain in my stomach. "I—it—who had the right to go into his apartment?"

The two detectives exchanged a glance. "The blood was near the door; it had begun seeping under the frame into the hallway. A neighbor saw it and called the police. It doesn't look good for him, Lena."

My mouth opened and shut again.

All I could see, for an instant, was blood—enough blood

to seep across floorboards and underneath a door. But what had been the origin of that blood? "A body," I said. "They must have found a body?"

"No—just the blood. But it's hers, and it's fresh. Which means that until recently, Victoria West was alive."

"Maybe she still is. Maybe she snuck into her old apart ment and somehow hurt herself. They should be checking the hospitals. They should be looking into all the reasons why blood would appear without a body, and why it would appear now, when things have finally died down." A thought occurred to me for an instant, but then flitted away. It had seemed important . . .

"They are looking into it. The first and best way is to interview her estranged husband, who just so happened to be in town recently. The prosecutor thinks it's enough to arrest him for, but he needs a judge to agree and to issue a warrant. I'm sticking my neck out telling him this much."

Something just didn't add up. Why didn't Doug Heller see that? Why was he looking at me with that infuriating pity in his eyes?

Sam West appeared, a travel bag slung over his shoulder. His face was carefully expressionless. I could only imagine what he was feeling. He said, "It's okay, Lena. I'll see you soon, I hope."

"Sam—we'll figure this out. Your lawyer will talk sense into them. They cannot arrest you for this!" My voice cracked on the last word, but I doubt anyone noticed, because they were already moving out the door.

He was escorted to a car by the Blue Lake Police, and I didn't say another word to him. I stood in his silent house, unable to think. With stiff fingers I picked up our breakfast dishes and washed them at West's elegant sink. I wiped my hands on a towel that hung nearby, then scanned the room and saw the nuts I had thrown on the floor, still lying there as reminders of the tiny scene I had caused. I bent to pick them up, crossed the room, and tossed them in a little black wastebasket that sat next to the counter. The garbage was empty except for a receipt I recognized—it said "BICK'S" in large blue lettering at the top. Without thinking, I picked it up and studied it. It was dated for the previous evening at six thirty-two P.M., when West had purchased only one item, listed as "Oster Waff Mk."

A waffle maker. After agreeing to look at Camilla's contract for me, Sam West had gone to Bick's Hardware and bought a waffle maker so that he could make me a special meal.

I stared at the receipt for a moment, then folded it carefully and put it in my pocket. I checked Sam's plants and did a quick scan of his house, then left and locked the door behind me.

11

Johanna hesitated to show the letter to Loli, the girl who had been such a friend to her, and in that instant, as Loli leaned forward, her blue eyes wide and curious, her fingers reaching for the paper, Johanna realized she didn't trust the other girl, and never really had. She slipped the letter into her pocket and made an excuse, and she did not miss the bitter expression on Loli's face.

—from *The Salzburg Train*

I BARELY HAD time to tell Camilla what happened before she had to leave for her doctor appointment. Her face was grim, though, when I told her about the new evidence that had been found in New York. "Blood?" she said, and then she grew quiet, occasionally shaking her head in disbelief. Her response satisfied me in a way that Doug Heller's had not.

Rhonda was at work in the kitchen, already making lunch for me and my eventual guest. I couldn't imagine eating or being a gracious host, and yet Lane Waldrop was going to show up regardless of my feelings. With a sigh I climbed the stairs to my room. I washed my face and combed my hair in the little bathroom, then went to my desk. Lestrade wasn't in the room; I assumed he had taken the morning to explore Camilla's house, which he had started to do on a regular basis.

I took Sam West's receipt out of my pocket and set it in the top drawer of the desk. Then I pulled out my laptop and tried to concentrate on Camilla's book and the scene she had asked me to reimagine. I had a good start, but even my scene needed some ramped-up suspense. I felt restless and certain that I couldn't concentrate, and then suddenly I realized I had written a great deal and that almost an hour had gone by.

Back down the stairs I went, straight to the kitchen, where I asked Rhonda if she needed my help. "Oh, I think just about everything is ready to go," she said. "Just go see if you think the table needs anything more. I pulled a few of those gorgeous roses out and put them in a smaller vase—it would be crazy to put them all out for your little lunch, right?"

I agreed with her. I went into the little dining room, where she had spread a white cloth and selected roses in two shades of yellow, then tucked them into an emerald vase at the center of the table. "This is beautiful, Rhonda!" I called.

She came in with a tray of canapés and set it down. "Thanks. It's refreshing to do some entertaining. It's been just Camilla for so long, and all of a sudden I have a dinner guest and a lunch guest. It's fun! I think you bring out a more social side of her."

"That's nice," I said absently.

She stopped halfway back into the kitchen and said, "I heard you two maybe had a visitor last night."

"What? Oh, yes. That seems like a long time ago."

"I hope the cops are on it. It's not a happy thought, that

someone is targeting an older woman who—for all they know—lives by herself."

I had not thought of this. No one in town knew that I was living with Camilla—just a handful of people, really. Allison, Doug Heller, Sam West, the people who worked for Camilla. And yet there had been those people in the diner who had seen me sharing a table with Sam West. He had assured me that I'd be the talk of the town. But what if I wasn't? What if, as far as any miscreant knew, Camilla was just an elderly writer who lived at the top of the hill? Might she be a target for hooligans? If so, why?

"Anyway, I've got a nice cold lunch laid out for you here, and a little dessert in the fridge. I have to leave early because my son has a doctor appointment. You'll be okay, right?"

"Of course. Thank you so much."

Rhonda shrugged. "No big deal. Like I said the other day, this is a great gig." She disappeared into the kitchen, then came out with her purse. "Just keep things locked up, okay? I don't like leaving you here alone, but—"

"I'll be here with two large German shepherds," I said, laughing. "And multiple telephones if I need to call the police." Although Doug Heller might be on the way to the airport—or would he let "Officer Dillon" do that alone? She seemed appropriately capable and even a bit mean. Would she go all the way to New York, or just make sure Sam West got on the plane? If she went, would Heller go, too? He certainly couldn't risk letting West get away, not after he broke protocol by telling him of the imminent arrest. Why had he done that, anyway?

"Well, good. We can't forget that a murder occurred here, way too close for my liking," Rhonda said.

This gave me a chill. For a while there, Blue Lake had seemed idyllic; now it seemed that every part of the town was tainted, and every person somehow cursed.

"Are you okay?" Rhonda asked, looking concerned.

"I'm fine. It's been—a weird couple of days."

"No joke. But when things get back to normal, you'll love it here. I promise." She gave me a maternal pat on the arm and a reassuring smile, then moved swiftly to the front door. "Have a nice lunch," she said and opened the door. Lane Waldrop stood on the other side, wearing a pair of brown wool pants and a cream-colored cowl-neck sweater with a long necklace of little pearls dotted with rhinestones. I was wearing the blue jeans and brown turtleneck that I had worn to Sam West's house.

"You look nice," I said. "I'm afraid I'm underdressed."

Lane laughed. "No you're not—I'm overdressed. But I'm so excited to be away from my kids, I can't even tell you. And I never get to wear nice clothes because of baby puke and stuff, so I figured hey, I'm going somewhere nice, I'm going to dress nice."

"Well, you look great. Rhonda made us lunch."

"Don't I get a tour?" Lane asked, her eyes on the stairs.

Her eagerness was surprising. What was it about this old "monstrosity," as Camilla called it, that fascinated people so much? Adam had wanted a tour, too, Camilla said.

"Well—I don't actually know the place that well. And I don't know if Camilla wants us upstairs. I can show you the rooms down here." I led her to the study, with its crackling fire, and the living room to the right of the main door, and then the kitchen and the dining room, with the breathtaking view of the bluff.

If she was disappointed not to see the rest, she hid it well. "This place is great," she said, gazing at a framed photo that sat on Camilla's hallway table. "It's got great bones."

"Yes—I'm not sure how old it is. I'll have to ask Camilla. The house came to her through her husband's family."

"That's cool." Her eyes were still wandering, soaking up the scenery.

"Would you like something to drink?"

Her gaze came back to me, and she smiled. "Oh, just a pop or something. What are you having?"

"That sounds good. Let me see what she has."

I dug two Diet Cokes out of Camilla's refrigerator, and we settled at the table and started munching on Rhonda's delicious little bites.

"Mmm! What's this?" Lane asked, biting into one and rolling her eyes with pleasure.

"I forget what Rhonda called it. Some sort of little cracker with mascarpone cheese and sprouts and something something."

"It's awesome. The best hors d'oeuvres I ever make are Ritz Crackers and Cheez Whiz."

"That's good, too. Rhonda seems to have a special gift for these fancy things."

"Obviously. Ooh—I have to try one of those little stuffed mushrooms. Yum. Clay would be so jealous."

"Clay—that's your husband? How did you two meet?"

She sat back and savored her food for a moment, then wiped her fingers on a napkin that Rhonda had set next to the plate. "He and I were high school sweethearts. Got married a year after we graduated."

"Wow. That's romantic."

"I suppose." She shrugged. "I love Clay, but I think my mom was right when she said we were marrying too young. You only see these things later—like when you're twenty-four and you already have two kids."

"They're great kids."

"Yeah. I can't complain. They're both healthy and beautiful, and Clay is beautiful, and we mostly get along great. So that's better than what most people have, right?" Her eyes were flicking around the dining room, noticing small details.

"I think it is better. And it doesn't matter what age you get married as long as you have a good relationship, right?"

"I like to think so. There really couldn't ever be anyone for me but Clayton. That's just how it is."

"Is he a good dad?"

"Oh, yeah. He does all sorts of stuff with the kids. Lets them ride on his tractor when he's mowing our yard, and takes them to the lake with their little life preservers on. Little Tommy has this inflatable duck that he rides on—it's just hilarious."

I munched on another cheese canapé, then sat back in my chair. "So you two went to Blue Lake High School?"

"Yup."

"Did you go there with Martin Jonas?"

Her eyes widened. "That's funny that you would know that. Yeah—Marty was a year ahead of us. Clay knew him because they took wood shop together. And I knew him because I was always with Clay, and Marty and he hung out together. I think Marty had a thing for me at one time."

"I wouldn't be surprised."

Her face was blank. "What do you mean?"

"You're a pretty girl. I'm sure lots of guys at your school had crushes on you."

She blushed slightly and shrugged, barely concealing a pleased smile. "I suppose. But they couldn't get anywhere near me. Clay's always been sort of possessive."

"So Clay must be upset—about Martin's death."

"He is. Although he and Marty didn't see each other much after high school. I wasn't interested in having my husband going out every night with those idiots, hangin' at the bowling alley and tellin' their tall tales and gettin' drunk."

"Does he have any suspicions about—what might have happened?"

She shook her head. "I don't think so. He was so shocked when he read Marty's name in the paper, you could have knocked him down by blowin' on him." She studied me for a moment, and her gaze moved to my left hand. "You're not married?"

"No."

"How come?" she asked. Somehow the question wasn't rude the way she asked it—it was rather flattering because her tone suggested it was impossible that the men of the world would have let me get away.

"I don't know. There was someone serious, but that ended almost a year ago."

"Yeah? What was he like?" Her naked curiosity was a surprise, and perhaps a refreshing change—but I imagined it would get old fairly quickly.

"He was two years older than I am. Dark hair, dark eyes. Handsome. Kind of brooding and aloof. And he was distracted, all the time. He was always absorbed in his job."

"Huh. What was he, a lawyer or doctor or something?"

"He's a botanist. He works as a researcher."

"A botanist. So that's—like—some kind of scientist?"

"A plant biologist, yes."

"Oh." She looked disappointed. "So how did it end?"

I shrugged. "One day I realized that I wouldn't ever be as important to him as I wanted to be. Or if I was, that he would never be able to show me. He didn't—express emotion very well."

"Wow, what a jerk. Clay is always grabbing me in these big bear hugs that go on forever. I couldn't live without those."

Now it was probably my face that looked envious, and the surge of jealousy that ran through me at her words was another surprise. Hadn't I just told Camilla that I wasn't interested in romance, and that I was happy just where I was? And yet the thought of a relationship in which one could find joy and security in a daily, heartfelt embrace—that sounded good to me.

"He sounds very devoted," I said. "Let me get our lunch." I stood up, taking the empty canapé tray with me. I claimed a new tray from the refrigerator, which held a graceful assortment of tea sandwiches that Rhonda had marked with tiny cards—cucumber and cream cheese; ham, brie, and apple; mortadella and watercress.

I brought it back to the table, along with a pre-labeled salad Rhonda had prepared, and listened to Lane's predictable oohs and aahs. She helped herself to some salad and said, "You know, my granddad was in this house a few times. He was a mechanic, back in the day, and I guess Mr. Graham's family hired him now and then to fix things. He knew how to fix everything. And at one time or another he was probably in every house in this town, just about."

"What a wonderful skill to have."

"Yeah." Her green eyes widened with a kind of excitement. "You know what he told me about this place? He said, 'That house has a secret, Laney! Graham House has a secret!'"

"What secret?"

She leaned forward. "He always told me he'd tell me one day. It was his little joke, to keep us in suspense. But he died, and he never did tell me." Her face was a mixture of sadness and resentment.

"Maybe he just meant it metaphorically. You know, like 'If houses could talk,' that sort of thing. Camilla is sort of mysterious."

Lane shook her head, impatient with me. "No. It was a secret that he learned as a workman here. A secret about the house itself. Don't you know what it is?"

I leaned away from the table, realizing with a jolt that Lane Waldrop hadn't been looking for a new friend—just for a way to satisfy a lifelong curiosity. "I'm afraid I don't," I said. I heard the coldness of my own voice, and suddenly I thought of Kurt. He had specialized in cold.

"Oh, don't get all mad at me, now. You can't blame a girl for being curious. Clay said I should have been a cat, because then I'd have eight backup lives when my long nose sticks into stuff that ends up being dangerous." She made a silly face.

I softened slightly. "You don't have a long nose."

"He just means, you know. Nosy. I am nosy—always have been."

"Well, it's good to know your weaknesses," I said with a tiny smile.

"I like you, Lena. I wish I had known you in high school.

We would have been best buds." She popped a whole sandwich into her mouth and chewed it, rolling her eyes and patting her stomach so theatrically that I laughed out loud.

"You're right, we would have, because you remind me a lot of the girl who was my best friend in high school. Her name is Allison; I'll have to introduce you sometime."

"That would be cool."

"Meanwhile, if this house ever reveals its secret to me, you'll be the first to know."

"Okay." She grinned. There was a little piece of cucumber in her teeth. Then her smile disappeared. "Man, you know who would have loved this? Marty. I told him about the Graham House secret a long time ago. This one night we were just sittin' and drinkin' and actin' big. Talkin' about what we'd be someday."

"What did you want to be?"

"A singer in a band, like half the kids at my high school. Or a movie star or something."

"And Marty?"

"He just wanted to be rich. His family always kind of struggled. It was sort of sad. He just always told me what he'd do for his mom and dad if he had money, and how he'd buy a huge house and a million cars and start investing in crazy stuff like travel to the moon."

"Not that crazy anymore," I said.

"I guess not. Poor Marty." Her face was genuinely sad, and she was subdued for the remainder of our little lunch. An hour later she stood up and said, "Let me help you clean this up. I only have a sitter for another half hour, so I'm going to have to go. Cinderella turning back into a pumpkin."

I laughed. "This isn't exactly a palace, Lane."

We walked into the kitchen and she set some plates on the counter. "No. It's just away. Sometimes away is as good as a palace, if you know what I mean."

I did know. "We'll get together again soon. Maybe we can see a movie some night when your husband can watch the babies."

She brightened. "That would be fun! Clay and I don't really do movies anymore. Not since you can get every darn thing on TV and the computer. We just sit in our house."

"It's a date, then. Text me the nights you're free, okay?"

"Okay. Thanks so much for having me over, Lena." She lunged forward and gave me a big hug—the kind she said her husband gave to her. "It's nice to have a new friend."

I walked her to the door and waved as she headed to her red Ford. "Drive carefully," I called.

I shut the door and realized that, for the first time, I was in Graham House alone. The dogs came snuffling over, and I let them out into the yard; they returned to the porch a couple of minutes later, and I let them in. A house with a secret, Lane had said. What could her grandpa have meant?

I shrugged at the dogs. "Not my problem. You know what? I have work to do." I finished cleaning up in the kitchen and went to my room.

I returned to the beautiful desk and spent some time investigating all of its drawers and cubbies. There was nothing so exquisite as a fine piece of furniture. With a pleased sigh, I opened my laptop. It was time to do some more work on the chapter in the Black Forest. I reread what I had, then started making changes here and there. I deleted the last four paragraphs and started something new. My conversation with Lane had given me an idea, and it would change the structure of the chapter entirely. Johanna Garamond was in the car with the man she loved, driving through the Black Forest. But the chase was not enough tension—there needed to be tension inside the car, between the two of them. This would layer the suspense and make the reader wonder which was the bigger danger—that they would be caught and confronted by the man behind them, or that the fragile love between them might be destroyed.

"Yes," I said, just as Lestrade came strolling up to see what I was doing. I barely noticed him as my fingers moved over the keys. I saw only the two people in a car, its headlights cutting the gloom of twilight in the forest, trees towering over them like sentries, arching above and linking their branches as though to prevent escape even through the sky. The woods were beautiful, yet sinister, and the road curled infinitely ahead, offering no relief . . .

By the time I had finished, it was dark outside and I could hear vague noises downstairs that indicated people were back in the house. I reread what I had written; it was good, and I was excited, this time, to show what I had to Camilla.

I got up and stretched, and suddenly questions I had been keeping at bay bombarded me. Where was Sam West and what was happening? Had Doug Heller thought about what I had told him? Did he truly believe Sam was guilty of killing his wife? Did Heller have total laryngitis now, after talking with that sore throat? Was Sam's lawyer going to sort this out and make them realize it was all a mistake? Was he going to find out what was really going on, so that Sam could come home where he belonged? Did Sam have people to talk to, people who would support him, in New York?

Of course he did. It was only in Blue Lake that he was a pariah, surely? New York should be full of family and friends who were in his corner. I remembered the way he had cleared his throat and changed the subject when I had asked about family, and it made me sad.

On a sudden whim, I took out my phone. I had called him at home the previous day; if it had been his cell phone, and not a landline, then I could text him, as well. I found his number and texted a message: *Are you okay? Let me know if you need any moral support.*

I couldn't think of anything else to say, so I clicked "Send."

I grabbed my laptop and headed down the stairs, seeking Camilla. I found her in the kitchen, drinking a glass of water and looking out the window. "Hello," I said.

She turned. "Hello, dear. How was your luncheon?"

"Oh—fine. I think Lane is a little bit starved for adult companionship. And a little bit in love with this house. It seems to represent prestige for her."

Camilla sniffed.

"How was your doctor appointment?" The question had been on my mind, because I feared that Camilla was sick and not telling me, and that our new arrangement would somehow be ruined.

"I'm fit as can be. Apparently I have good genes. Both of my parents have longevity. My father died at age ninety-four, and my mother, if you can believe it, is still alive."

"Is she? Where does she live?"

She set down her water glass; her expression grew fond. "In England. She's ninety-one and still on her own; she has a cottage by a lake and some very caring neighbors. I Skype with her. And I see her twice a year."

"She must be proud of you."

"She is. She's proud of all three of her daughters."

"Oh—you have sisters! I read that once, in one of your interviews. I think I know their names: Philippa and—don't tell me—Sybil."

Camilla's brows rose to her hairline. "My goodness. You have done your homework."

"I have. Camilla, I have two things to tell you."

"Yes?"

"One: I'm craving one of those cupcakes. And two: I'm ready to show you what I've written—whenever you have a chance."

Her face brightened. "Let's combine those into an impromptu meeting. You get the cupcakes, and hand me that laptop. Where will I find it?"

"It's the document already open—just click the Word icon."

She sat down at the kitchen table, opened my chapter, and began to read. I busied myself with the cupcake plate—there were two left—and concentrated on getting napkins and little forks so that I didn't scream with the tension caused by wondering what she would think.

Finally I set everything on the table and darted out of the room. I went into Camilla's study and did a couple of jumping jacks and ten push-ups, then ten crunches. Exercise alleviates tension, my father had always said. And he was right. My heart was beating faster, but I felt better, more ready to face whatever Camilla had to say.

I waited a few more minutes, then returned to the kitchen. Camilla had pushed my laptop aside and was daintily eating the sailboat cupcake with a fork. I sat down across from her.

"It's good," she said. "Very good. Very exciting, in fact—the idea of her telling him a secret, blossoming out the tension in an unexpected way—I like that. It will involve me going back, though, and planting the seeds of this revelation. We have to know all along that Johanna has a secret, so that when it comes out at this least appropriate of times, we will have known it was coming."

"Yes—that's the only dilemma."

"Not a dilemma at all! This is doable. I need to think on it, but I am grateful, Lena, because you've pinpointed the area that was a problem, and you've written us a way out of that problem."

Us, she said. *Us*. As in Camilla Graham and me, writing team.

"Now," she said, cutting off another piece of her cupcake. "I have another problem to run past you. It's the ending. Johanna and her Gerhard must flee the Black Forest. Initially I pictured them wandering through the mountains, finding the freedom to pursue their love. But that's a bit laborious, isn't it—time-intensive and uncertain. And too reminiscent of the ending of *The Sound of Music*."

I giggled.

"So I was thinking: what about another train? They're in the south, but they could take a night train—say from Freiburg to Hamburg—it would take what? Six, seven hours. Then they are right on the North Sea."

"The train would create powerful parallel structure—a train out of Austria at the beginning, a train out of the forestland at the end. But then what?"

"Somehow they would have to be smuggled out from there. Remember that Gerhard has family with money. He could have someone—that long-lost brother, maybe—make arrangements. I have to work that out."

For some reason, I thought of Sam West and his wife, who wanted to metaphorically sail away from her problems. Why not make that metaphor real? "They could sail away," I said.

"Sail?" She took off her glasses and leaned in to study my face. "Sail on a boat? What sort of boat—oh my goodness. Yes. A yacht, Lena!"

"Yes. If the brother has money, he might have one, right? Weren't yachts all the rage in the 1960s among the wealthy? Or am I just imagining that?"

"They sail away," she repeated dreamily. "Perhaps that's more evocative of the freedom I want them to feel, and the reader to feel, at the end."

"Oh, yes, Camilla! I agree. That would be wonderful! My only regret at the end is that we really don't see them get to the place that we know they're going. If we see them boarding a boat, we know they are free. And there can be so much imagery about the freshness of wind and sky and water. How beautiful!"

"Good. Then here is your next task—yacht research. This is happening in 1965, remember, and things were different then. Travel, and politics, and perceptions about wealth. But yachts? Yes, they were very much around."

"I love it. I'll start tonight."

She sat back, her face contented. "We make a good team, Lena London."

"We do, Camilla Graham."

"You haven't even touched your cupcake."

"That is the best evidence you'll ever have that your

novels are better than sugar to me," I said. "But I will eat it now."

AFTER I E-MAILED my new draft to Camilla, I put my laptop away upstairs; I planned to start my yacht research that very evening, and I was excited to have a specific plan. I would write up a sheet of facts for Camilla, and she could pick and choose from all the information (and images culled from the Web) that I could summon.

When I went back downstairs, I found Camilla marching toward her desk with a determined expression. "Camilla? Before you start on your new notes, I wanted to tell you two things I forgot to mention."

"Oh?"

"Yes—just something Lane Waldrop said. Her grandfather was apparently a very popular handyman in Blue Lake. She said he was in everyone's house, including this one, and he had told his grandchildren that this house had a secret. It was the suspense of her childhood, and he never got to tell her the secret because he died. Apparently he enjoyed holding the knowledge over them, if there was any knowledge at all."

Camilla pursed her lips. "It would have been unprofessional of him to reveal it. He had the sense to know that."

"You remember him?"

"Oh, yes. His name was Mr. Haney, and she's right—everyone used his services. He was very good, and charged reasonable prices."

"But—there was no secret?"

"Not exactly. What was the second thing?"

"What? Oh. She said that Martin Jonas knew there was a secret, too, and that he, like Lane, had always wanted to know what it was."

"My goodness. Well, now that we're the writing team of Graham and London, and now that you already know significant secrets of my life, why not share the so-called secret of my husband's manor house? Come here, my friend."

She walked to the back of her study and pointed to the window. "Go over there and take a look at the scenery."

"All right." I walked to the window and glanced out at the bluff and the blue line of lake. "What now?"

"There's a heating vent in the floor there at your feet. Do you see it?"

"Yes."

"On the right there's a little dial for opening and closing the vent."

"Yes."

"There's another dial on the left—about an inch away from the vent itself. Slightly larger. Yet you don't really notice it, do you? It blends in."

"Yes—it doesn't open the vent?"

"No."

I turned to look at Camilla, who smiled at me with twinkling eyes. "Go ahead and turn the dial," she said.

I squatted in front of the vent and rolled the dial mechanism toward me until I heard a loud click. The sound had come not from the floor, but from an area to my left, where a corner hutch bookcase tucked against two walls. Now one of those walls seemed unproportional. I stood up and walked to it; I pushed it slightly, and it moved farther. It was a doorway, and the darkness behind it emitted a lavender scent.

"There you are," she said. "The only secret this house has, that I know of. Go on through. There's a light just there, near your right hand."

I flicked on the light and walked into a narrow little room lined with shelves. On one side were jars of canned fruits and extra dry goods like sugar and flour and spices. On the other wall were, predictably, more books. The walls stretched for perhaps fifteen feet, and at the back of the space were a couple of folding chairs. "I don't know why we put those there. It's a fun little hiding place, but the heat and air-conditioning don't reach here as well, so it's often a bit too warm or cold. But it's handy for extra storage. I keep my little air fresheners in here so that my books won't grow musty."

"There were times," I said, gazing around, "that I couldn't find you—or that I thought I'd seen you in your office, and then you weren't there."

"I dart back here now and then to claim a book I need. Or a jar of something to give to Rhonda for dessert. That jelly in the cupcake? Homemade raspberry preserves."

"This is an impressive secret! Sort of a cliché, but still impressive. I never would have imagined it. Why did your husband's family have this room?"

"Oh, who knows?" she said, brushing some dust off the spines of books. "The house is very old. It may well go back to the late eighteenth century, the local Realtor has told me. In any case, some claim it might have been a sheltering place for runaway slaves. Indiana has many registered sites on the Underground Railroad."

"Wow."

"But James—that's my husband—felt that it was more likely connected to bootlegging in the twenties. No one will admit to anything, but he thought his grandparents made their share of bathtub gin. He figures maybe they stored it in there. Anyway, in the modern era it is nothing but a storage space, devoid of excitement or intrigue."

"It's still amazing. And that dial hidden in plain sight—a sophisticated touch."

Camilla grinned. "Have we seen enough? Because it's rather drafty out here."

"Of course. And thank you for sharing."

We left the room, and I slapped my head. "Camilla! Last night, when we thought there were intruders—could they have been—?"

"No. I checked there while you were turning on lights. The dogs did seem interested in that corner, but there was not a soul inside, and nothing had been disturbed. Besides, you saw that the room is self-contained, and one can enter only from the inside."

"Hmm. It's weird, anyway."

"Yes. But I believe I've had enough real-life mystery for one day. I only want to spend time on my fictional one."

"Fair enough. Is Rhonda coming back tonight?"

"I gave her the night off. I figured we could be fun and order a pizza. Would you do that for me, Lena? You can decide what to put on it."

"Of course. I'll have them deliver it in—two hours?"

"Perfect. See you then."

I waved and went upstairs. I could do some yacht research and share it with Camilla while we ate.

I grabbed my phone and put it on my desk so that I would remember to order the pizza in time. I held it in my hand for a moment, then clicked on text messages. I had one.

My heart was pounding when I clicked on the message that said "Sam West."

His response was short: *Appreciate the support. You have persuaded me to stop smoking, but I have picked a very stressful time to do so. Keep sending good thoughts.*

I sat for a moment, staring at his message, then turned it off and stared at nothing. What was happening to him right now? Were the police interrogating him? Was he being besieged by the media? Was anyone on his side? At least he had a lawyer waiting for him. Hopefully that person was vocalizing the "innocent until proven guilty" idea, as well as the "innocent until proven a crime" notion. And what about the investigator that West had hired? He must have turned up enough, after all this time, to cast doubt on their suspicions.

With a sigh, I turned on the computer and started Googling articles about yachts, especially yachts in the 1960s. Soon I was immersed in a world of beautiful people in pressed white clothing, with sun-kissed skin and smiling faces, as though the problems of humanity didn't touch them in their special bubble of wealth and celebrity. Here were film stars and directors, pausing for a swim while filming some famous movie; here were multimillionaires, squinting into the glare of cameras as though the world's admiration were their due; and here were people that no one knew, but who through a series of golden decisions had been lifted into the upper strata—that little-known tip of society where yachting was just one way to spend a long, leisurely summer.

By the time I finished my evening's notes, I knew one thing for sure: these were people who lived a long way from everyday life.

12

"We have to go," Gerhard whispered in the darkness of her room.

"Go where?"

His face was grim. "I don't know."

"Why must we go?" she murmured, still half asleep.

"Because if we don't, they'll kill us."

—from *The Salzburg Train*

I WOKE THAT night at midnight, not certain why, my heart pounding. I grabbed for my phone and pressed it on to give a dull illumination to the area around my bed. I had heard something, but what was it? Lestrade, too, was awake, standing in the middle of the bed, his hackles raised, his eyes on my bedroom door.

"What's going on?" I whispered to him. I slid reluctantly out of bed and grabbed the cow doorstop that I had just put back earlier in the day. A snuffling sound in the hallway had me asking, softly, "Who's there?"

A slight moaning and scratching answered me, and I slowly opened the door to find Rochester and Heathcliff there, without Camilla, their paws busy against the bottom of my door. "What do you guys want?" I asked softly. "How did you get out?"

I glanced down the hall to see that Camilla's door was slightly ajar. Somehow these two had escaped. Now they looked up at me and ran halfway down the hall, then looked back.

"I get it. You have to go, right? Give me a sec." I went back inside to get my robe and slippers, then grabbed my cell phone and turned on the flashlight app. It created a great deal of light for the stairway.

The dogs and I moved downstairs in relative silence. I felt protected with them nearby, and they seemed eager to get to the entrance. I opened the kitchen door, as I had seen Camilla do many times, and let them into the yard. The wind must have been strong, because the trees on the bluff were bending their dark silhouettes against a slightly lighter sky, and a ghostly sighing sound could be heard behind the glass door. I waited for a while, peeking into the refrigerator, running a finger across Rhonda's shiny stove, peering at some notes Camilla had put on the kitchen bulletin board. The dogs did not return.

"How long does it take to do your business?" I said aloud, feeling nervous.

After another five minutes I decided that I needed to take Lady Macbeth's literary advice and screw my courage to the sticking-place. Making sure the door would not lock behind me, I crept outside into the cold, burrowing into my robe as I padded across the grass, calling softly for Rochester and Heathcliff. "Hey, guys! Come on back and we'll warm up inside. I'll even give you some food. Come on, doggies!" I had covered the length of the back of the house, and now I turned the corner, wishing I didn't have to search in the dark.

"Heathcliff!" I called a bit louder. I sensed motion to

my left and turned with a sense of relief, only to see a dark form coming at me fast.

"Hey!" I yelled, but it was already ramming into me, hard, and I was suddenly flat on my back on the ground, the wind knocked out of me and the stars the only thing in my line of vision. While I tried to regain my breath, my muscles clenched with panic, I heard whispering voices and felt the pounding of footsteps vibrating on the ground and into my back. Someone was there, but they were going away. I had walked into something that I wasn't supposed to see.

As the voices grew distant, I tried to make out what they were saying, but could only hear disjointed words. "Ray," perhaps, and "Before the dogs come back." Where had the dogs gone? Had they done something to the dogs?

My panic increased. What if they came back? What if they intended to do more than just knock me down? I closed my eyes and willed myself to be calm. My breath was returning in small, gasping bits, and I struggled to a sitting position, looking around for my phone light. It was still there beside me, lighted side down. I grabbed it and dialed 911. An operator asked what my emergency was, and I told her, in a panicked voice that did not sound like mine, who I was, where I was, and that intruders had just knocked me to the ground. "And I can't find my dogs," I said. "I don't know what's happened to them!"

Her voice was calm and soothing, and she assured me that someone would be out presently.

I clicked off the phone and stood up. Something touched my leg and I jumped approximately three feet into the air. "Darn it, Rochester! Where were you all this time?"

The dog did me the courtesy of looking guilty, as did

his brother, who sidled up next to him. "Where the heck were you guys, seriously? Did you happen to see the jerks who knocked me down? Did you think you might want to use your training to stop them?" I heard the crazy pitch of my own voice and paused to take some deep, calming breaths. "Anyway, I'm glad you're both okay."

I started limping toward the back door. The violent fall had done something to one of my knees, and my back felt as though a disc or two had jolted out of place.

I opened the door and gingerly moved through, followed by the dogs, who seemed ready to go back to bed after their nocturnal adventure. I went to the stove and started heating water for tea. By the time I found a tea bag, I saw red and blue lights in the driveway. I moved swiftly to the front door and peered out; Doug Heller stood on the steps.

"Lena?" he asked when I opened the door. His voice was a little stronger tonight. "Are you okay?"

"No. I let the dogs out and they didn't come back, so I went outside and someone ran out of nowhere and knocked me down. Just slammed into me."

"Don't cry. Come on—let's go in."

"I'm not crying," I said angrily. "I'm just mad."

"Turn a light on; let me see if you're hurt."

I flipped on the living room lamp and blinked in the light. Doug Heller narrowed his eyes as he studied me. He fingered my cheekbone. "Looks like you'll have a bruise there. He body-slammed you?"

"Yeah. I was so surprised I didn't know what was happening. In retrospect, I think he hit me hard. I landed on my back," I said, turning around.

"Ah. The dirt tells the story."

"And this is my favorite robe. Because it's my only

robe." Heller had been right; I was sort of crying, but it was a release of tension more than anything.

"Hey—is that a teakettle I hear? You go make some tea. I'm going to have a look around. I'll meet you at the back door."

I nodded and locked the front door after him, then went to the kitchen and fumbled with the box of tea bags, finding one and plunging it into my mug of boiling water. I indulged myself with sugar and cream and sat down, taking a few bracing sips. Heller appeared about fifteen minutes later, and he joined me at the table, looking wide-awake and comfortable, as though this were a lunch date. "How's your tea?"

"It's good. I put a lot of sugar in it."

"Good. You feel a little better?"

"Yeah."

"Do you think you need a doctor?"

"I don't think so. I'm just going to be sore."

"So let's take this from the top. Why were you outside?"

"Because I let out gosh darn Rochester and Heathcliff, and they didn't come back. I didn't think Camilla would take too kindly to me losing her dogs in the middle of the night, so I went out after them."

"Okay. And where did you get knocked down?"

"I was turning the corner. I got to the end of the house on the back side here, and I turned around the corner to the west wall, and suddenly there it was."

"It?"

"Just this big black form, coming at me. And then I was looking at the sky."

Doug Heller grinned at me. "Beautiful night for it."

I sort of wanted to punch him, except that I did feel a little better after he joked about it.

"Yeah."

"So there's no way you could identify this guy?"

"No. But it was more than one."

He sat up straighter. "Why do you say that?"

"There was whispering. Talking in low voices—I couldn't make them out. And then they took off. Boom boom on the ground, like they were running. I felt it through my back, which was pressed against the dirt. And there was a smell—yes, I think I smelled something weird."

"Pot, maybe?"

"In all honesty, I don't know what pot smells like. Maybe. It had a weird incense smell. But there was something else, too. Some kind of cologne on top of that smell. Something kind of cheap, like Brut or Old Spice."

"And the other night, when our guys came out here—you didn't see anyone then?"

"No—Camilla was just alerted by the dogs. They wanted to come downstairs, and they ended up standing— Oh boy."

"What?"

"Nothing—well—I don't know if I'm allowed to say."

"Lena, I'm trying to help here."

"Well, I was having lunch with Lane Waldrop. You know her?"

"Yeah. I know Clay, at least."

"She said this place had a secret, and she had always been curious about it, and that she had told Martin Jonas, and he had been curious, too."

Heller's eyebrows went up so high they disappeared under his blond hair. "And what is this secret?"

"Well, I didn't know when I talked to Lane. But later Camilla told me about it. Listen, I don't know if I have permission to—"

Heller stood up and folded his arms. "A man assaulted you, Lena. Tell me all the information or I'll arrest you for not cooperating with the police."

"You wouldn't dare."

"Lena!"

"Okay. But swear you won't tell Camilla's secret to anyone."

"I swear."

I led him into Camilla's study and turned on the light. We walked to the window and I showed him the dial near the heat vent. He turned it, then looked to his left , as I had done, when he heard the click that unlatched the wall mechanism. He stared for a moment, his face a picture of surprise. "No way," he said, and then he disappeared into the little room. I switched on the low-wattage light and he studied the shelves in the dimness, along with all the corners of the space. "And there's no chance that any of these walls also magically opens?"

"No—this is self-contained. So I can't imagine it would have anything to do with the people outside."

Heller ran his hand over a few canning jars, his face thoughtful. "So let's recap: a man is shot to death a few hundred yards from this room. Subsequently, on two different nights there are intruders who are found in your backyard, also adjacent to this room."

We left the room, and I shut it. I started walking back toward the kitchen, and Heller followed me. I returned to my cup of tea.

Sitting down, I said, “We never found intruders the first time—just a fifty-dollar bill and a gray scarf.”

“Uh-huh. There are people in town who knew this house had ‘a secret.’ One of those people was Martin Jonas.”

“Yeah, but those could all just be unrelated ideas. You know—what’s that old term from the list of logical fallacies?—post hoc ergo propter hoc—‘after this, therefore because of this.’ It’s faulty thinking.”

“Is it, Lena? Here’s another little tidbit for you. Based on the inside of this house, it would seem that this little room would jut out like a porch, and therefore be visible from the outside. But look at that back wall—it’s smooth and even all the way across. No additions or porch-like protrusions. What does that tell you?”

“Um—what?”

“That something else must be right next to that room, keeping the wall level across the back of the house. The room is only about twenty feet, but the back of the house has to span about sixty or more. So what’s in the rest of the space?”

I shrugged and took a sip of my tea.

“We’re coming back here in the morning with a team.”

I sat up straight, alarmed. “You can’t! You just said you wouldn’t tell anyone the secret! How are you going to keep the town from knowing if you go barging around her house?”

Doug Heller’s face was a mixture of surprise and belligerence. “Lena! You could have been badly hurt out there. For some reason, people are returning to this house at night, and it is not unlikely that it has something to do with the death of Martin Jonas. I’m not going to avoid investigating just because it might seem impolite!”

I slumped in my chair, and a soft voice behind me said, "I thought I heard something down here. Hello, Doug. What am I missing? Is this a midnight rendezvous?"

I whirled to face Camilla, who smiled sleepily at me and said, "Is there enough water for another cup of tea?"

I jumped up to make her a cup, and she saw my disheveled appearance and dirty clothes. "What's happened? Is that a bruise on your face? Lena, what's going on?"

Doug Heller leaned against the counter and folded his arms. "Lena called 911 about an hour ago. She went out after the dogs and got body slammed by a person or persons unknown. She ended up on her back and they took off."

"Oh, no! Lena, are you all right?"

"Yes, I'm fine. I was just shocked and frightened, but I'm okay now. Doug investigated. Camilla, I have a confession."

"Oh? No, sit down, I'll make my own tea."

I returned to my chair, not knowing how to approach the topic of the secret room, and Doug Heller snorted with impatience.

"Camilla, this is an assault and possibly a case of breaking and entering. It might also relate to the death of Martin Jonas. So I persuaded Lena to tell me about your secret room."

"I'm sorry, Camilla," I said.

She turned to me, her face creased with worry. "Oh, who cares about that stupid room? Lena, you could have been killed! What if they had been carrying knives, or guns?"

Doug Heller looked pleased. "Exactly. Which is why I'll be back early in the morning with a team. We'll comb that yard for any evidence, and we'll look for another secret entrance from the outside. Based on the view from the backyard, Camilla, there is no logical way that room can exist unless there are other hidden spaces against that back wall. Did you ever consider that?"

Camilla blinked at him, an Earl Gray tea bag dangling from her hand. "I'm afraid I have no sense of spatial reasoning. I never have had. Rooms are rooms."

Now he was impatient. "Lena, is there anything else you need to tell me about tonight? Anything else you noticed?"

"No—except—wait." I thought back to the whispering, urgent voices. One calling to the other, both making a quick retreat. "I think I heard the name Ray."

Heller's brows creased. "I don't know of any Rays who hung out with Martin Jonas."

"But this doesn't have to have anything to do with Martin Jonas."

"True. We'll look into it."

"Well, whatever. That's all I can remember."

Heller sprang away from the counter and clapped his hands. "Well, then. You two can go back to bed. We'll be here early tomorrow—you can rest assured we will get to the bottom of this."

"Thanks, Doug," Camilla said.

"Is there any word on Sam West?" I asked.

He turned to scowl at me. "It's not my job to keep track of Sam West. We escorted him to New York, and now I assume they are questioning him. What's your obsession with that guy?"

Camilla looked shocked. "He's our friend, Doug. This has all been very stressful for him."

Heller looked from one of us to the other and shook his

head. "You ladies might be making some dangerous assumptions. For my part, I'm glad he's safely out of town and not right down the bluff from you."

I stood up, tired of looking up at them from my chair. "And yet the one time I get attacked is when Sam West is not here. So I guess he's not the only person in town that you should be suspicious of."

"Excuse me for caring about your safety," Heller said, his eyes on me, his voice cold. "And Sam West can thank me for giving him a heads-up and letting him walk into that police station under his own steam rather than being hauled out of here and becoming a sound bite on the ten o'clock news."

"Yeah—why did you do that for him, if you suspect him of murder?" I asked.

Heller said nothing.

Camilla touched his arm. "We appreciate all that you do, Doug, including coming out here at this ungodly hour. We are lucky to have you, and so is the town of Blue Lake."

Heller nodded, still looking at me, and then turned and walked to the door. "Thanks, Camilla. I'll be here in the morning. Lock this door after I leave."

He left quietly, and Camilla re-latched the glass door. Then she turned to me. "He's a good man," she said.

"So is Sam," I told her.

"Agreed. Don't you ever wonder why Doug gets so angry about Sam West?"

"What do you mean?"

"Maybe his anger is partly defensiveness."

"You mean—because he knows West isn't guilty?"

"Doug has to keep an eye on Sam. That's his job. But I think there might be some questions in his own mind about the whole thing, and yet it's not his case, when all is said and done."

"No, I guess not."

Camilla looked at the tea bag that still dangled from her hand. "Do you want more tea?"

"No, thank you—one was enough to calm me down. I'm going back to bed. I'm sorry we woke you up."

"You didn't. I think I sensed that the dogs were gone, and then I looked up and saw that my door was open. I had to investigate after that."

The dogs in question were sitting in the doorway, their heads drooping. It seemed we were free of intruders at the moment, and the canines were standing down.

I moved toward the door, and Camilla said, "Lena?"

"Yes?"

"Doug wants very much to impress you."

"I know. Good night, Camilla."

She waved at me, and I left the room. Upstairs I headed for my bed, but a thought came to me, unbidden, and sent me to my laptop. Sam had mentioned, in our last conversation, a woman named Taylor who had been his wife's best friend. She had a blog, he had said.

Quickly I searched for "Taylor Brand blog" and got an immediate result: a web diary called *A Fashionable Life*, which featured a header picture of a tall, dark-haired woman—clad in a strange, asymmetrical gown and sporting Cleopatra eye makeup—leaning against a brick wall with a disinterested expression.

Lestrade leaped up to sniff the computer. "Blech," I said to him.

I scrolled through the blog entries, noting that Taylor enjoyed talking about Taylor, and that she also talked a great deal about her friend's disappearance. On the side of her blog was a little virtual badge that said "Justice for Victoria" over a strikingly beautiful picture of Sam's wife.

I clicked back to the week that Victoria West had disappeared and found that her friend Taylor had much to say on the matter. Her September 28 post said, "I am still reeling from the disappearance of my good friend Vic, and wondering if anyone has any information about her. The last time I saw her we were having lunch in Chelsea. She was upbeat and hyper as always, full of plans and ideas for her business and her future. She said she needed a break from it all, but she never would have taken a break without telling me where she was going, or leaving me contact information. That's how I know Vic has met with foul play."

While I sensed that Taylor Brand did in fact miss her friend, I found it strange that she had posted a sad picture of herself with the entry about the missing Victoria. I glanced down at the comments section; there were 115 responses to the post. I began to scroll through them. Many were just a few words: "Sorry to hear this, Taylor," or "We're thinking of you, hon."

Some were critical of her post. "Why don't you spend your time looking for her instead of feeling sorry for yourself?" one rude poster had written. Another wrote, "You look terrible in that picture."

I wondered why Brand hadn't deleted the obnoxious comments—maybe she hadn't read any of them; but wasn't the point of the post to see if anyone had news about Victoria?

I kept reading. The seventy-fourth post, from "Anonymous," said, "If the cops want to find Vic West, they should follow the money and the drugs."

What money? Sam had said that his wife had declared bankruptcy before she disappeared. And what anonymous person would know anything about it? Had the police investigated this claim? Or was this poster just another malcontent, an Internet troll who liked posting negative things for the fun of it, and who assumed that all famous people were wealthy and addicted?

And what drugs? Had Mrs. West truly been forming an addiction? What did it all have to do with the word "Nikon"? Had someone photographed her taking drugs? Or perhaps she had photographed someone, and was blackmailing them! What if Victoria West had gotten herself in danger, perhaps for money to fuel a drug habit?

A wave of exhaustion suddenly washed over me, and I dragged myself back to bed. Lestrade followed. As I lay inert, he sniffed at my face, purring loudly.

"Stop purring. You're keeping me awake," I complained, and then I fell deeply asleep.

13

On the first night, they stayed in a small tent, deep in the silent forest. Gerhard promised her that she would not have to hide forever—just until they had a plan.

"I don't mind," she said. "There are things that I prefer about this existence."

His smile flashed white in the darkness. "Yes? What is preferable about this gypsy life?"

"You," she said.

When he leaned in to kiss her, she thought for the first time that her dream might be resurrected.

—from *The Salzburg Train*

I WOKE AT eight the next morning and stayed under the covers for a while, not liking the blustery sound of the wind against my window, but preferring the soft, purring mass that was Lestrade, who was warming my left side. I looked around the room, with its watery sunbeams and its bright white walls. I had come to love it in a very short time—my special space inside Camilla Graham's home—but today it brought me no comfort. Too many conflicts dominated life here in Blue Lake, and I needed to find some resolution.

In a sudden burst of remembrance, I realized that Doug Heller and his team were probably downstairs at that very moment, and that propelled me out of the comfortable bed. I showered and dressed quickly; before I ran downstairs I sent another text to Sam West. *Are you all right?* I didn't know if he'd answer, or if he even had leisure time to read his messages, but I felt, especially after reading Taylor Brand's critical rhetoric, that he might benefit from hearing a friendly voice.

Doug Heller continually warned me against Sam West, and yet my own instincts about the man, aside from my first rather unpleasant encounter with him, were that he was innocent. Could I be missing some glaring reality? Could it really be that West was a sociopath who could smile at me and feed me waffles while knowing the location of his dead wife's body?

I shook my head and ran down the stairs. Camilla was there in the kitchen, eating some fruit and drinking tea. "Good morning," she said brightly. She wore a crisp white blouse with a pair of blue wool slacks. "I hope you were able to go back to sleep last night."

"I was."

She studied my face. "Your injury is less noticeable today, but it still makes me cringe. To think that someone was just outside, rushing out of the darkness to protect—what? What would prompt that sort of violence?"

"I assume Doug's people are out investigating?"

"Yes. They've been there for about an hour, tapping and pounding and putting things in evidence bags. I haven't heard a report yet."

My eyes wandered around the room; my legs felt jumpy. "I think I'll walk the dogs. Is that all right? I might go into town."

"Fine, dear. They'll enjoy it, and I'm sure you'll like the fresh air."

"Yes. Thanks, Camilla. Just let me know when you want to meet again—I've already started on my yacht research, but I need to do more."

"I'm still going through your last notes. You can call today a research day, and a recovery day. I feel somehow responsible . . ."

"You're not. Only one person is—or maybe two. I'm confident Doug will figure this out soon."

"Go walk and enjoy it, and I'll have a warm drink ready when you return."

I bundled up against the cold, then wrestled with the dogs, who started leaping around when they saw the leashes, and finally clipped the leads into place. "Okay, geez. Help a person out," I told them. They did not seem repentant.

We made our way down the bluff; we stopped at Sam West's house. I entered with his key and checked on all of his plants, watering the ones that seemed too dry. I brought in his mail and set it on his kitchen table while the dogs roamed around his house, sniffing and snuffling.

I checked all of his locks and made sure that the timers on his lamps were set properly; if someone was lurking around Camilla's property, they might be more than tempted to do some damage to a beautiful empty house like Sam's. Better that they not know it was empty, although all they had to do was watch the news to know of Sam's plight. It had been a top story that morning, both on television news and online: "New York Investor Sam West Returns for Questioning," said one website's headline, while another said, "West Confronted with Blood Evidence in New Twist."

I looked around, satisfied that, at least in West's peaceful, lovely home, all was well. The dogs and I went back outside, and they dragged me the rest of the way down the hill, where we started making our normal trek down Wentworth Street. As I had been on my first visit, I was lured by the delicious aroma of Blue Lake Coffee. Camilla had promised me a hot drink, but suddenly I really wanted the store-bought kind. I tied the dogs up to a "No Parking" sign near a hydrant. They sat peacefully even as the cold wind ruffled their thick fur. "Be right back," I said. "I want some java."

I went inside, where it was delightfully warm and fragrant, and got into a line of about four people. Some customers sat at oaken tables, chatting peacefully while they sipped coffee and munched on muffins or scones. A few others sat in corner booths under a sign that said "Free Wi-Fi" and tapped away at laptops while occasionally guzzling their caffeinated beverages.

I shifted my gaze to the menu above the counter, which had a surprising variety of choices for coffee. Someone had walked up behind me; I decided to ask for a recommendation. I turned, ready to confide my confusion, and came face-to-face with the man that I had suspected of killing Martin Jonas—the red-haired man that Heller had called Dave Brill. "Hello," I said, but my voice didn't come out friendly, as I had initially intended.

He looked surprised that I was speaking to him. "Hey," he said.

"I know you, don't I?" I asked, feeling bold.

"I don't think so." He looked around, as though for an exit.

"I do. I saw you a week or so ago, talking to Martin Jonas in Bick's Hardware. You were telling him he needed to do something for you."

"Who *are* you?" he asked. He had the bleary eyes of a man who had not slept well.

"My name is Lena London. What's yours?"

He narrowed his eyes at me. "Are you a cop or something?"

"No. Just a Blue Lake resident."

"Huh. I don't remember seeing you."

"You were there, though. With Martin Jonas. I understand you sell comic books."

His eyebrows shot up. "What?"

"Don't you sell comic books? I was interested in buying some."

"You?" he asked, almost jeering. "I'm guessing you couldn't even name a comic book."

He was wrong there. My brilliant former boyfriend had been obsessed with them, and I had learned more than I'd wanted to. "I could name plenty. Not so much in DC, although I've read my share of those. I'm more of a Marvel person."

"Huh," he said. He was not a good conversationalist. He was looking restless again, as though he might try to make a run for it if I looked away.

"I'm looking for the Daredevil series from 1964."

A slight beam of interest glowed in his eyes. "That's kind of rare. Are you looking to start with number one? Those first ten are hard to keep in stock."

"Which is why I'm looking for them. Love that Matt Murdock," I said with a fake smile.

"It's a pretty good series. I've got big Hulk and Spider-

Man collections, but not much Daredevil right now. You have anything to sell?"

"Not here in town. I have stuff back in storage in Chicago," I lied.

"I'm always looking for new series. What all have you got?" he asked.

"Next," said the person at the counter. It was a teenage girl with an eyebrow piercing and a friendly grin. "What can I get you?" she asked.

"Hang on," I told Dave Brill. I gave my order for a standard Colombian roast, nothing fancy, and the young barista looked disappointed. She nodded, though, and set about getting my order ready.

Dave Brill was lingering behind me, perhaps dreaming of finding that elusive comic book that might be in my possession. "So was Martin a part of your comic book business?" I asked him.

"How do you know Marty?" he asked.

"Just through mutual friends."

"Like who?" He looked downright suspicious now.

"Lane and Clayton Waldrop," I said.

This surprised him; he thought about it, then nodded a few times. "Okay, that's cool. I know Marty went to school with them and everything."

"So how do you know Marty?"

He shrugged. "We met down at Terry's Bowling Alley."

Of course. The legendary bowling alley that Marge Bick had called "unsavory."

The barista put my coffee on the counter and I paid her. Then I turned and Dave Brill moved up to the counter. As he did, I got a whiff of his scent—Old Spice, with something else underneath it. A bolt of fear had me remembering the night before—the terror of being knocked to the ground by an unknown force.

I stared at the side of his face while he ordered a complicated latte. He needed a shave. "So you and Martin probably know Ray, right?"

His head turned swiftly toward me, his eyes wary. "How do you know Ray?"

Oh, boy. "Just another set of mutual friends."

This he clearly did not believe. Perhaps Ray didn't have any friends. He narrowed his eyes at me. "What's your name again?"

"Lena."

He nodded. "You want to buy some comic books, you can find me online. Dave Brill. I have a website called Small Town Comics. Meanwhile, I'll tell Ray you said hi."

"You do that. Thanks, Dave!" I waved and started toward the door.

He called after me, his voice nervous. "Whose dogs are those?"

I turned and met his eyes, which were strangely pale. "They're mine," I said. "Or at least they belong to my employer, Camilla Graham. You probably know her—she lives at the top of the bluff."

His eyes widened just enough, and his nostrils flared just enough, that I knew I'd hit the bull's-eye. I managed to walk steadily toward the door and to appear cool and unconcerned while I set my coffee on a blue bench and untied the dogs, then reclaimed my drink and walked—oh so casually—toward the hill. I had been planning to investigate the town, but now I intended to go straight back to Graham House, find Doug Heller, and tell him my instincts had been correct—the red-haired man had probably killed Martin Jonas, and he had been at Camilla's last night.

By the time I got to the end of the street I was running; I looked back once to see that Dave Brill was on his phone and talking animatedly. I turned back and kept up my pace. The dogs were happy as could be; they rarely got to run, and they tore up the hill as though they were chasing a particularly elusive squirrel.

When I finally got to Camilla's I was out of breath and perspiring. I let go of the leashes so the dogs could wander in the yard. Doug Heller was standing near the front porch, pushing some hair out of his face; the wind seemed bent on obscuring one of his eyes. Now that I had arrived, I realized how very cold it was. My mind had been occupied with other things.

I made eye contact with Heller and held up a hand, indicating that I wanted to speak with him. I heard a car coming up the bluff, speeding and careening. I had almost reached Heller when it pulled into Camilla's yard. I turned to see the anxious face of Lane Waldrop peering out of her station wagon.

"Lena," said Doug.

"Lena," Lane called, stepping out of her car and smiling in a tentative way. "Can you talk for a minute?"

Camilla appeared and gathered up the dogs; she glanced from Doug to Lane to me, looking bemused. The wind lashed against us; I took a bracing sip of my coffee and walked toward Lane. "What's up?" I said.

Again, her smile seemed hesitant. "I got a break from the kids and I thought I'd check to see if you want to do something. See a movie or whatever." Her eyes flicked past my shoulder to Doug Heller, who answered a ringing phone with a brusque "Heller" while uniformed officers milled back and forth behind him.

I was distracted, wondering what the call was about, and Lane said, "Is everything okay? You look like you could use a break."

"Uh—I actually can't right now. I have to talk to Detective Heller about something, and then I'm committed to working with Camilla today."

Lane looked disappointed and also reluctant to leave. Her visit dovetailed so perfectly with my realization and Dave Brill's phone call that it seemed as though my life were being orchestrated by a silent conductor.

"Okay. I guess I'll go then. What are the police here for?"

"Oh, they—" I stopped.

"Lena?"

"Hang on," I said. I was thinking—about the fact that Lane had driven up the bluff at an almost crazy speed, like a woman with a mission. About Lane telling me that she knew the house had a secret, and so did Martin Jonas.

I studied her attractive face, slightly freckled, and her wide and curious green eyes. I was being ridiculous; surely she had no connection to the mysterious Ray. Except that—Clay. Her husband's name was Clay. Was that what I had heard whispered in the darkness? Had Clay Waldrop been there? Had Lane been there, as well? Had Martin Brill been reacting, not to the name Ray, but the fact that I had gotten it wrong? He had admitted he knew Clay, and also a Ray. What if Clay were indeed the mastermind?

There on the gray and windy bluff, my suspicion trumped my budding friendship. I faced her with my hands on my hips. "They're here because someone was trespassing last night. I ran into them and they knocked me down." I pointed to my cheek, and Lane seemed to grow pale. "So I have to go talk to Doug Heller. I'll catch up with you another time, Lane."

"Oh, that's cool. I'm sorry to hear that, Lena. I'll text you soon, okay?"

I nodded, and she got back into her car, did a U-turn, and exited the driveway.

Heller approached. "What did you find?" I asked.

"Plenty. Are you okay?"

"I think Lane there might be involved. Because I know Dave Brill is. I saw him at the coffee shop, and he smelled the same as he did last night. And then I mentioned that I lived at Camilla's, and he got a panicky look on his face. Then he made a phone call, and ten minutes later Lane came tearing up here, asking if I could go somewhere with her."

Heller put a hand on my shoulder. "Take a deep breath, Lena. We're on top of this. If they're involved, we'll get them."

"Why—what *did* you find?"

"Another entrance, and another section of room that abuts your little hidden book room. This one has something special, though. And this is probably the real secret that everyone has been talking about. Come here, I'll show you."

He led me to the side of the house and pointed out a nearly undetectable handle built into the gray siding. "Don't touch," he said. "They're dusting for prints. You can just peek in there." I peered into a narrow little room, similar in shape to the one inside. "So?" I said. "This is nothing special. And there's not much in here, aside from what look like—what—gardening tools?"

"Right. But look to your right. See that dark square on the floor? It's a door."

"A door to what? The ground?" Then it hit me. "No! A tunnel?"

"You got it. A little dirt path that goes right under your backyard and straight to the lake. Handy, right? Explains why the boat you saw Jonas board was right there. They could take their product, hop on the boat, and drive to whatever dock was closest to their customers."

"Customers for—?"

"Drugs. That little tunnel houses a tiny laboratory for packaging and processing—mainly coke, we think. That's what we found in plentiful amounts."

"Cocaine?"

"Yes. And a backpack full of money. That might explain your wayward fifty-dollar bill."

"So—they've been coming here at night to run a *drug* ring?"

"Yes."

"Oh my God! This is why we didn't hear them, whenever the dogs would react to something. They weren't next door, they were underground!"

"Pretty soundproof, as far as we can tell."

I shook my head in disbelief. "Is Camilla okay?"

"She's fine. She took the dogs in. She says she's going to make some tea."

"So how are you going to catch them? If they know you found their stash, they're all going to run."

"I'll round them up right now. We want Brill, maybe Lane and Clayton Waldrop—but we need the big man. If that's Clay, great. Then we might have everyone we need. Hang on, I have to send out some cruisers." He walked away, talking into his phone.

Still reeling, I walked into the kitchen, where Camilla stood pouring tea from a china pot into flowered cups. "Sit down, dear. I swear, when I hired you this was still a boring old house in which nothing much had ever happened. Your arrival was apparently like the shaking of a hornet's nest. Or at least it happened parallel to the shaking."

I sighed and sat down in a chair. "I don't blame you at all—but what a very strange week this has been," I said. "I feel so tense, I find myself suspecting everyone of wrongdoing. Speak of the devil," I said, as Adam Rayburn loomed up in the doorway.

"Hello, all. Doug Heller said I could come in. Camilla, are you all right?"

"I'm fine, Adam. I'm learning that I am more of a resilient person than I once imagined. But of course I have a strong young roommate who inspires me." She handed me a cup of tea, and I added milk and sugar. "What brings you here?" Camilla asked. "And would you like tea?"

"No, not today. I have to get to work, but I just wanted to check in on you because of the, uh—proximity of Martin's murder to your place. But here I find that Doug is making great strides in finding the perpetrators, is that right?"

Rayburn leaned forward, his eyes wide and curious. He was making me feel as paranoid as Lane had done.

"He seems to be on the right track," I said. "I'm not sure how much we're at liberty to disclose right now."

"Of course. Of course." Rayburn grew brisk. "Camilla, you promised you would come out to the restaurant this week for a meal. Would Thursday suit you?"

"Oh, my. Yes, I think so. I'll check my calendar and call you. Thank you so much for the invitation, Adam." She poured her own tea, holding the pot gracefully in her slender hands.

He gave her a long and rather strange look, then nodded at me. "Well, good-bye, then. Let me know if you need anything."

After he was gone, I took a sip of tea and looked at Camilla, whose face grew thoughtful. "Camilla, is it just me, or does everyone in town seem to be showing up in your yard lately?"

"Day and night," she added.

"I think I need a distraction. I'm going back to my yacht research."

"Wonderful. If you ever need the library for that, it's less than a mile away. Turn right at the foot of the bluff instead of left, and right again on Elderberry."

"Thanks. I'll start with my laptop, but I might just go there to clear my head." I finished my tea, thanked Camilla, and made my way upstairs.

Back in my haven of a room, which felt toasty warm today—perhaps Camilla had cranked up the heat—I found no Lestrade, but a welcoming desk and a magical genie known as a laptop computer.

I opened my notes folder, where I had already started several files for yachts of different eras and for general observations about yachting culture, as well as the speeds at which yachts could travel on the navigable inland waterways of Europe. Generally, yachts were not fast. For Camilla's purposes, however, the yacht didn't need to be—it just had to provide an avenue of escape, of traveling to a new world.

I tapped a fingernail on my keyboard for a minute, trying to think of specific search terms. I had already tried "yachts of the 60s" and "yachting culture past and present." I had also simply Googled "yachts" and "yachtsmen." The latter had provided a colorful list of names and faces from the early twentieth century to the present—names like Vladislav Bogomolov, Zephyr Kalahalios, N. Leandros Lazos, Albrecht Iverson. It was like reading names of Olympics participants. I had found only one woman yacht owner of note—Helen "Flip" Flannery—who had struck oil on her tiny retirement property in 1974 and promptly cashed in for a life on the water.

I typed in "yachting life" and then clicked "Images." More of the same: big yachts, small yachts, old and new yachts. On a sudden whim I typed "yachts" and "Nikon." If I expected some amazing solution to the disappearance of Sam's wife, I was disappointed. What I got were yachts. I scrolled through these, noting down the ones that seemed vintage and the ones that seemed to be from the present day. A large and colorful picture caught my eye; I clicked it and saw that it was from a magazine called *Yachting Life*. The article was about a yacht festival in the Greek Islands at which people adorned themselves and their boats and sailed from place to place, eating and drinking and making merry. As bacchanals went, it looked to be as carnal as Mardi Gras and as flamboyant as Carnival. The pictures, though, were beautiful to observe, and I clicked through a slideshow of them, drawn in despite the ridiculous display of wealth. Here were men and women sharing champagne in the moonlight, surrounded by tiny Italian lights; here was a man leaping into the water in the briefest of bathing suits, looking fit, tanned, and trim. Here was a woman sitting on the edge of a yacht, her thick hair blowing in the wind, her summery smile lazy and indulged. She was lovely and exotic, from her cloud of hair to the mole on her chin, which almost seemed drawn on to add an aura of distinction.

I pushed my computer away with a sigh. Why had I typed "Nikon"? It was a separate issue, a problem for the police, and certainly not a part of my research for Camilla. The fact that I had done so was evidence of my distraction.

I took out my phone and checked my messages; perhaps Sam had answered my text from the previous night. I had two messages: one from my father, and one from Sam West. I read my father's first, suddenly afraid to read Sam's. My dad was simply checking in, asking me to call when I got a chance. Tabitha had loved my card.

I clicked on Sam's message and read: *My lawyer tells me that my arrest is imminent. Don't stop believing in me, Lena.*

Stunned, I sat for a moment, listening to the wind hurl itself against the pane. Lestrade pushed my door all the way open and wandered in to wash his paws in a single beam of sunlight.

How could they arrest him when it wasn't clear what had happened? How could they haul a man in for murder when there was no body? But of course it had been done before, and the public was seemingly clamoring for Sam West's punishment. What a monster society could become when it concentrated its hate on one individual.

"Dammit," I said. I ran to my bed and leaped on it, then lay facedown, defeated. I felt absolutely helpless. What, really, could I do for him, except believe him?

I recalled the last moment I had seen him, right before Doug Heller and his associate had barged into the house. He had been on the verge of telling me something; he had said, "Lena," with an urgent look. What had he been about to say?

A phone rang in a distant part of the house; it was Camilla's landline. Curious, I moved away from my desk and went downstairs, leaving Lestrade to his bath. Camilla stood at her desk, nodding as she listened to the caller. "Yes, I understand. Wonderful. That will be quite a relief. No—I'll ask Bob Dawkins and his son to take care of it today, before night falls." She listened, then laughed. "Yes, his son is horrible," she agreed.

Then she turned to me. "Doug says that Clayton and Lane Waldrop both have an alibi for last night. They were at a family wedding party until two in the morning. They were quite surprised to be called in, but are cooperating fully."

"Huh," I said. I was relieved, because I had not wanted to believe that Lane was involved, and yet somehow I still felt suspicious. The timing of Dave Brill's phone call and her careening ride up the hill had been more than coincidental, I was sure. What was Lane hiding? Was it only the "secret" that kept her returning to Graham House?

Camilla didn't seem to notice my hesitation. "Dave Brill

is another story. Doug is convinced that he is involved, and he is detaining him at the station, but Brill won't say a word and has summoned a lawyer."

"How's he paying for the lawyer?" I asked.

"A good question. Maybe whoever is still at large will be helping with that."

"Huh," I said again.

Camilla leaned back on her desk. "Meanwhile, I need to call Bob Dawkins and arrange to have the disgusting drug facility sealed off. Or padlocked or some such thing. Doug's people are confident that there are only two entrances—one at each end of the tunnel. My husband would be horrified to know his house had been used for something so sordid."

"It's terrible—and unbelievable—that they could do it right under our noses. With the dogs inside, your well-trained dogs, and yet somehow they barely ever made a sound. Until the last couple of nights. Maybe they usually entered the tunnel from the lake side, in which case you wouldn't hear anything and the dogs wouldn't be awakened. For whatever reason, in the last couple of weeks they must have occasionally entered from the side of your house. Or exited there. Something that would make enough noise that the dogs would be alerted."

"Are you suspicious of something in particular?"

"No—it just all seems strange, starting with the death of Martin Jonas. Assuming he was a member of this group, this drug gang, why would they choose to kill him? I mean, what motive would they have? Was he about to turn them in?"

"Or could he have somehow cheated someone out of

their purchase, and so they hunted him down and killed him?" Camilla said.

"He was so close to the house, and to the boat. So of course they must have confronted him either going into the tunnel or coming out of it."

Camilla paled and held up her hand. "Doug did tell me something about that. Apparently they found blood inside the tunnel, near the lake doorway—entrance—whatever one might call it. The theory is that perhaps Martin was shot in the tunnel, but that he escaped long enough to run a few yards down the beach."

"Poor guy. And yet he chose to hang out with those people—Brill and whomever else might have been involved. He made bad choices; deadly choices."

With a sigh, Camilla nodded her agreement. "What surprises me is that they're having such trouble tracing the boat. The people involved in this don't seem smart enough to make those kinds of arrangements—an elaborate computer trail and an alias."

"No, they don't," I agreed. "So who could have been their connection? Are you thinking there's some kind of local mastermind? Or at least some friend or family member pulling the strings?"

"I don't know that Martin had many friends or acquaintances in this town. His family is in Boone Lake—about an hour from here."

"There's the restaurant, though. He worked there, so he knows people there. Waiters, waitresses—"

"And Adam," Camilla said.

The room was silent as we both thought about this.

I said, "Adam does come over here fairly often, doesn't he?"

Camilla nodded. "And he wanted that special tour of the house. He even jokingly asked me if it had any secret passageways."

"And yet—it couldn't be Adam—could it?"

Camilla's face looked briefly sad and vulnerable, then determined. "He invited me for dinner at the restaurant. I think I'll go tonight. You shall be my guest, Lena. Let's ask Adam Rayburn some questions."

"I'm with you. Let me run upstairs and change."

14

"Hans is coming with a car. He'll leave it at the place with the twelve pines. Then you must run."

"Not you?"

"I'll take you to the border, and we'll contact the police."

"You won't come with me?"

He studied her face as though memorizing its features. "If only I could, Johanna."

—from *The Salzburg Train*

GREEN GLASS HIGHWAY seemed to glitter in the last rays of the setting sun, and Wheat Grass stood like a stylized piece of driftwood on the shores of Blue Lake, its beige walls glowing artfully with landscaping lights, its tall windows glinting. Pots of purple mums sat in each window well, and as we walked through the large doorway, I spied a stone fireplace in the back of the large main room, flames crackling behind diners who were focusing on their plates and their generous glasses of wine.

"Nice place," I murmured to Camilla.

"Yes. It's been a Blue Lake staple for years. James and I used to come here once a week."

"So you've known Adam a long time," I said. A waiter appeared to claim Camilla's attention.

"Two for dinner?" he asked smoothly.

Camilla nodded, and the white-shirted man led us to a table by a window, blue now with night and flickering with candles that sat on the ledge. "This is beautiful, Camilla. I don't recall ever being in a restaurant like this."

"It's refined, but not so expensive that an average family can't eat out here. I never know how Adam does it." We settled into our chairs, and she said, "Or maybe I do. I don't know anymore. Everyone in town seems sinister to me these days."

"I was thinking that same thing this afternoon! Perhaps we are paranoid." I looked around at the other diners. They were strangers; who knew what secrets lurked behind their doors? The idea cast a pall over my thoughts, and the room seemed to grow darker.

Camilla was clearly in a similar frame of mind. "And yet a man is dead, and his body was in our backyard. We didn't imagine poor Martin lying out there in the rain."

The waiter appeared again. "Good evening, ladies. I'm Grant, and I'll be your waiter this evening. Here's a pitcher of our famous cucumber water. Try it and you'll be gasping for more." He grinned at us with extremely white teeth, and I wondered if he were an aspiring actor.

"Thank you," I said. "May I also have a Diet Coke?"

"Sure thing. And for you, Ms. Graham?"

"Oh, my, you know my name. Just the water is fine. Have I met you, Grant?"

"No, ma'am, but I've read all your books and I am a fan! I recognized you from the book jacket."

I leaned toward him slightly, pleased to find another Graham fan. "What's your favorite book?"

"Oh, it's hard to choose. Maybe *Death at Seaside.* They're all great."

"You are too kind," said Camilla, glancing at her menu.

Grant hovered. "I actually have one of them in back. I don't suppose—would it be intruding if I—"

"I'll be happy to sign it, dear, if that's what you mean."

"Thanks! That would be so great. I'll wait until you're finished with your meal and everything. Let me get those drinks!"

Camilla held up a hand. "Would you tell Adam Rayburn we're here, please?"

"Mr. Rayburn? Uh—sure. Sure thing." He darted away, and I studied my menu, suddenly hungry again.

"I think I'm going to start with soup. They have split pea. The weather is so unfriendly today, isn't it?" I asked.

"Blue Lake wind chills break weather records every year. And we're famous the world over for our record snowfalls."

"Wow—something to look forward to."

She laughed. "I'll have soup, too. And maybe this cod sandwich."

"And I'll go with the Reuben."

When Grant returned, we gave him our orders and handed him our menus. Seconds later Adam Rayburn almost burst out of the back, his eyes raking the room. He saw us and brightened, then immediately seemed to deflate. I was starting to think that Rayburn might be the weirdest person I'd met in Blue Lake—and that was saying a lot.

He made his way to our table and grinned. "You made it! Is Grant taking good care of you ladies?"

"Oh, yes. Would you like to join us for a moment, Adam?" Camilla said.

He glanced at his watch, then at the door to his kitchen. "Perhaps for a moment, yes. I—we had agreed on Thursday, and tonight I have a bit of a—"

"We won't keep you long. It's just that we've had some interesting things happening up at the house, as you know. First Lena received unexpected visitors. Then she was nearly mowed down in the night by an intruder in the darkness. Doug Heller came to investigate and found that we have been housing the equivalent of a drug lab in our home, and the only man we've linked to the crime so far has mysteriously gone silent and hired a lawyer. Doug says he's hired someone expensive."

"Unbelievable," said Adam, shaking his head as he took a seat at our table.

"Martin Jonas was killed, perhaps by the very people running this lab. We're wondering, Lena and I, if he had a crisis of conscience. Perhaps some members of his group didn't want him to have a conscience. Or perhaps they had a conscience, too, but felt trapped by circumstances. Perhaps they made a mistake long ago, and have had to cover it up ever since." Her look was searching, incisive.

Adam nodded. "That may well be. Poor Martin."

"So we were trying to think of something that might connect it all. Who knew Martin Jonas? Who could provide Martin Jonas with a cover that might conceal his 'real' job? Who might be wealthy enough to pay for Dave Brill's expensive lawyer so that Dave wouldn't be tempted to share information with the police?"

"And what did you decide?" Rayburn asked, his eyes flicking to the kitchen as a waitress came out with a full tray.

"Well . . . you came up as a possibility."

Rayburn's eyes returned to us, wide with shock. We had all his attention now, and Camilla met his gaze. I admired the way she held her ground, although a red mark appeared on each of her cheekbones.

"I—?" He left his mouth open, as if uncertain what sounds should come out of it. "Are you suggesting that I had something to do with the death of poor Martin?"

"We're trying to put together a puzzle," I said.

He didn't even look at me. His eyes were on Camilla. "And you think that I, the wealthy restaurateur, might spend a large sum to silence a low-life drug dealer?"

For the first time, Camilla seemed to falter. "I didn't think it, until Lena and I were talking, and we realized how often you had been coming over. And how curious you seemed about the house, what Doug was doing—what the police were doing. How—present you were."

Rayburn barked out a short laugh, but his eyes held something like despair. "Oh, yes. I've been present. I've been present for longer than you've even noticed, Camilla. I've used every possible excuse to get your attention, as a matter of fact."

I saw it all then in a flash of insight. Rayburn bringing over a bottle of wine "so you can see if you like it." Rayburn with a sheaf of flowers that he insisted were extras. Rayburn asking for a tour of Camilla's house. Rayburn asking Camilla to dine with him at his restaurant.

Camilla saw it, too, and her cheeks flamed with embarrassment or some emotion I could not name. "Oh," she said. "I see."

He slumped back in his chair. "I thought enough time

had gone by. He's been dead almost three years, Camilla. I thought that was—an appropriate period of mourning. I thought maybe you—might have room in your life."

Suddenly I was a most uncomfortable third wheel. I slid to the edge of my chair, hoping to escape, but Camilla said, "Do stay there, Lena. Don't be silly." She had regained some of her composure, and now she flashed a gaze at Adam Rayburn. I wasn't sure if it held disdain or pity or gratitude, or a mixture of them all.

"Adam, perhaps we can talk about this later. I intend to keep our date for Thursday, as we planned. I apologize that we—seem to have misinterpreted your actions."

Rayburn had endured enough. He stood up, and his emotions, too, seemed a jumbled mixture. He was angry, but his eyes were still hopeful, I thought. "Yes, later. Good night, Camilla." His voice was cool, and he walked away without looking back.

I stole a glance at Camilla, who sat in silence, processing the interaction. I gave her time. Our soup came, and I studied mine with great concentration, blowing on it and taking a first delicious sip out of my spoon. After a couple of minutes my eyes returned to Camilla, and she sent me an almost mischievous smile. "Do you know, Lena, that in my youth I had more than one man in love with me?"

"Apparently you have one now, as well."

"Will wonders never cease," she murmured. "How blind was I? I had briefly suspected, after he had dinner with me the other night—"

I remembered how she had looked almost dreamy and happy at our little cupcake date. That had been the night she'd had dinner with Rayburn.

"—and then I told myself I was being a fool."

"Trust your instincts, Camilla."

We grew silent again. Grant brought our sandwiches, and we tasted them and proclaimed them delicious. I finally said, "Do you feel anything for him?"

She shrugged. "I don't know. We've always been friends—he and James and I. So we—have a certain intimacy that goes back many years. And he's a good-looking man."

I had never thought about this, but in many ways Rayburn was, in fact, attractive. "Yes," I agreed.

"But, Lena, I'm sixty-nine years old. I think I've passed the expiration date on things like love and romance and all the drama they entail."

"Have you? Because a man just walked angrily away from your table, holding his heart in his hand. You had just hinted that you thought he might have conspired in a murder. If that's not drama, I don't know what is."

"Oh, my."

"And if you have your mother's longevity, then you have several more decades to contemplate the way Adam Rayburn seems to feel about you."

She studied me for a moment with her intelligent eyes.

Then, finally, she said, "I will give that some serious thought. Now eat your sandwich. If Adam didn't have something to do with the death of Martin Jonas—and I am most relieved to realize he did not—then we still need to know who did."

"Yes. I wish all of this were over. Or that it had never happened at all."

She nodded and waved to Grant, our waiter, who was standing near the kitchen doorway. Camilla made a motion to suggest she wanted to pay the bill, and Grant disappeared.

"Camilla, you must let me pay for dinner. You've treated me to everything since the moment I got here."

Instead of arguing with me, she studied me again. I realized I was growing to love Camilla's face, especially her shrewd eyes. "All right. Thank you, Lena. That is most generous of you."

"Hardly generous, but a nice opportunity to thank you—for everything. Despite everything that's happened in this town, I love it here, and I love Graham House, and I most especially love working with you. In some ways—I hope you don't mind my saying it—you remind me of my mother."

"Why would I mind? It's a compliment, I'm sure. And where is your mother residing these days?"

"She died, years ago. Cancer. My father is remarried and lives in Florida."

She put a hand on one of mine. "You must miss her very much."

"I do, but the pain isn't fresh anymore. Sometimes, now, I'm just happy to think of her. And that she's with me all the time."

"I know she is. Because if I were your mother, I would certainly want to visit you after I died. You are a very loveable young woman, Lena London."

Grant appeared at our table to find me dabbing at my eyes with my cloth napkin. I held up my hand for the check, and he gave it to me. While I was signing the charge slip, he produced a worn paperback for Camilla, along with a pen that said "Wheat Grass" on the side. The book was, in fact, *Death at Seaside*. I hadn't read that one in a while, and seeing the cover, with its tossing waves, made me want to rediscover it.

Grant was effusive in his gratitude. "Thank you so much, Ms. Graham! It is such an honor to meet you, and I'll treasure this inscription. I wish I had brought one of my hardbacks."

Camilla smiled. "Have Adam bring a few to me at the house. I'll sign them and send them back. He can be our courier."

"Oh my gosh—thanks! It truly is an honor. I just want to say—your books just—transport me to another time and place. I hope you write a million more."

Camilla thanked him again, I handed him the leather folder with the signed charge slip inside (along with a healthy tip for Grant), and we gathered our coats. Apparently, though, Grant wasn't finished speaking. "Oh, and I just wondered what you thought of your notorious neighbor!"

"I'm sorry?" Camilla's voice was cold now. A queen displeased by a subject.

"Oh—it's just—Adam mentioned once that Sam West was your neighbor. I wondered what you thought about the latest news. You being a mystery writer and everything."

"What latest news?" I said sharply.

"That he's been arrested. I just heard it on the radio. They said they have enough evidence to prosecute him for the murder of his wife."

15

For a long time she existed without living, working at the local bakery and paying the baker's wife half of her wages for a cot in the room behind the business and for meals twice a day. She waited for a word from Gerhard, or for any sign that he was still alive and perhaps coming for her. Despite all of her vigilance, when the sign came, she was not ready.

—from *The Salzburg Train*

We listened to the car radio and heard the dreadful details. Sam West had been taken into custody early that evening. Police were not saying what evidence they possessed, but they were confident that West would be found guilty of his wife's murder when the case went to trial—and the state's attorney did intend to prosecute Sam West to the fullest extent of the law. West's lawyer, in turn, said the arrest was a travesty of justice, and that if he had anything to do about it, West would soon be free.

"Ridiculous," Camilla said. "Poor Sam."

"I need to text him," I said. My head felt strange, as though it were filled with roaring ocean waves.

"You can't, dear. If he's under arrest, they take those things away, don't they?"

"Oh, God. This is terrible. What can we do, Camilla?

Can't we do something for him? You're famous. What if you gave the police a comment, saying you are confident that Sam West is innocent?"

"My dear, that would accomplish nothing at all. No one cares what an old novelist thinks. The police are supposedly basing this on evidence, though I find the appearance of the blood quite suspect."

I turned to her. "Yes! So do I! Why do you think so?"

"Lena—please. We can't help him if we don't live. Keep your eyes on the road and try to calm down."

I had driven us in my car, and now I stared ahead into the darkness, feeling foolish. "I'm sorry. I just—this is such bad news. I don't know what to do with it."

"Neither do I. But Sam has a good attorney and a fine mind. He's trying to work this out, too. He has been for a year."

"But now the whole world will be against him. You know how willing people are to believe the news headlines. To think the worst."

"And why don't you think the worst? What makes you defend Sam so strongly?"

I stole a glance at her and saw curiosity in her eyes. "Because—because I met him. And I saw his pain and misery, but I didn't see cruelty or jealousy. And when he spoke of his wife—he was worried about her. That's authentically innocent. If he had killed her, he'd want to place the blame on her, or deny that a crime had been committed. That's what the others do—the men who really did kill their wives. I've seen their faces on television, and I've seen Sam's face, and Sam's is good."

I felt on the verge of tears again.

"I agree, Lena. I couldn't have put it better myself."

We pulled onto the gravel road that led to her house, and I realized that I hadn't checked on Sam's house recently. The thought of doing it in the dark didn't appeal to me; I made a note to check it the next morning and water all of his plants.

"He has plants, Camilla. He cares for them and . . . nurtures them."

"Yes."

"I'm curious, though. Why isn't his family speaking out on his behalf? Surely they can't believe he's guilty?"

Camilla sighed. "So he didn't tell you that part of his history."

"What?"

"It's sad. I'm not sure you can handle much more sadness."

"What is it?"

"When Sam was twenty-two, his parents and his younger sister boarded a plane bound for Massachusetts; they intended to visit some colleges. She was seventeen, and starting to plan her future."

"Oh, no."

"The plane crashed. It was Flight 427—do you remember that, on the news? But you would have been only about, what—twelve or thirteen years old."

"Everyone aboard was killed. I do remember. They were searching the water for survivors."

"Sam was orphaned, and Wendy was his only sibling. But this is what I want you to see—he's remarkably strong, Lena. He's weathered it all and remained a good person, under the veneer of cynicism."

I parked in front of the house and stared at its dark outline. "Thank you for telling me."

We went inside, and the dogs greeted us with their predictable merriment. Camilla said, "I'll let them out."

"I think I'll head upstairs, Camilla. Thank you for your company."

"Thank you for dinner," she said. "Things will look brighter in the morning." Her expression was comforting, and yet I was not comforted.

Upstairs I found my room empty—Lestrade was on some evening prowl. I sat at my desk and gazed at my notes, my laptop, my phone.

I picked up the cell phone and sent a text to Sam West. I didn't know if he could read it, but I wanted him to know he had my support. In a world of people out to believe the worst of him, I believed the best.

Restless, I dialed my father's number. He picked up on the second ring and said, "There's my long-lost girl! How's the new job going?"

"Oh, Dad," I said, half in tears.

"Whoa! Take a deep breath. Let me get my glass of wine. Okay, there we go. Now start at the beginning."

I talked to him for two hours: about Camilla, about Martin Jonas, about Doug Heller, about Allison, about Sam West.

"Wow," he said at last. "And I thought things were complicated with your plant scientist."

"Kurt?" With surprise, I realized that Kurt had practically been wiped from my memory banks by a couple of weeks in Blue Lake. "Yeah, you're right—Kurt was ultimately less complicated. But also less worthwhile."

"Do you want us to come up there? We can stay in a local B and B or something. Just be around for moral support. Tabitha would love that. She misses you as much as I do."

"You are the sweetest dad in the world. Maybe we can plan something like that for spring. It's too cold right now, and it's getting colder. You guys stay warm in Florida, and let me finish this first project for Camilla, and then—yes, I would love it if you came up here."

"You just let us know. We can take vacation days and make arrangements on short notice."

"I will. And thanks, Dad. I feel better just talking to you."

"Meanwhile, I have to be a father and say that a murder was committed in that town, and I'd prefer if you don't wander around alone. If you go out, go with other people. Okay? Will you promise me that?"

"I promise, Dad."

By the time I hung up I did feel more peaceful, and more optimistic that things would resolve themselves. Martin Jonas' killer would be caught, and Sam West's lawyer would prevail.

In the meantime, I had my own job to do, and perhaps it would be best if I focused on that. I looked out into the darkness and saw that it had begun to rain. In a burst of visuals, I recalled the storm that had brought me to Blue Lake: the bulging clouds, gray over tossing water; the anxiety over my meeting with Camilla; Doug Heller, blond and handsome on the side of the road; Martin Jonas facedown on the sand; and Sam West, his blue eyes concerned, standing in the drizzle and thinking his private thoughts.

16

One thing Johanna had learned since boarding the train in Salzburg—oh, how long ago it now seemed—was the power of instinct. It was her instinct that told her that she was no longer safe in the baker's house, instinct that persuaded her to creep down the stairs in stocking feet before the sun rose, and instinct that sent her, for a third time, out into the world alone.

—From *The Salzburg Train*

THE NEXT DAY it was cold, yet bright; a few wayward leaves had pasted themselves to my bedroom window, reminiscent of a child's art project cut from paper. I showered, dressed, and poured food into Lestrade's bowl. He was still sleeping off his nighttime revels, whatever they had been, and he snored lightly at the foot of my bed.

Downstairs, too, things seemed more cheerful. Rhonda was in the kitchen making something that smelled delicious, but wouldn't tell me what it was. "It's a surprise," she said. "Just go sit down in there."

I headed for the dining room, but by way of the front hall, so that I could retrieve Camilla's morning paper. I opened the door and grabbed it from the porch; Bob Dawkins and his awful offspring were finally painting the porch they had repaired. I forced out a "Good morning," which Dawkins answered in a gruff voice. His son merely sneered at me.

"Wow," I said under my breath, retreating into the house.

"That guy is the worst," I told Camilla as I sat across from her at the dining room table. I pointed at the stairs and she nodded.

"They both are, really. The apple doesn't fall far. But I must say they do excellent work, and they charge a fair price."

"Just like Lane Waldrop's grandfather—what was his name—Mr. Haney?"

She nodded, brushing a strand of silver hair behind her ear. "Oh, yes, Mr. Haney. He was quite good. But he had much more charm than those two. He was charismatic, and a born storyteller. Perhaps that's why he was so fascinated by this house and its hidden parts. I'm sure he spun the mystery into quite a tale for his grandchildren. No wonder little Lane was fascinated."

"Wait—if his name was Haney . . . does that mean that her name, at one time, was Laney Haney?"

"Oh, dear. What a name to saddle a child with! No wonder she married young. Although Waldrop itself is not particularly graceful, is it? Let's hope Haney was the mother's maiden name, and not Lane's surname."

We giggled, but I could tell that Camilla, like me, had other things on her mind, and we were each making an effort to divert the other.

"Have you—heard from Adam today?"

"No. I don't expect to. We'll need a bit of time to process last night's interaction. We were both taken by surprise."

"Yes, I suppose so." I tapped my fingers nervously on the table. "I had some new ideas about the Black Forest scene last night. And if you could give me some work—any other scenes in particular you'd like me to focus on—I'd be happy to do it."

Camilla nodded. "Yes. Perhaps we both need the distraction of work." Neither of us mentioned Sam or Martin Jonas, but their names hovered in the air.

Rhonda came in with a tray of something hot and fragrant. "Here we go—homemade waffles, Rhonda-style!"

She put a large waffle on each of our plates, then pointed to the syrup, butter, and cream on the table. "Help yourselves," she said.

Camilla was effusive in her thanks, and I made some grateful noises.

"Lena? Are you all right?"

I took a bracing sip of my coffee. "I—suddenly feel a little bit queasy. I'm not sure I can eat this, but I don't want to offend Rhonda."

Camilla took a bite of hers. "Mmm. Delicious. But if you absolutely can't—there is a way to dispose of it that will make everyone happy." She tipped her head in the direction of the dogs, who sat in the doorway, ears alert, not exactly begging, but ready for any sign of human largesse.

I slipped most of my food to them while Camilla managed, serenely, not to notice.

"Are you running any errands this morning, Lena?" Camilla asked, sipping some coffee.

"I was going to mail a letter to my father. Did you need anything?"

"I have a small list; I'd appreciate the help, if you're already going."

"Of course. I may as well go now. Let me grab my jacket."

Rhonda walked past us, also with a coat on. "I'll be back to make lunch, Camilla. My son is getting that award today, as you know. But I have everything ready, and I should return by twelve thirty."

"That's fine. You two run along and I'll get some writing done."

A few minutes later I was at the door. Camilla met me there with her wallet and a small list. "This should cover it; let me know if it doesn't. They should have it all right there at Bick's Hardware."

"Of course. Bick's has everything."

I looked out the screen door and watched Rhonda driving away in a little pickup truck. The breeze seemed to have intensified, and despite the sun that shone on the new porch paint that the Dawkins duo were assiduously applying, the air smelled like rain. I wondered if another storm were coming.

"You can't come this way," said Dawkins the lesser, squinting at me as he held up his brush. Dipped in a deep gray tint, it looked like eagle talons in his hand. "The paint's still wet."

"Oh, right—I forgot. Didn't Rhonda come out this way?"

"We sent her around back."

Camilla appeared next to me. "That's fine, Lena. I'll walk you out. I need to call Doug. I thought he took away all evidence of that terrible drug ring, but I found some more this morning, and I want to share it with him. It might just give him the break he's looking for."

I spun around, surprised. "You didn't tell me that at breakfast."

She blushed slightly. "We were speaking of other things. I'll tell you all about it when you come home."

"All right." I studied her face; there was something she wasn't telling me. "I'll get going then. Out the *back*," I said loudly, so the Dawkins duo could hear.

I made my way outside and down the back porch, then around the house and down the path, past Sam's sad and empty house and down, down the pebbled path of the bluff. At the bottom of the hill I turned left on Wentworth, remembering that Camilla had told me the library was in the other direction. Perhaps I would have time to explore it soon . . .

But first I had errands to run. I marched to Bick's and moved to the back wall, familiar now with all the clutter and the strange assortment of goods. I greeted Marge, who was leaning on her counter with a tranquil expression, peering through her cheaters at what looked like a romance novel.

"Hi, Marge. I'd like to mail this, please." I handed her my letter and suffered her nosy glance at the address.

"How is your dad doing?" she asked.

"He's fine. I'm just sending him an update; I do it every week or so. We e-mail, too, but he likes letters."

"Don't we all? They're so much more personal." She tossed the letter into an outgoing bin and said, "Anything else I can do?"

I looked at Camilla's little list. None of the objects were particularly personal, so I felt I could show it to Marge. "Can you tell me what aisles these items are in?"

She took the paper and squinted at it. Her cheaters didn't work very well. "I'll do you one better—I'll write the aisle numbers down next to each one. This for Camilla?" I nodded. "She wants a box of nails—that's in our hardware section—aisle twelve. Then she wants a legal pad—that's in stationery, aisle two." She jotted down a few more things and handed me the paper.

I thanked her, retrieved Camilla's items, and returned to pay for them. Marge smiled at me while she punched things into her register. She had no scanner, so she actually had to punch in the amounts manually. Bick's was like a visit to the twentieth century. "So, you're quite the popular young lady here in town," she said.

"I'm sorry?"

"Well, you've made all sorts of friends, haven't you? After just being here a short time. And I say good for you."

Were people gossiping? What friends had I made, exactly? "I'm not sure what you mean," I said, forcing a smile.

Marge began placing my items in a paper bag. "Well, the other day you were here with the Waldrop girl. You seemed thick as thieves." She smiled at me with slightly crooked teeth. "Then, the word was that you had breakfast with Mr. West."

I said nothing. I watched her hands as they finished packing. Marge seemed immune to my lack of response.

"And of course Mr. Bick and I were wondering about another young man in town. We thought maybe there was a romance brewing."

"I certainly seem to have been the subject of conversation around here," I said, my voice cool.

"Oh, not just out of pure gossip. Mr. Bick happened to see someone leaving your place at a surprising hour, and he happened to mention it to me. And then we just wondered—maybe a romance."

My cheeks felt suddenly hot. I put my hands up to cool them. "That is certainly not true. He happened to be at my place because I called in an emergency, and he came to respond. We had an intruder, actually."

Marge's eyes widened. "Why in the world would he come if you called about an emergency?"

"Because Doug Heller is on the police force," I said, my voice crisp. I was tired of defending my life to her.

Marge Bick's eyebrows rose, and her lipsticked mouth opened slightly. "Who's talking about Doug Heller? I was talking about Ray."

I heard every sound in the store in a weird rush of sensation. People chattering in the aisles; ceiling fans squeaking on their hinges; Mr. Bick flicking the switch on a paint mixer, which whirred and thumped on the wood floor.

Ray.

"I'm sorry; I think we're at cross-purposes. I don't know anyone named Ray, and I certainly didn't invite anyone named Ray to my home."

Marge paused, a finger on her chin as she gave this some deep thought. "Well, that's funny. Horace says he saw Ray coming out of your driveway at one, two in the morning."

"Ray who, Marge? Who is this Ray person?"

She barked out a laugh of disbelief. "Everyone knows Ray. He works with his dad all over town, doing odd jobs. Ray Dawkins."

"Oh my God!" I said.

Bob Dawkins' horrible son. Ray Dawkins. The Ray who had been there when I was knocked to the ground. The Ray who had probably killed Martin Jonas. A terrible chill ran up my spine. Had poor Martin Jonas seen horrible Ray Dawkins' sneering face as his last sight on earth?

And now he was at Camilla's house, and Camilla was home alone. She would be safe, I supposed, as long as she didn't suspect him. But—what had she said, as I was leaving? That she had more evidence to give to Doug Heller—evidence implicating the unknown killer. And Ray Dawkins had been sitting right there, with the door open!

I had left Camilla alone with a killer.

"I have to go," I said, putting a twenty-dollar bill on the counter and grabbing my bag with numb hands.

"But, hon, you've got change coming," she said.

"I'll come back for it—I have to hurry," I said, and I ran.

I flew down Wentworth toward the path at the foot of the bluff. Why, why, had I never once asked about the horrible son's name? Because he was as invisible as a mailman or a telephone worker; he was background music.

Now he was in the foreground, and a whole lot of things came into focus, starting with the easy access he would have to his lair at Camilla's because he always found reasons to be on her property. If anyone ever questioned him, he could usually say that he was working on a job for her. And Camilla, in her generosity, had probably gone out of her way to make new jobs so that the Dawkins family could keep working.

Camilla. What sort of evidence had she been talking about? Why hadn't I asked her about it at the time? I had assumed she was safe in her own house, but I was wrong, wrong! And now, perhaps, I had left her, old and frail, with a heartless murderer who feared exposure.

A new and more terrible thought occurred to me: Martin Jonas had been shot to death, and Heller and his investigators had never found the gun. Did that mean Ray Dawkins still had it? Was it on him right now? How could Camilla possibly defend herself against a loaded weapon?

I paused on the pebbled path, catching my breath, then ran again. If I could just get to her before Dawkins made his move—because surely he would make a move—then I could lock the doors and call Doug and the whole thing would be over once and for all.

I tore up the last of the bluff, my calves screaming from the uphill run, and stopped dead in the center of the yard. The old van that the Dawkinses drove was gone; had they left? Was Camilla all right? I set the bag down, fumbled for my phone, and dialed with trembling fingers.

"Heller," Doug said.

"Doug, I know who Ray is."

"What? Who?"

"Bob Dawkins' son. He was here today. He overheard Camilla say something about evidence she had—"

"What evidence?"

"I don't know, it's just something she said. But now their truck is gone, and she was alone here, and I'm going in to see if she's all right."

"Do *not* do that. Wait for me; I'll be right over." He hung up in my ear, and I lifted the bag and propelled myself forward, up the newly painted, still-sticky porch and through the front door, which was unlocked.

That was the first bad sign.

The second was that the dogs were nowhere to be seen.

In fact, the house was eerily silent. "Camilla?" I called softly. "Camilla, are you here?"

I heard a creaking sound; I wasn't in the house alone, but a strong instinct told me that it wasn't Camilla who was sharing the space with me. I was in the hall, fair game for anyone who might dart down the stairs or out of a doorway. I peeked into her study, which seemed empty. On a sudden impulse, I moved swiftly toward the vent and turned the dial. I heard the satisfying click and rushed to the wall.

The door slid quietly open and I went inside. I didn't flip on the light. I closed the door almost all the way, leaving just a crack through which I could observe the room, but hopefully which would not allow someone to notice the aperture from the study itself.

I waited, breathing hard, listening to the drumming of my own heart. I remembered being a child in a game of hide-and-seek, waiting painfully for someone to discover me, fearing detection, wanting to go to the bathroom, dying of suspense. I hoped I wasn't breathing too loudly.

Another creak, louder this time, and a form came into view. It was Bob Dawkins' horrible son; how had I not noticed how sinister he was, how evil his face looked? He was only feet from my hiding place, and he wore the look of a hunter; he paused every now and then to listen, his entire body still, and then he would creep forward again on silent feet. He paused once at the windowsill; he picked something up and put it into his pocket. Was he robbing her now? I couldn't focus on that, because Dawkins was coming closer. Would he see the slight crack in the wall, or the wallpaper that was now not flush with its opposite panel?

His focus, though, seemed to be on my supposedly invisible hiding place.

I realized with sudden dread that I had trapped myself. Assuming he figured out my location, I had nowhere to go.

I pressed my eye to the tiny crack in the door and tried

to suppress my breathing. Dawkins was acting strangely, tapping at the wall behind Camilla's desk. In an instant I saw the truth: he suspected a secret door, and he would tap until he found the hollow place. He was coming right toward me.

A look around the room behind me reminded me of its contents: books and canning jars. I moved silently toward the jars and picked a heavy-looking one labeled "Strawberry Preserves." Slowly, I edged back toward the door and peered out again, almost letting out a scream when I saw that he was directly in front of me, his eyes scanning. I stepped away from the wall, fearful that he would see my eye against the tiny crack. How had he not seen the little aperture in the wall? Was it that well hidden from his side?

A door slammed somewhere in the house. "Lena?" I heard Camilla say.

His chin came up; his eyes narrowed. His hands had both been at my eye level, reaching toward the wall. Now one of them flicked to his side and came up with something that gleamed in the sun. *A knife.* He was holding a knife. He was going to hurt Camilla. Perhaps he had already done so? Where was she? Where were the dogs? Were they already dead or hurt? Where was Doug Heller? I was on my own with a man who had killed someone.

On an impulse of horror and rage, I kicked the door outward, catching him in the forehead. "Ouch! Son of a—" he yelled, grasping his head with both hands. His knife clattered to the floor.

I leaped forward and kicked it out of the way.

"You," he said. "You stupid cow. You're the reason the cops came here, aren't you?"

"What are you doing in this house? Camilla isn't here."

"Where's the evidence she has for the cops?" he said, looming over me. "Give it here, or I'll hurt you. I'll hurt you both."

He crowded into me, pushing me back against the wall; his hands wrapped around my throat. I felt the weight of the strawberry preserves, still in my right hand, and I swung the jar up and against his head, hard.

"Ouch!" he yelled again, staggering backward. Then he let loose with a stream of swear words, some of which I didn't even know, but which sounded particularly filthy. His head was bleeding. He touched it, then looked at his hand. He sent me an evil glance. "I'm gonna kill you," he said.

"You are not going to touch her," said Camilla's voice. She stood in the doorway of the office, a shepherd on either side of her. The dogs, showing their teeth, looked alert and ready to attack; I was especially pleased to see them. "Unless you'd like me to give my dogs the order to pin you down."

He sneered at her. He truly was stupid, because he said, "I'll take my chances," and lunged for his knife.

Camilla said one quiet word, and the dogs rushed across the floor with a whooshing sound, then clamped down their jaws on his flesh with a noise that sounded like "snarf." Heathcliff had his calf, and Rochester had his right arm.

Camilla's voice was calm, but I could see that she was frightened. "They'll just hold you like that, unless I have to give them the order to bite. It's up to you," she said.

Dawkins' horrible son swore some more, and called Camilla and me some names that neither of us had ever been called, and I could see that Camilla was tempted to give her dogs the order.

Then we heard a sound at the front door. Camilla leaned

out of the study doorway and said, "Hello, Doug. Please do come in."

Doug Heller walked into the room and took quick stock of the situation. "What's he doing in here? Did he hurt either of you?"

"He threatened to kill Lena. Perhaps he would have tried, if the dogs and I hadn't come in at that moment," Camilla said.

"He was looking for the evidence Camilla said she had against the leader of the drug ring. He threatened to hurt me if I didn't give it to him," I said. "I hit him—that's why he's bleeding. First with the door, and then with a canning jar."

"I'm suing her," Dawkins said from the floor. "That was assault."

"Shut up," Heller said. He took out a pair of handcuffs and pushed Heathcliff out of the way so that he could attach them to Dawkins' wrists.

"Ray Dawkins," he said, "I am arresting you on suspicion of the murder of Martin Jonas, and for the possession, manufacture, and sale of illegal substances in the state of Indiana. Anything you say can be used against you in a court of law . . ." As he Mirandized Dawkins, the man on the floor scowled at Camilla and me.

"You don't have to say the whole thing. I know it from TV shows," Dawkins said irritably. "I also know that I get a lawyer and that if I don't say a word then you have nothing on me."

I saw something poking out of his pocket and I ran forward to retrieve it. "Except this," I said. I held up the gray scarf. "Doug, your guys found this on one of the nights these guys visited their drug lair. They gave it to Camilla, and she held on to it, waiting to find out if it belonged to anyone she knew. And when Mr. Dawkins here saw it on the windowsill just now, he shoved it into his pocket."

"That don't mean anything," Dawkins sneered. "I'm here all the time, fixing stuff. I probably lost it then. You got nothing on me."

Doug smothered a laugh. "We've got plenty on you, idiot. We've got fingerprints which I'm thinking will match yours, and we've got your stupid drug lab, and we'll probably have Dave Brill's testimony in a plea deal. We have the fact that you broke into this house today, armed with a weapon, and threatened to kill Miss London. And we have whatever Camilla found."

We looked at her, expectantly. She shrugged. "Oh, I didn't find anything. I just suspected this young man, so I figured I would send Lena out of harm's way and take myself out with the dogs and see if he took the bait. Which he did." She looked at Ray Dawkins, the horrible son who had turned out to be a horrible criminal. "Why in the world did you choose my house for your illegal hideout?"

He shrugged and shared his chronic sneer. "I'm not saying I did, but why wouldn't I? There's no better hiding place than that tunnel, which I seen when we boarded it up, and you're just an old woman. No one would suspect it, and you couldn't do a thing."

I was furious on her behalf, but Camilla looked amused. "Perhaps you'll rethink your decision in your jail cell."

Doug said, "Camilla, call off your hounds so I can get this guy back to the station."

She clapped for the dogs, who jogged over to her, and she patted their heads. I was sure they would get a special treat for dinner tonight.

"That's a pretty nasty bump, Ray. Did you fall?" Doug asked dryly as he marched his prisoner across the room.

"She just told you she hit me! Arrest her, why don't you?" Dawkins attempted to point at me with his cuffed hands. "And I'm going to sue. I'm going to sue her, and your stupid-ass police force."

"Oops," Doug said, as he bumped Dawkins' head into the door frame. "That was an accident. Please go on about your lawsuits."

"Police brutality!" Dawkins yelled. "I'll sue for that, too."

"I'm sure these ladies will countersue," Doug said. He turned to us and said, "Thanks, girls." And he winked. I didn't think men still winked, but Doug Heller did it, and it looked attractive. He went through the door, but poked his head back in. "Are you two okay?"

"Yes," Camilla and I said in unison.

We thanked Doug and waited until the door shut.

I ran to Camilla and we hugged each other. "I was afraid he would hurt you," I said.

"I felt the same. I didn't think you'd be back so soon. I thought I could take out the dogs, leave the house unattended, and let him fall into the trap. Then I would call Doug—which I did—but he told me you had just called and were planning to check on me. Then I was terrified!"

I patted her hair, which was a bit disheveled. "Why did you suspect him?"

"It dawned on me just this morning, as I saw him painting with his father. I've seen Bob Dawkins do work all over town, but his son isn't always with him. Here, though, the son was always along. I studied him while he worked, and saw that his eyes kept darting to the side of the house, and the padlocked hiding place. Then I realized he had opportunity and motive, assuming he had a falling-out with Jonas. He's around the same age as both Jonas and Brill, which would explain how they all met one another. You told me that Martin Jonas knew the house had a secret. Apparently they figured it out.

"So I decided to say something about evidence and see what he would do. I stood by the window after you left, watching them. When it was time to leave, he sent his father off alone, saying he was going to walk to a friend's house. That's when I took the dogs out and waited."

"You were taking a risk, Camilla. I can't believe you put yourself in such danger!"

"I ended up putting you in danger, which is the last thing I wanted to do. And look what a tough fighter you are! Everyone should have you on her side. Or his side," she added with a hint of a smile.

I gave her an extra squeeze before I let her go. "I think this means it's over, right? Things will go back to normal now."

"You never knew what normal was, poor thing." She looked around the room with sudden distaste. "Let's get out of here. We'll go somewhere. Would you like to ride out to Lake Michigan, or the Dunes? Or perhaps we can go somewhere for a nice lunch—food to warm the soul. Or should we see what's playing at the movie theater? That might be just what we need."

She went to her computer and saw that the town theater, which specialized in showing "oldies but goodies," was in the midst of a Golden Era week and currently showing a Katharine Hepburn classic: *Bringing Up Baby.*

Camilla Graham looked up at me from her desk chair.

It could have been a picture on the jacket of one of her books. "How does that sound, Lena? Would you like to see a movie with me?"

I told her I would like it very much.

And that is why, only an hour after Bob Dawkins' horrible son was arrested for the murder of the ill-fated Martin Jonas, I found myself sitting in a movie theater and sharing a large popcorn with my idol, Camilla Graham, who sat with perfect posture in her seat and looked like some elegant, adventurous aunt that I might dream up for myself.

In the midst of our laughter at what was a very funny movie indeed, I had a sudden thought. "Camilla," I whispered, "what about the boat? What did they use it for? Why couldn't they trace it?"

She thought about this, then nodded. "We'll ask Douglas in the morning. He's a bit busy today, don't you think?"

She patted my hand and then left hers there, sitting lightly on mine.

17

On her own again, she wondered who might be out there, in the large disinterested world, to offer aid. It was a sobering thought to realize that, upon reflection, she had no true friends.

—from *The Salzburg Train*

THE BOAT, DOUG Heller told us while we all shared coffee and rolls at Willoughby's the following morning, had been a purchase made on craigslist and paid for in cash. Martin, who had been gifted in technology, had created the false persona of Darren Zinn in order to avoid detection. Zinn had a real post office box which occasionally received mail.

"Why didn't they just do their business on the boat, then? Why involve Camilla?" I asked, poking at my cinnamon roll.

"They did use the boat all the time, at first. But they didn't like having it out in the open and risking witnesses every time they boarded. Then a couple of years ago Ray Dawkins was doing a job with his dad, repairing some siding on Camilla's house that had been knocked off by a storm. He discovered the little lever that opened the door entirely by chance, and soon enough he found not just the room, but the tunnel. That was when they relocated the boat to a dock near Camilla's place, and they figured they had the perfect location. The tunnel was basically soundproof. They visited it only in the wee hours of the morning, and they used the boat to make their deliveries at various docks around Blue Lake."

"Disturbing," Camilla said, sipping her coffee, "not just that they were there, but that I never suspected. It explains some of the dogs' behavior, though." She looked at me. "That night they woke you up wasn't the first night they'd gone down there to the office, sniffing around. And yet I never heard a thing. To be honest, if Martin hadn't been killed, I doubt I would have thought twice about it. I would have figured I had vigilant dogs who were perhaps overeager. Or that they smelled a deer or a raccoon or something."

"Thank God the tunnel has been found, and exposed, and the proper people have been arrested," I said. "You did a great job on this, Doug."

His face reddened slightly, and he swept some crumbs off the table, his eyes cast down. "All in a day's work."

"Not really. You came to Camilla's place at all hours, more than once, despite all the other things you had to do. We're in your debt."

"We are, Doug," Camilla said warmly.

"You've been helping me since the second I came to town," I said.

Camilla leaned forward. "I haven't heard this story!"

"He got my cat out of his hiding place in my car so that I wouldn't be late for my date with you. My interview, I mean." Doug finally met my eyes with his wise brown ones. "So I guess you owe me one, Lena."

"I guess I do." I grinned at him. "Meanwhile, what will happen at the station?"

Doug stretched and yawned. "Don't know, don't care. Today is my day off, and my colleagues will be handling things for the time being. Dawkins has already been transferred out of our jurisdiction, to the county lockup."

"Well, you should enjoy the time with a good book. I recommend the novels of Camilla Graham."

Doug brightened. "That's a great idea. I've read two of them, but there are lots more I still need to read. What do you recommend?"

"Have you read her first? *The Lost Child*? In many ways that's my favorite."

"Mine, too," Camilla said.

CAMILLA AND I agreed to meet and work that afternoon, so I spent the rest of the morning at Allison's house, since she too had the day off and we hadn't found much time to hang out together. Now we lounged lazily on her couch while I filled her in on the last of the Martin Jonas story.

"It's unbelievable. First that this sort of crime would happen in idyllic little Blue Lake, but then that those guys were so cruel and heartless."

"Not so unbelievable, I guess. All you have to do is read the headlines every day."

"No, don't get all depressed on me. This is our fun day!" Allison said with her usual bright and happy demeanor. "What should we do? Make chocolate chip cookies? Take a walk outside? Get addicted to a Netflix series? What are you doing?"

I was scrolling through pages on my phone. "Talking about headlines got me thinking. I want to see what they're saying about Sam West today."

Allison jumped up and put her hands on her hips. "What is it with you and this guy, Lena? He's been arrested, for gosh sakes! What more evidence do you need that he's guilty?"

"Guilty of what? They don't even have a body. For all we know his wife is still alive."

Allison gave me a pitying look—the kind that Doug Heller had given me on the day he took Sam away.

"You don't believe me? When have you ever known me to be illogical?"

She sat back down on the edge of the couch. "Never."

"Something doesn't fit, Allie. I've never once thought he was guilty—not once. Camilla doesn't think so, either. And when you read this blog that one of her friends wrote—hang on. Can I use your laptop?"

"Sure."

I set down my phone and went to her computer, where I pulled up the blog called *A Fashionable Life*. Allison moved next to me, curious.

I pointed to Taylor Brand. "This was her best friend—or so she says."

"She seems kind of into herself," Allison said.

"That's what I thought! But look—here's the post she put up right after Mrs. West disappeared." I showed it to Allison and watched her read it.

"So what? She's upset."

"But she says that Victoria had talked about getting away. And look at the comments down at the bottom. This anonymous person said that they should "'follow the money and the drugs.'"

Allison snorted. "Yeah—and another anonymous person says that he's a wizard and he put a spell over everyone so they could no longer see her. Look—it's right here." She pointed to another comment.

I sighed. "The fact is that no one knows the truth, including the cops, which means they have no right to be holding Sam West."

Allison's hand on my shoulder was gentle. "They have *evidence*, Lee."

I said nothing.

She scrolled up the blog, waving her hand at all the entries. "Look at this—so many times she posted about her friend. Don't you think if Victoria were still out there she would have contacted Taylor?"

"I don't—wait! Go back. Two or three entries back—I want to see that picture. The one with their heads together. There. I've never seen that picture before."

Allison studied the image. "So? She looks a little different, doesn't she? Neither of them have any makeup on. What, do grown women still have slumber parties?" she said scornfully. Then her face changed, in typical Allison fashion, and she beamed at me. "We should have a slumber party!"

I laughed in spite of myself. "Wait—don't scroll away. There's something about this picture that's so familiar . . ." I leaned in. It was a shot of Victoria West and Taylor Brand, both looking a few years younger, their heads together in a typical "girlfriends" pose. Brand's dark hair contrasted with her friend's reddish, silky locks. They looked as though they had taken the picture in the early morning, or on some weekend getaway that didn't involve glamour. It was a rather sweet picture in its innocence and sincerity. West's face looked different than it had in other pictures I had seen. "Oh my God. Allie. Oh, God."

"What?" She leaned in. "What's going on? It's just a picture, Lee."

"Wait. Wait." I minimized the blog and started Googling some of the search terms I had used days earlier. "It's got to be one of these. There was this festival, this giant festival full of boats . . ."

I felt Allison staring at the side of my face, but I kept looking. "No, it's not this site. Okay, wait—I think it's this one. But if this is the case—oh my God—these search terms themselves could be a clue! Yeah—see these people? It's this big yacht festival. I was researching it for Camilla. It's got to be here—I know I saw it—okay, here. Here it is. That's her. Look at this woman."

I pointed out the woman I had seen while doing yacht research; she had reminded me of Sam West's wife, but I hadn't really thought about it at the time. And I hadn't really thought about what I'd typed in to bring up the image until I recalled it today. "Look, Allie."

Allison sat stiffly. "She's a woman on a yacht."

"Look at her face. Let me zoom in." I did, and then I moved the image to the side of the screen and brought back the blog picture. "Look at them together."

She leaned in closer. "Wow. They do look similar. But lots of women look like that. Red-haired, beautiful, snooty-looking. Straight teeth, good skin, blah blah. That's how they end up on yachts."

"Look at the mole. Or I guess it's more of a birthmark, right? That's what I see now in the picture of Victoria West. A little birthmark on her chin, almost shaped like a heart. Now look at the woman on the yacht."

Allison's eyes widened. "It's not just the birthmark. One of her teeth is slightly crooked. Do you see it, there? And there." She pointed at the yacht page, then looked at me. "What have you found here?"

"I've found Victoria West."

She shook her head sadly. "But it doesn't matter. Maybe she was off on some yacht years ago, but why would that matter now?"

My heart pounded in my chest; I was barely conscious of my words as I said them. "Look at the date on the website. That yachting festival happened eight days ago. That's Victoria West. She's alive, and she was in Greece one week ago."

We stared at each other in silence for a minute. "What now?" Allison asked.

I stood up. "Doug Heller has the day off. I'm going to pay him a visit."

HELLER ANSWERED HIS door wearing sweats and holding a beer. "Lena? What's going on? Is something wrong?"

"No. Can I come in?"

"Sure." He stepped back and allowed me into his kitchen, which was small and bright and spare.

His blond hair was slightly mussed, and his gold brown eyes were more than curious; I could see, at a glance, that he wondered if I were pursuing a romantic liaison.

"I need you to look at something."

"With pleasure," he said, grinning at me.

I smiled back, nervously. "On the laptop." I set it up on his little wood table and brought up the two windows. "I need you to look at these images."

He focused in and frowned. "Victoria West. Why, Lena?"

"Just hear me out, Doug. First of all, would you agree that this is the same woman?"

He sat and studied the pictures with close attention. Whatever he might think about Sam West or my "weird" obsession, he was still a cop first, and I was showing him evidence.

Finally he leaned back. "I would say yes, this is the same woman. The mark on the chin is distinctive, as are a couple of other facial features."

"Okay. Then consider this. The picture on the left, according to the blog, was taken in 2014. The picture on the right was taken last week."

"What?" He had been looking at me, but now he grabbed the laptop, pulled it closer, and clicked around to look at the posted dates. "This is impossible. How would they not have found this?" Then he looked suspiciously at me. "How did *you* find this?"

"It was an accident. Sam told me that his wife used to say she wanted to sail away from it all. I guess in my mind I thought of yachts, because she hung around with a wealthy set. So then Camilla was asking for ideas about her book, and I said what about yachts, and then I was doing research for her. It was just the vaguest thought that became a link. Just something she once said, and something I pictured, and then a website. Total serendipity. Sort of."

"Meaning?"

"Well, I was using all sorts of search terms relating to yachts. But I guess I still had Sam's wife on my mind, so one of the things I Googled was 'yachts' and 'Nikon.'"

"Why?"

I shrugged. "It was on my mind. It wasn't related to Camilla's book, but it was in my head, how she said she'd sail away, and how she had been typing the word 'Nikon' into her phone. So I just typed them both in at one point, and that's what came up."

"Why? What's the connection? What's Nikon?"

"I have no idea. But it brought me that picture."

"Unbelievable," he said.

"Doug."

His eyes met mine. We were both still leaning over the computer. "What?"

"You know what. Sam West has been done an injustice. By the police. By the public. By you. For more than a year now. And he's sitting in jail."

He nodded, his face half shame and half disbelief. "Yeah, okay."

"So now it's time to set things right. How do we do that?"

He leaned in and kissed me softly on the lips. I pulled back, surprised, and he smiled. "Okay, I get it. *We* don't do anything. I do. And it will take a large portion of my day off, so I'll ask you to skedaddle."

"I could stay, and—"

His face grew stern, remote, cop-like. "This is police business, Lena. I'll update you when I can."

"Okay. Thanks, Doug."

"Thank you, Lena. It looks like you just saved a man's life."

Before I had even closed the door he was on the phone.

18

She walked toward the river, not certain of her destination. Her only conscious thought was that everything was lost: her past—her family—her love—and she had no way of retrieving what had once been hers. When the man stepped in front of her on the dirt path, she almost screamed, but her voice froze in her throat and she stared, in shock. It was Gerhard. Somehow, against every predictable outcome, he had found her again, and in a rush her life came back to her.

—from *The Salzburg Train*

CAMILLA AND I worked in her office the next morning, trying to find momentum after the strange events of the past week. Doug had called the previous evening, but had stayed on the line only long enough to tell us that "things were in motion" and he couldn't divulge more. I tried watching CNN for information, but so far there were no headlines, so we buried ourselves in work for several hours until Camilla yawned and stretched. "I think the dogs could use a walk. Would you like to come along, get a bit of fresh air and a stretch of the legs?"

"I don't think so. I was hoping Doug would call . . ."

She smiled. "All right, then. You keep the lamp in the window, as it were, and I'll get these fellows some exercise. Do me a favor and close the door after us." She put the leashes on the happy shepherds, and they all marched out the front door. They would have yanked her right down the stairs, but Camilla said something stern under her breath and they both settled down, adapting to her more quiet pace. "See you soon!" she called over her shoulder.

I was about to close the door, but I saw a car pull into the driveway. Adam Rayburn emerged, looking more casual than I'd ever seen him in a pair of faded jeans and a gray hooded sweatshirt. He said something to Camilla with an urgent look on his face, and she replied, putting what looked like a comforting hand on his arm.

His expression changed to one of incredible relief, and he pulled Camilla into a big hug. I didn't think she would like that sort of thing, but she was laughing when he let her go. She said something else to him, looking up into his face, and he smiled.

I realized he must have read the Martin Jonas story in today's newspaper—an update including the arrest of Ray Dawkins and the surprising confession of Dave Brill. (Doug had told us he talked to get a more lenient sentence.) The story had contained some details about the day of Dawkins' apprehension, including the fact that he had broken into Camilla's house and confronted her and "her assistant" as they were at work. It wasn't particularly accurate, but it was close enough.

Adam must have read about it that morning and driven out to see Camilla for himself—to be sure that she was intact and none the worse for wear. I remembered his face at the restaurant, stricken by the idea that Camilla would ever suspect him of something terrible. And looking at him now, with his kind and smitten smile, it did seem rather ridiculous.

Adam lifted one of Camilla's hands, with a dog leash still in it, and kissed it. Camilla, always so reserved, beamed at him and said something in his ear.

Then the two of them went walking down the driveway, each holding a dog, speaking easily to each other and looking perfect together.

I sighed and closed the door.

CAMILLA AND ADAM came back half an hour later only to leave again, bound for lunch. "Rhonda left some mouth-watering sandwiches," Camilla called to me. "Eat as many as you like, Lena."

I felt too restless to eat. I paced around for a while, studying the paintings on Camilla's walls. I went upstairs and fed Lestrade. I came back downstairs and fed the dogs. I took my camera out to the back porch and photographed the lake and then Camilla's house; my father had asked me to e-mail him some pictures, and I hadn't gotten around to it yet.

I came back in and paced some more before I realized I was going stir-crazy. I put on a jacket, determined to go down the hill and into town. If I got enough exercise I would probably get rid of the nervous feeling inside me.

The wind was cold on my face when I started down the driveway. The autumn trees were losing their color now, some stripped bare by the last storm. Soon it would be November, and the cold would set in. Blue Lake was most likely quiet in winter, as people holed up in their houses under mounds of snow, waiting for the warm months and a chance to enjoy the water. I thought of my father and Tabitha in Florida. What would they think of it here? I could arrange for them to visit me soon, now that the worst was over . . . I saw an unfamiliar black car ascending the hill and I darted behind some trees in a sudden return of the paranoia Camilla and I had felt for days.

The car stopped before reaching our driveway; one of the backseat doors opened and a large bag was thrust out, followed by Sam West, looking thinner and more vulnerable. His brown hair blew around in the wind as he reached in to pay the driver and send him a polite wave. The car made a U-turn and went back down the hill. West hesitated, looking first at his driveway and then at the road that led up the bluff toward Graham House. Toward me.

I stepped out from behind the trees and started to walk toward him. Even at this distance I was able to lock eyes with him. He started to move toward me, and then I was running. When I was three feet away, he said, "Lena," and I threw myself against him. His arms wrapped around me instantly, possessively. "Sam, I'm so glad you're home," I said, and then I was kissing him, and he was kissing me back as the cold air blew around us.

For a long moment there was only the feeling of his mouth on mine, my hands in his hair, his warm palms on my lower back. "Sam," I said again, only a centimeter away from his face.

"I didn't know," he said, looking slightly stunned. "I hoped, but I didn't—" He shook his head.

"Now you do." I smiled at him.

"I thought maybe you liked the cop."

I moved back a few more inches so that I could study his features. “Doug?”

He smirked. “I guess I’ll have to call him that now. He’s suddenly turned decent in the last twenty-four hours.”

“He knows he was wrong. He’s making amends. Did they—mistreat you?”

He rearranged his arms around me and sighed. “It wasn’t so bad, except for the hopelessness. The feeling that I was being sent away for something that I didn’t do, that I would never know what had happened to Victoria, and that I would never be able to explain to anyone, especially you.”

I brushed a stray eyelash from his face. “Now they all have to apologize to you. The whole world, all your critics, all those nasty people who were willing to believe the worst.”

He shook his head. “I can’t believe it. And I have you to thank, Lena. You showed up here, only weeks ago, and I yelled at you like some ogre, and every day after that you made my life brighter and brighter, and then you saved it.”

“It was just luck.”

“Luck that I met you.” He pulled me back against him in a sudden spasm of emotion and squeezed hard. “You want to know something? That day you and I had breakfast together? I followed you, Lena. I wasn’t going to go into the damn town and face all the endless stares. But then I saw you go drifting by with your bright face and your happy walk, and I couldn’t resist. You were like a siren.”

I laughed, surprised.

“So I pretended that I meant to go into that stupid little restaurant, and luck was with me again, because your date canceled and I got to have breakfast with you. It was the best day I'd had in a long time."

"That's sweet," I said, smoothing out some frown lines on his face.

"I was afraid you were too young for me, and I saw the way Heller looked at you. But then, just as I was feeling bummed about it, you called me on the phone. Your voice perked me right back up. There's something about you, Lena. You're like an elixir. Every time I was exposed to you, I felt a little more of my life returning."

"And then you made me waffles," I said. "With a brand-new waffle maker that you bought just for me."

He looked surprised. "A detective, huh? But of course you are. You found Victoria when no one else could." He kissed me again. I slid my arms around his neck and kissed him back, and then I pulled away slightly and breathed in the scent of him, my nose on his cheek. He said, "How did you find her, Lena?"

"It was a weird coincidence. I don't think I would have seen the picture if not for the conversation we had at breakfast—the one at your house. You told me that Victoria said she wanted to sail away, and somehow that image stayed with me. You thought it was an image of escape, but subconsciously I guess I thought that it might be more than that."

"Hmm."

"So Camilla and I were working on the book, and I ended up suggesting that the characters escape on a yacht. She liked it, so I was doing online research, looking up yachts with various search terms. I saw that picture and didn't recognize her in it. But later I saw Victoria on her friend's blog, in a picture I hadn't seen before, and it reminded me so much of the yacht photo."

"Yes—I saw them both."

"But here's the crazy part—the thing I Googled, that made those particular pictures turn up? Were the words 'yachts' and 'Nikon.'"

Sam stiffened. "What? Why? What does it mean?"

"I have no idea. That's the next step, right? To figure out what Nikon is, then use it to find Victoria."

"That's good information. I need to get inside and pass it on to a couple of people."

"Not yet," I said, snuggling against him. "Do you know I thought you were a horrible person when I first met you?"

"I was horrible. I'm sorry."

"But I thought you were handsome, too. I still do."

He kissed my hair. "I thought you were very pretty, and sweet. Especially when you made that disapproving face at me."

"I disapproved." We stared at each other for a while without speaking, sending messages in silence. "So what happens now?" I finally said.

He sighed and pushed me away, gently. "That's the bad news. Nothing happens, Lena. Not until this is sorted out. I'm not going to drag you into this controversy, and I don't want nosy reporters hunting you down and calling you 'Sam West's lover' in the tabloids."

I started to protest, but he held up a hand. "No. This isn't over. You know what I went through, Lena; you understood better than anyone, and that's why you'll understand that I'll do whatever is necessary to keep that kind of evil away from you."

"Sam—"

"They'll be here soon, the vultures. I'm surprised they're not here now. But of course they don't know I'm back yet. They'll find out, and they'll come. So nothing is going to happen right now, for your sake."

"I can handle myself. You know I'm strong."

"I know, and I hope you'll wait for me. Maybe it won't take long. The police are on it, and now my own investigator has something to go on. The problem is that the man who took that picture was just taking crowd shots. He didn't know Vic or who she was with, and now that crowd has dispersed. The festival is over, and everyone went sailing away. We know she's alive, but we don't know where."

"So?"

"So we need that information. One image does not put me totally in the clear. To be honest, the DA in New York didn't want to let me go, not even after they had the pictures, because he said it wasn't enough evidence."

I made a scoffing sound.

He laughed. "They had a special hearing yesterday, and my lawyer—Don Fraser is his name—really earned his money. Don wiped the floor with that DA, and later he told me he really enjoyed it. Don's believed in me all along, and yesterday was vindication for both of us. He put up both photos on a big screen; then he Skyped with the man who had photographed Victoria. Ultimately it was more than enough for the judge."

"God, I hope so!"

He shook his head, still seemingly amazed by it all. "What I really can't believe is that she let me go through all this. That she was going to let me go to jail."

"Maybe she didn't know."

His face hardened. "She must have known when she provided a bunch of her own blood to help frame me. I can't get over that part. It was her blood, Lena. And officials are estimating the blood was there before the picture on the yacht was taken, not after. So she didn't lose it as a result of foul play. What does that leave?"

"Oh, the *blood*! I think I never wanted to believe that evidence existed."

He looked down at me, his brows raised. "Why did you believe me, Lena? When no one else did? Without even knowing me—why did you believe?"

"Because it was clear that you were telling the truth."

He stared at me for a moment, then said, "Unbelievable."

"You look tired, Sam. You should go take a nap. I'll come with you."

He laughed and looked half tempted, then shook his head. "No. You are going home." He kissed me again, softly, and said, "Promise you'll wait for me, Lena?"

"I promise. But if it takes too long, I'll risk the paparazzi. Maybe I'll call them myself and give them a piece of my mind."

He laughed. He backed away slightly, his eyes on me, and picked up his bag. "I'll see you later. Maybe Camilla can invite me for dinner sometimes."

"She will."

He waved and turned away, then turned back. "Hey—guess what? I gave up smoking. That's another way you saved my life. I haven't had a cigarette in three days."

He offered me a crooked smile that almost sent me running back to him, then turned and walked to his driveway, where he disappeared into the trees.

19

They decided they would take the night train, far into the north country, where no one would recognize them. Gerhard had some money stowed away with which he purchased tickets, and they boarded under a large gold moon, round as a wedding ring.

"It's not over," Gerhard warned as they entered their compartment.

She breathed more freely as she tucked against his side. "But we're together now. That's all that matters, even in the face of danger."

—from *The Salzburg Train*

SAM DIDN'T HAVE long to wait. Two nights later Camilla invited him for a celebratory dinner, along with several other Blue Lake residents, including Allison and John, some of the closest neighbors from houses along the bluff, a few of the people that Sam had said he "didn't despise," select members of Camilla's knitting club, and Detective Doug Heller of the Blue Lake Police Department. The two men greeted each other awkwardly in the foyer, shaking hands without making much eye contact. Camilla was dressed in a regal blue silk blouse and gray slacks; she moved among us as we stood in her library making rather stilted conversation with the other people at her party.

Rhonda, too, was dressed up, with a white blouse and a black skirt and an heirloom cameo choker. She whisked in and out with trays of hors d'oeuvres, which I snatched more frequently than I usually would, keeping a nervous eye on Sam, who was surprisingly kind to the people who approached him, some with genuine compassion or remorse, and some with bald curiosity.

Sam looked healthier now; I had texted him regularly to make sure he was eating, and once I had sent a giant pizza to his house. He made a point of not looking at me too often, and I was trying to do the same with him. I tore my gaze away from his conversation with two of the knitting club ladies and saw that Doug Heller was watching me with a wry expression. He stood in the corner of Camilla's study holding a vodka lemonade. He moved toward me and clinked his glass against mine—a Diet Coke and cherry juice on ice.

"I get it," he said softly. "You had a lot of extra motivation pushing you to help West. Right? You're into him."

"Don't use your detecting skills on me."

"It doesn't take much detecting. Anyone in here just has to look at your face."

"I need to be more diplomatic, I guess."

"Why?"

"He doesn't—he won't—be involved until it's over. He doesn't want the press near me."

"Then he's smart. And considerate." His words were complimentary, but his face looked resentful.

"I want you to know that I really appreciate—"

He held up a hand; he looked impatient. "Yeah, I know."

"Doug. If it hadn't been for Sam—I would probably have wanted you to ask me out."

"I sort of got that impression. So I just need him out of the picture, right?"

I smiled, because he was joking over his hurt feelings. "What's next for you? I assume there won't be any more murders in Blue Lake."

"Probably not. This isn't a murder kind of town."

"You did a good job on the case; you're a good cop." He bowed his head at the compliment and took a sip of his drink. I studied him for a moment. "Do you think you'll stay here? Or will people try to recruit you into a big city?"

He shrugged. "They do try, sometimes. Right now I'm happy here. I grew up in this town. Everyone should work in a place that feels like home, right?"

I ran an affectionate hand over the arm of Camilla's purple chair. "Absolutely. I couldn't agree more."

I looked up to see Sam West had finished his conversation with the knitting ladies; before he left the room, he sent me a secret smile.

BY TEN O'CLOCK everyone was gone, but Camilla had requested that both Doug and Sam stay behind. She asked the three of us to join her in a little sunroom that jutted out beyond the dining room. I had never sat there before, as Camilla and I preferred the intimacy of the kitchen table or the formality of the dining area. This room, surrounded by large windows with views of the darkened forest around us, felt odd, and there was a certain tension as Camilla waved us to the table and we took our seats, sending unspoken questions to one another in the form of raised eyebrows.

"Please, I won't keep you long," Camilla said, putting

a pot of coffee in the center of the table. Rhonda had already left, but she'd set the table first and put out a round green serving plate covered with slices of pumpkin bread.

I poured myself a cup of coffee and looked at Camilla, who had carried in her laptop. "I asked you all here because we all still have a job to do for Sam."

Sam looked more surprised than any of us. "Camilla—you've done plenty for me. And I thank you for this very nice party. It turns out that people in Blue Lake aren't that bad after all."

Camilla waved his comment away with some impatience. "No, no—they owed you tonight, and they owe you a lot more. Don't think twice about that. What I mean is, your mystery is not solved, and as you told us, the district attorney in New York is still pacing around, trying to figure out how to get you back in jail."

Sam shrugged. "He can try."

Camilla opened her laptop. "We can try, too. We can find Victoria and end this once and for all. It's our job."

Doug pushed his mug toward me, and I filled it. He said, "Camilla, with all due respect, it's not our job—it's the job of the police in New York City. We have no jurisdiction over this case."

She looked disappointed. "Doug. You know better than anyone that no one out there is going to find Victoria West. How hard will they even try? They want Sam more than they want her, because he made them look bad by being innocent."

Sam barked out something like a laugh, then took a piece of bread and crumbled it on his plate. "And I took great pleasure in it."

Doug's face was stubborn. "I know that Sam is your

friend, but why exactly do you think we can do what the police can't?"

Camilla smiled. "*You* are the police, which is why you are a necessary member of this team. And while you may think Lena and I are expendable, I would argue that we are the most important of all."

"Why is that?" I asked.

"Because we are writers."

No one knew what to say to this. Camilla sighed. "We have *imaginations*, and imagination is what is needed when plain old police work hits a brick wall. Sam would still be in jail if Lena hadn't followed her rather whimsical inclinations. Isn't that true?"

"It is indeed!" Sam said warmly. "You may be right, Camilla."

"I am right. And Sam, of course you are needed because you know Victoria. How she thinks, what she likes, how she might act in a given situation."

Doug still wasn't on board. "What exactly are you suggesting, Camilla?"

She nodded. "I am suggesting that the four of us find Victoria West, and soon. It's not just a matter of keeping Sam free. There is a more urgent component to this puzzle."

Now she had everyone's attention. She looked back at her computer and clicked with her mouse for a moment. "When Lena told me about the picture of Victoria, I studied it. In fact, I saved the picture from the website to my own files. Then I played with it in Photoshop, manipulating the image."

We stared at her. I had never exactly considered Camilla a throwback to another era, but even I had not anticipated the extent of her computer savvy.

"Why?" Doug asked.

"Well, I couldn't see it well, so I cropped it so that I could see her better—so that just her face filled the screen. And then I played with that image a bit. Zoomed in and out. That's when I found it."

In a sudden, mutual movement, we all leaned closer to her. "Found what?" Sam said.

She turned the laptop toward us. There was Victoria West's face in close-up, smiling at us. "Here's the picture as we've all seen it," Camilla said. "But look what happens when you cover everything but her eyes." She zoomed in until only Victoria's eyes were visible on the screen.

I gasped. "That's a different picture," I said.

"No," Camilla said. "Same picture, without the distraction of the smile. We were all focusing on the smile, weren't we? Perhaps all people would. But what do you see in those eyes?"

"Fear," I said. It was obvious now, in the window that Camilla provided. Victoria West's green eyes were creased with unhappy lines, and her brows were low over them, clearly expressing distress.

Sam made a guttural sound in his throat.

Doug said, "What the hell?"

Camilla widened the shot again to include her smile. "At a glance she is a happy woman on a yacht. But when you isolate the eyes, you see the truth. This woman is afraid. We need to know why. And there's a very real chance, Sam, that your wife needs rescuing."

AFTER MUCH DISCUSSION, we agreed with Camilla. Victoria West was potentially in danger, but we had no evidence of that other than her eyes in a photograph. Sam, after a close study of the picture, grudgingly agreed. "This does make her look afraid. And I've seen her afraid many times. She insisted on watching horror movies, for one thing, even though she disliked them, and this—it's authentic fear. I am amazed that you found this, Camilla."

"There was something wrong about the image. It bothered me. Now I know what it was: a basic disagreement between the top half of her face and the bottom—and of course the top is in shadow, which makes it even harder to see."

Doug nodded, looking interested. Once again, the cop in him could not resist this new mystery. "So the question is, what's she afraid of? She's on a yacht, she doesn't seem to have been physically abused or starved. She's wearing what looks like a designer bikini. What's the threat?"

"That is the question," Camilla said, sighing and closing her laptop. "Along with many others. One: where has she been? Two: why did she let the world believe Sam committed murder? Three: did she have the option of telling the world otherwise? Four: is she being held against her will? Five: is that why she is afraid, or is it some other reason? Six: what is Nikon?"

Doug leaned back in his chair and played with his coffee cup, his face moody. "This is troubling. Camilla, I admit, at first I thought you were really out in left field, but—I agree with almost everything you said. Except one thing. I'm not convinced the word 'Nikon' is important."

"Why?" I asked.

He shrugged and turned to West. "You said it was something you saw on her phone, right? But we type all sorts of pointless things into our phones, especially when we're texting people. It could be nothing at all. She could have asked a friend what sort of camera she recommended."

West nodded. "True—but that doesn't explain her reaction when I happened to read the word over her shoulder. She acted like I'd invaded her privacy. Like she had a secret."

"I think it's worth pursuing," I said. "And frankly it's the only clue we have to pursue, aside from chasing down the yacht, which apparently no one knows the name of, and that's the one thing the police probably are doing, at their own pace."

"Which could be glacial," Doug said. "Depending on how much they want to find this woman."

Sam looked solemn. "They want to find her—or find out it was a misunderstanding, and the woman isn't Vic at all. There are some pit bulls in the DA's office who really want my blood."

"Blood," I said.

They turned to me. "What?" Doug asked.

"They said the blood on the floor in Sam's apartment was Victoria's, but did they test it for drugs?"

Everyone looked at me blankly. "Why would they do that?" Doug asked.

I pointed at the computer. "Camilla, can I borrow that?"

She slid it across the table, and I opened it up and did a quick search for Taylor Brand's blog. "Remember this blog?" I said, showing them the picture. "It's the one with the picture of Victoria that made me realize she was the woman on the yacht. But there's another post—one that her friend Taylor made around the time Victoria disappeared. Here it is. And all these people made comments underneath. One of them, from an anonymous poster, says this: 'If you want to find Victoria West, follow the money and the drugs.'"

Sam's brows creased, but Doug shook his head. "So what? That's an anonymous poster on the Internet. That means nothing."

"Maybe. But if someone has been detaining her, wouldn't that be one way to do it? To drug her, or keep her addicted to drugs? I don't know a lot about it, but ever since I read that post I've wondered . . ."

"It would at least be worth checking, wouldn't it?" Camilla said, her face thoughtful. "If the girl were being drugged, and that blood contained her DNA, then they would be able to determine the drug content as well. Sam, did they give you any information about the blood?"

Sam rustled himself out of some deep thoughts and said, "No. But I will certainly be asking through my lawyer. And you should all know that I have a private detective named Jim Harrigan who's been looking for Victoria for the last year. He has the picture, too, and he's currently in Greece, trying to get information. I'm going to tell him everything we came up with."

Camilla nodded. "Meanwhile, keep us privy to the reports he's giving you. We may get new insights into the whole thing." She poured herself a cup of coffee and held up the mug in a sort of grim toast. "We'll solve this for you yet, Sam. It's the least we can do."

We all nodded agreement, including Doug Heller, who made eye contact with Sam, his expression grave and slightly remorseful.

* * *

HALF AN HOUR later both men departed and Camilla and I cleared away the dishes and the leftover bread. "Camilla, you are amazing," I told her. "We never would have had this revelation if you hadn't sensed something amiss. It's so subtle, really, when you see the photograph as a whole. But when you study the discrete elements—it's fascinating."

"We can say the same thing of your searching online. You and I have, perhaps, that extra sense, attuned to the things that others might not notice. We seek a solution, and our minds are helping us do that."

I noticed that, despite the late hour, Camilla was walking with a bright energy, and her eyes were glowing. "Camilla—you certainly are spritely this evening. Is this due to a certain lunch with Adam Rayburn?"

She grinned. "Lunch was very nice, but I must confess it's not Adam that has me feeling so energized right now." She rinsed out the coffeepot and started to dry it with a dish towel. She turned to me, pot in hand, and I saw her young self in her face.

"The fact is, Lena, there's nothing so exciting as a real mystery—I've always thought so! Don't you agree?"

20

They met Hermann Josef at the harbor at midnight. The long-lost brothers embraced, and Gerhard took Johanna's hand and helped her board the Pontoporeia, *named for a sea nymph, while a mass of stars glimmered above them. The air was fresh and cold, but their hearts were warm as they contemplated life together in a new land, young and free, with their lives yet to unfurl before them.*

As the yacht made its slow, graceful way out to sea, Johanna gave silent thanks that she had summoned the courage to board the Salzburg Train, the first step in a journey that had led her to this place, these people, this chance.

Now another journey would begin, and she had chosen her direction.

—the ending of *The Salzburg Train*

CAMILLA HAD ORDERED me to sleep in the next morning, assuring me that she would do the same. "It's the first day you haven't had some terrible stress weighing down on you, and I want you to relax. Daydream, enjoy the scenery out the window, pet that purring ball of fluff who keeps getting under my feet," she had said with a smile. "Doug will be doing the morning shift on our latest project, so we have some time to ourselves."

I woke and did as she advised, stretching out under my warm covers and studying the little cat face of the sleeping Lestrade. The trees outside, growing bare but still adorned by some colorful and determined leaves, bowed to me with the pressure of the wind. I lay back on my pillow and closed my eyes, luxuriating under my comforter. Everything would be better from this point on. I would find ways to spend more time with Sam; my father would come to visit me and tour Blue Lake; Camilla would finish her novel and I would see its publication; and soon, very soon, we would solve the mystery of Victoria West.

My eyes opened again. It was no use; I wouldn't be falling back asleep. It was best, despite my determination to lie in, to get up and start my day. I reached for my phone and sent a quick text to Sam: *Good morning. I'm thinking of you.*

I set the phone down, climbed out of bed, leaving Lestrade to his slumbers, and headed for the shower. Camilla had replenished the fragrant French shampoo, and I indulged in this and some lavender soap while I gazed at distant Blue Lake, and the vast sky above it, through the small shower window.

Downstairs I found coffee and warm muffins on the dining room table. Rhonda was chopping vegetables for a lunch soufflé and singing a song to herself that I thought might be from a musical. I peered into the kitchen and waved at her; she lifted a hand, still singing. I returned to the table and sipped at hot coffee, enjoying the sunlight that speckled the tablecloth.

Camilla did not appear, but I could hear her voice in the office, murmuring into her phone. It sounded like a business call. I glanced at my watch: nine thirty, which meant it was ten thirty in New York.

I took one of the muffins, fat with blueberries, and ate it appreciatively. Then, in a moment of pure decadence, I ate another one. I poured more coffee and took my mug out of the room, down the hall, and to Camilla's doorway. I peered in; she was off the phone, but studying something at her desk.

"Good morning," I said.

She looked up and beamed at me. "Oh, good morning! My goodness, if this is what you call sleeping in, you could never be accused of self-indulgence."

"I couldn't sleep. But I'm having a lovely morning. Look at the sky today! And Rhonda has already made me fat and complacent."

Camilla laughed. "Come in, come in, Lena. Pull up the purple chair. I have some questions to ask you. And we have work to do."

It was quite familiar now, sitting across from Camilla at her large desk, settling into the stuffed chair and readying myself for creative dialogue. "Of course. We need to talk about Victoria. And work on the book, too," I added hastily.

She nodded. "Let's do book business first, because I have some pressing deadlines. I've gone over the scene you wrote in the Black Forest. I made my own changes, but it's largely yours. I'm wondering if you might look over a few more scenes in the same way. Discussing them with me, giving me your own take on them."

I leaned forward. "Of course! I love collaborating with you."

She nodded, pleased. "I thought you would say that, and I made some decisions based on your past performance."

The words sounded flattering, yet I felt a stab of fear.

This sounded like an assessment. Was I going to be reviewed? I had been distracted lately, worrying over Sam, badgering Doug, chasing ideas about Martin Jonas and Sam's wife . . . I had never really had a chance to prove myself under normal conditions. Camilla had acknowledged that yesterday, though; she had told me that she feared I would think Blue Lake was always a place of conflict.

"Uh—what . . . ?" I began.

She pulled a document from a folder nearby. "I just printed this. They sent it from New York this morning and want to know if I need any changes. It's the cover for *The Salzburg Train.*"

"Oh, how exciting!" I said.

She handed the paper to me. "Tell me what you think."

It was beautiful, and the colors were close to what I had imagined: a purpled, twilight view of a delightfully old-fashioned train emerging from a bricked tunnel with a backdrop of beautiful Austrian countryside. The sky was a mixture of blue, lavender, and orange—a poetic vision of day turning to night. The title was one line, spread across the sky, and Camilla's name was stretched across the bottom, white letters against the dark terrain—

"Oh my God," I said.

"Do you like it?"

"Camilla—this isn't right. I—this isn't necessary."

"I think it is, Lena. I think we must make our collaboration clear; who knows how much more you'll do, as the years pass? And you could be publishing your own books in a year or two. This will help with that, don't you think?"

I stared at her, my mouth open, my eyes warm with tears.

My gaze dropped back to the cover, the beautiful cover, the bottom of which read "Camilla Graham," and underneath that, in slightly smaller letters, "with Lena London."

I traced my name with one finger. "It's beautiful. Wonderful. But you can't do it. It will make people think that you need someone to help you write your books, and you don't. This book was the best yet! People will get the wrong idea."

Camilla shook her head. "No. All sorts of writers work with collaborators. It doesn't mean they've lost their gift. It means they're open to nurturing new talent." She leaned forward. "I have loved working with you, Lena. I hope you feel the same."

"I do! You know I do. I—I don't know what to say."

"Will you approve the cover?"

"If you think—"

She shook her head.

"I mean, of course I love the cover. I—I'll try to earn that credit, Camilla."

"Of course you will earn it, and have earned it."

"Thank you." I wiped at my eyes.

"We will need to do some interviews together. Tour together, although not extensively. I've made it clear that I'm too old to travel the world on tours. Some select cities in the U.S. and England, mostly."

"I've never been to England." My lips felt numb.

"Oh, it's lovely. I can show you my favorite places."

"Camilla."

"Yes."

I set the picture down on her desk. "I need to hug you now."

To my surprise, the cool and reserved Camilla Graham

laughed, clapped her hands, and moved swiftly around her desk, her arms open.

I barreled into them, resting my chin on her shoulder. "You are everything I ever dreamed you would be," I said. "And you have no idea how much I fantasized about meeting you, the person who created so many beautiful worlds for me."

Camilla kissed my cheek. "You are such a sweet child."

I stepped away from her. "Will we be working today? Or will we be sleuthing?"

She nodded. "A bit of both. We need to go back over this new edited version—see what we find, and what we might want to change. My editor needs the changes back within the next two weeks."

"Of course. I'll spend all day on it, every day. It's been—a little distracting around here."

"Yes, indeed. But you can't work on the book all day. As we established, Mrs. West is in danger. Doug will be involving the police, one hopes, and yet I fear they don't have the imagination for it. That's where we come in."

I nodded, accepting this even as I worried that it wasn't true, that we wouldn't be able to help them find Victoria.

"But first, I have one more thing for you."

"Camilla, really," I protested. "You've already given me a gift I can't repay."

She went back to her desk and opened a drawer. She pulled out a book, which she held out to me. It was a hardback copy of *The Lost Child*; it looked like a first edition. "I was signing some books for that waiter from Wheat Grass; Adam brought them over for me, and I did promise, didn't I? While I was doing it, I thought it made sense to sign this one for you. No one understands my characters as you do, Lena, especially Colin, my sweet boy. You saw him best of all."

She handed the book to me, and I accepted it with reverent hands. "Thank you," I said. It was all I could muster.

"You're welcome."

"I'll be ready to work in just a minute. I just want to put this in my room," I managed. I escaped upstairs and leaped on my bed, clutching the book like a talisman. I lay for a while, staring at the ceiling, trying to absorb all that had happened.

Then, tenderly, while Lestrade purred beside me with his eyes closed like some wise sphinx, I opened the cover. "To Lena," it said. "In some ways, you are like the child I never had." It was signed "Camilla."

Surely I would wake up and it would all have been a dream: coming to Blue Lake, meeting Camilla, confronting a murderer, meeting Sam West, finding the image of Victoria West, meeting Doug Heller, finding a hidden tunnel. Befriending my idol and finding that I had become as important to her life as she was to mine.

With a sigh, I took the book to my desk and laid it down carefully. I would have to find some beautiful bookends, or a display rack, for something so precious.

On a whim, I picked up my phone. I had a return text from Sam. It said: *Me, too. Keep texting me—it brightens my day.*

I wrote back: *Camilla just told me she'll put my name on her next cover.*

Then I dialed my father; there was no answer, so I left him the same message, with a bit more detail, in a voice too high-pitched to hide my excitement. My father would understand; although it was my mother and I who had shared a love for Graham novels, my dad was the one who had always remembered to buy them as birthday and Christmas gifts for us both. He would understand the significance of seeing his daughter's name on one of those book covers.

HOURS LATER CAMILLA and I sat at the dining room table, poring over corrections and making notes. It was painstaking work, but we had found that we could work well together, mainly in a companionable silence, occasionally consulting each other with questions or ideas.

Finally Camilla sat back and removed her glasses, rubbing her eyes. "Oh, my. That might be all I can do until I take a break."

"Okay," I said. "Would you like to walk the dogs? Head down to the lake? Hike in the woods, maybe?"

She put her glasses back on; her eyes were still bright, despite the bleary work of editing.

"I'll let the dogs into the yard for now. We can walk them later. Right now, Miss London, we have some different work to do." She pushed her manuscript away and leaned toward me, her expression conspiratorial. "We have a real-life mystery to solve."

"Yes," I said, thinking of the man down the bluff whose future depended on resolving his past. "We do."

Camilla Graham placed her hands on the table, palms down, and directed her intelligent gaze at me. "So, Lena. Let's put our heads together and find Victoria West."

Keep reading for an excerpt of
Julia Buckley's Undercover Dish Mystery . . .

THE BIG CHILI

Available in paperback from
Berkley Prime Crime!

My chocolate Labrador watched me as I parked my previously loved Volvo wagon and took my covered pan out of the backseat; the autumn wind buffeted my face and made a mess of my hair. "I'll be right back, Mick," I said. "I know that pot in the back smells good, but I'm counting on you to behave and wait for your treat."

He nodded at me. Mick was a remarkable dog for many reasons, but one of his best talents was that he had trained himself to nod while I was talking. He was my dream companion: a handsome male who listened attentively and never interrupted or condescended. He also made me feel safe when I did my clandestine duties all over Pine Haven.

I shut the car door and moved up the walkway of Ellie Parker's house. She usually kept the door unlocked, though I had begged her to reconsider that idea. We had an agreement; if she wasn't there, or if she was out back puttering around in her garden, I could just leave the casserole on the table and take the money she left out for me. I charged fifty dollars, which included the price of ingredients. Ellie said I could charge more, but for now this little sideline of a job was helping me pay the bills, and that was good enough.

"Ellie?" I called. I went into her kitchen, where I'd been several times before, and found it neat, as always; Ellie was not inside. Disappointed, I left the dish on her scrubbed wooden table. I had made a lovely mac and cheese casserole with a twist: finely sliced onion and prosciutto baked in with three different cheeses for a showstopping event of a main course. It was delicious and very close to the way Ellie prepared it before her arthritis had made it too difficult to cook for her visiting friends and family. She didn't want her loved ones to know this, which was where I came in. We'd had an agreement for almost a year, and it served us both well.

She knew how long to bake the dish, so I didn't bother with writing down any directions. Normally she would invite Mick in, and she and I would have some tea and shoot the breeze while my canine lounged under the table, but today, for whatever reason, she had made other plans. She hadn't set out the money, either, so I went to the cookie jar where she had told me to find my payment in the past: a ceramic cylinder in the shape of a chubby monkey. I claimed my money and turned around to find a man looming in the doorway.

"Ah!" I screamed, clutching the cash in front of my waist like a weird bouquet.

"Hello," he said, his eyes narrowed. "May I ask who you are?"

"I'm a friend of Ellie's. Who are you?" I fired back. Ellie had never suggested that a man—a sort of good-looking, youngish man—would appear in her house. For all I knew he could be a burglar.

"I am Ellie's son. Jay Parker." He wore reading glasses, and he peered at me over these like a stern teacher. It was a good look for him. "And I didn't expect to find a strange woman dipping into Mom's cash jar while she wasn't in the house."

A little bead of perspiration worked its way down my back. "First of all, I am not a strange woman. In any sense. Ellie and I are friends, and I—"

I what? What could I tell him? My little covered-dish business was an under-the-table operation, and the people who ordered my food wanted it to appear that they had made it themselves. That, and the deliciousness of my cooking, was what they paid me for. "I did a job for her, and she told me to take payment."

"Is that so?" He leaned against the door frame, a man with all the time in the world. All he needed was a piece of hay to chew on. "And what *job* did you do for her?" He clearly didn't believe me. With a pang I realized that this man thought I was a thief.

"I mowed her lawn," I blurted. We both turned to look out the window at Ellie's remarkably high grass. "Wow. That really was not a good choice," I murmured.

Now his face grew alert, wary, as though he were ready to employ some sort of martial art if necessary. I may as well have been facing a cop. "What exactly is your relationship to my mother? And how did you even get in here, if my mom isn't home?"

At least I could tell the truth about that. "I'm Lilah

Drake. Ellie left the door unlocked for me because she was expecting me. As I said, we are friends."

This did not please him. "I think she was actually expecting *me*," he said. "So you could potentially have just gotten lucky when you tried the doorknob."

"Oh my God!" My face felt hot with embarrassment. "I'm not stealing Ellie's money. She and I have an—arrangement. I can't actually discuss it with you. Maybe if you asked your mother . . . ?" Ellie was creative; she could come up with a good lie for her son, and he'd *have* to believe her.

There was a silence, as though he were weighing evidence. It felt condescending and weirdly terrifying. "Listen, I have to get going. My dog is waiting—"

He brightened for the first time. "That's your dog, huh? I figured. He's pretty awesome. What is he, a chocolate Lab?"

"Yes, he is." I shifted on my feet, not sure how to extricate myself from the situation. My brother said I had a knack for getting into weird predicaments.

I sighed, and he said, "So what do we do now?" He patted his shirt pocket, as though looking for a pack of cigarettes, then grimaced and produced a piece of gum. He unwrapped it while still watching me. His glasses had slid down even farther on his nose, and I felt like plucking them off. He popped the gum into his mouth and took off the glasses himself, then beamed a blue gaze at me. Wow. "How about if we just wait here together and see what my mom has to say? She's probably out back in the garden, picking pumpkins or harvesting the last of her tomatoes."

I put the money on Ellie's table. "You know what? Ellie can pay me later. I won't have you—casting aspersions on my character."

"Fancy words," said Ellie's son. He moved a little closer to me, until I could smell spearmint on his breath. "I still think you should hang around."

I put my hands on my hips, the way my mother used to do when Cam or I forgot to do the dishes. "I have things to do. Please tell Ellie I said hello."

I whisked past him, out to my car, where Mick sat waiting, a picture of patience. I climbed in and started confiding. "Do you believe that guy? Now I'm going to have to come back here later to get paid. I don't have time for this, Mick!"

Mick nodded with what seemed like sympathy.

I reversed out of Ellie's driveway, still fuming. But halfway home, encouraged by Mick's stolid support, and enjoying the *Mary Poppins* sound track in my CD player, I calmed down slightly. These things could happen in the business world, I told myself. There was no need to give another thought to tall Jay Parker and his accusations and his blue eyes.

I began to sing along with the music, assuring Mick melodically that I would find the perfect nanny. Something in the look he gave me made me respond aloud. "And another thing. I'm a grown woman. I'm twenty-seven years old, Mick. I don't need some condescending man treating me like a child. Am I right?"

Mick was distracted by a Chihuahua on the sidewalk, so I didn't get a nod.

"Huh. She's pretty cute, right?"

No response. I sighed and went back to my singing, flicking forward on the CD and testing my upper range with "Feed the Birds." I started squeaking by the time I reached the middle. "It's tricky, Mick. It starts low, and then you get nailed on the refrain. We can't all be Julie Andrews." Mick's expression was benevolent.

I drove to Caldwell Street and St. Bartholomew Church, where I headed to the back parking lot behind the rectory. I took out my phone and texted I'm here to Pet Grandy, a member of St. Bart's Altar and Rosary Guild, a scion of the church, and a go-to person for church social events. Pet was popular, and she had a burning desire to be all things to all people. This included her wish to make food for every church event—good food that earned her praise and adulation. Since Pet was actually a terrible cook, I was the answer to her prayers. I had made a lot of money off Pet Grandy in the last year.

"She'll be out here within thirty seconds," I told Mick, and sure enough, he had barely started nodding before Pet burst out of the back door of the church social hall and made a beeline for the adjoining rectory lot. Pet's full name was Perpetua; her mother had named her for some nun who had once taught at the parish school. Pet basically lived at the church; she was always running one event or another, and Father Schmidt was her gangly other half. They made a hilarious duo: he, tall and thin in his priestly black, and she, short and plump as a tomato and sporting one of her many velour sweat suits—often in offensively bright colors. In fall, you could often spot them tending to the autumnal flower beds outside St. Bart's. At Christmastime, one of them would hold the ladder while the other swayed in front of the giant pine outside the church, clutching strings of white Christmas lights. Pet was utterly devoted to Father Schmidt; they were like a platonic married couple.

As she marched toward my car, I studied her. Today's ensemble, also velour, was a bright orange number that made her look like a calendar-appropriate pumpkin. Her cheeks were rosy in the cold, and her dark silver-flecked hair was cut short and no-nonsense. Pet was not a frilly person.

She approached my vehicle, as always, with an almost sinister expression, as if she were buying drugs. Pet was very careful that no one should know what we were doing or why. On the rare occasions that someone witnessed the food handoff, Pet pretended that I was just driving it over from her house. Today she had ordered a huge Crock-Pot full of chili for the bingo event in the church hall. Everyone was bringing food, but Pet's (my) chili had become a favorite.

I rolled down my window, and Pet looked both ways before leaning in. Her eyes darted constantly, like those of someone marked for assassination. "Hello, Lilah. Is it light enough for me to carry?"

"It's pretty heavy, Pet. Do you want me to—"

"No, no. I have a dolly in the vestibule. I'll just run and get it. Here's the money." She thrust an envelope through the window at me with her left hand, her body turned sideways and her right hand scratching her face in an attempt to look casual. Pet was so practiced at clandestine maneuvers that I thought she might actually make a good criminal. I watched her rapid-walk back to the church and marveled that she wasn't thin as a reed, since she was always moving. Pet, however, had the Achilles' heel of a sweet addiction: she loved it all, she had told me once. Donuts, cookies, cake, pie, ice cream. "I probably have sweets three times a day. My doctor told me I'm lucky I don't have diabetes. But I crave it all the time!"

Pet reappeared and I pretended that I was about to get out of my car to help her. I did this every time, just to tease her, and every time she took the bait. "No!" she shouted, her hand up as though to ward off a bullet aimed at her heart. "Stay there! Someone might see you!"

"Okay, Pet." She opened my back hatch and I spoke to her over my shoulder. "It's the big Crock-Pot there. Ignore the box in the corner—that's for someone else."

"Fine, fine. Thank you, Lilah. I'm sure it will be delicious, as always." She hauled it out of the car, grunting slightly, and placed it on her dolly. Then, loudly, for whatever sprites might be listening, she said, "Thank you so much for driving this from my house! It's a real time-saver!"

I rolled my eyes at Mick, and he nodded. Mick totally gets it.

I waved to Pet, who ignored me, and drove away while she was still wheeling her prize back to the church hall. My mother played bingo there sometimes and probably would tonight. We were church members, but we were neither as devout nor as involved as was Pet. My mother called us "lapsed Catholics," and said we would probably have to wait at the back of the line on our way to heaven, at which point my father would snort and say that he could name five perfect Catholics who were having affairs.

Then they would launch into one of their marital spats and I would tune them out or escape to my own home, which was where I headed now.

My parents are Realtors, and I work for them during the day. I mostly either answer phones at the office or sit at showings, dreaming of recipes while answering questions about hardwood floors, modernized baths, and stainless steel kitchens. It isn't a difficult task, but I do lust after those kitchens more than is healthy. I have visions of starting my own catering business, experimenting with spices at one of those amazing marble islands while a tall blue-eyed man occasionally wanders in to taste my concoctions.

Mick was staring at the side of my face with his intense look. I slapped my forehead. "Oh, buddy! I never gave you your treat, and you had to sit and smell that chili all through the ride!"

Mick nodded.

We pulled into the long driveway that led to our little house, which was actually an old caretaker's cottage behind a much larger residence. My parents had found it for me and gotten me a crazy deal on rent because they had sold the main house to Terry Randall, a rich eccentric who had taken a liking to my parents during the negotiations. Taking advantage of that, my parents had mentioned that their daughter would love to rent a cottage like the one behind his house, and Terry had agreed. My rent, which Terry didn't need but which my parents had insisted upon, was a steal. I'd been in the cottage for more than two years, and Terry and I had become good friends. I was often invited into the big house for the lavish parties that Terry and his girlfriend liked to throw on a regular basis.

I pulled a Tupperware container out of my tote bag—Mick's reward whenever he accompanied me on trips. "Who's my special boy?" I asked him as I popped off the lid.

Mick started munching, his expression forgiving. He made quick work of the chili inside; I laughed and snapped his picture on my phone. "That's going on the refrigerator, boy," I said. It was true, I doted on Mick as if he were my child, but in my defense, Mick was a spectacular dog.

I belted out a few lines of "Jolly Holiday" before turning off the sound system and retrieving Mick's now-clean container. I checked my phone and found two text messages: one from my friend Jenny, who wanted me to come for dinner soon, and one from my brother, who wanted me to meet his girlfriend. I'd met lots of Cam's girlfriends over time, but this one was special to him, I could tell, because she was Italian. My brother and I, thanks to a wonderfully enthusiastic junior high Italian teacher, had developed a mutual love of Italian culture before we even got to high school. We immersed ourselves in Italian art, music, sports, and film. We both took Italian in high school, and Cam went on to get his PhD in Italian, which he now taught at Loyola, my alma mater. We were Italophiles from way back, but Cam had never met an Italian woman. It was I who had won the distinction of dating an Italian first, and that hadn't ended well. But sometimes, even now, when I found myself humming "*Danza, danza fanciulla gentile*," I could hear Miss Abbandonato saying, "*Ciao*, Lilah, *splendido*!"

She had told us, in the early days of our classes, that her family name meant "forsaken," and I had remembered it when I, too, was betrayed. *Abbandonato.* How forsaken I had felt back then.

I turned off my phone and smiled at Mick, who was still licking his chops. We climbed out of the car and made our way to the cozy little cottage with its green wood door and berry wreath. Home sweet home.

I grabbed my mail out of the tin box and unlocked the door, letting Mick and me into our kingdom. We had hardwood floors, too, at least a few feet of them in our little foyer. The living room was carpeted in an unfortunate brown shag, but it was clean, and there was a fireplace that made the whole first floor snug and welcoming.

My kitchen was tiny and clean, and between my little dining area and the living room was a spiral staircase that led up to a loft bedroom. Every night I thanked God for Terry Randall and his generous heart (and for my savvy parents, who had talked him into renting me my dollhouse cottage).

As I set my things down, my phone rang.

"Hello?"

"Hi, honey." It was my mother. I could hear her doing something in the background—probably putting away groceries. "Are you going to bingo with me tonight?"

"Mom. Bingo is so loud and annoying, and those crazy women with their multiple cards and highlighters . . ."

"Are what? Our good friends and fellow parishioners?"

I groaned. "Don't judge me, Mom. Just because I get tired of Trixie Frith and Theresa Scardini and their braying voices—"

"Lilah Veronica! What has gotten into you?"

"I don't know."

"Sweetie, you have to get out. Dad thinks you have agoraphobia."

"I don't have agoraphobia. I just happen to like my house and my dog."

"What song is in your head right now?"

My mother knew this odd little fact: I always had a song in my head. There was one in there when I woke up each morning—often something really obscure, like a commercial jingle from the nineties, when I was a kid—and one in my head when I went to bed at night. It was not always a conscious thing, but it was always there, like a sound track to my life. My mother had used it as a way to gauge my mood when I was little. If I was happy it was always something like "I Could Have Danced All Night" (I loved musicals) or some fun Raffi song. If she heard me humming "It's Not Easy Being Green," she knew I needed cheering up. Nowadays my musical moods could swing from Adele to Abba in a matter of hours. "I don't know. I think I was humming Simon and Garfunkel a minute ago."

"Hmm—that could go either way."

"Don't worry about it, Mom."

"You haven't spent much time with young people lately. You need to get out on the town with Jenny, like in the old days when you two were in college."

"I'm planning just that next week. We've been texting about it. But, Mom, I'm not in college anymore. And neither is Jenny. She's busy with her job, I'm busy with my jobs—plural. And if you are subtly implying that you want me to meet men, I am not ready for that, either."

My mother sighed dramatically in my ear. "One bad relationship doesn't mean you can't find something good."

"No. It just means I'm not *interested* in finding a man right now. I think I'm a loner. I like being alone."

"I think you're hiding."

"Mom, stop the pop psychology. I have a great life: a growing business, a nice house, a loving family, and a devoted dog. People who saw my life would wish they were me."

"Except no one sees your life, because you hide away from the world in your little house behind a house."

"Right. With my agoraphobia," I said, choosing to find my mother's words amusing instead of annoying. She had found me this house, after all.

"Come with me tonight. I heard that Pet will be making her chili. It's my favorite," said my mother, who was one of only three people who knew my secret.

"I guess I'll go," I said. "But only because I'm hoping your crazy luck will rub off on me and I'll win the jackpot."

My mother had won two thousand dollars at bingo six months earlier. She came home beaming, and my father groused about the fact that she went at all. Then she pulled out twenty hundred-dollar bills and set them in his lap. Now he didn't say much about bingo, especially since they'd used the money to buy him a state-of-the-art recliner.

What I could do with two thousand dollars. . . . I gazed around the kitchen and indulged a brief lust for gourmet tools, an updated countertop, or even a new stainless steel refrigerator—the wide kind that accommodated large pans.

"Great!" said my mother. "Do you want to come over now and we'll hang out together before we go? I have a couple of Netflix movies. One is a Doris Day. Remember how we used to watch her when you were little, and have our tea parties?"

I laughed. "I do remember. And as I recall, you developed quite a crush on Cary Grant after watching *That Touch of Mink*."

"Oh yes," my mother said. "My secret crush."

"It's not secret. Dad knows about it and hates it."

She giggled. "Your father is attractive when he's jealous."

"*Anyway.* I have to pass on the movies—I need to walk Mick. I have one last delivery, and then I'll be there for our bingo date."

"Okay." Her voice had brightened since I'd agreed to go. My mother was an innately cheerful person.

I grabbed a water bottle from my fridge and hooked Mick's leash to his collar. We went outside, through Terry's amazing backyard, with its plush furniture and giant stone birdbath, down his driveway, and out onto Dickens Street, where we walked at a leisurely pace and admired the Halloween decorations. The evening was cold and dark, yet somehow cozy because of all the glowing yellow and orange lights, and the occasional jack-o'-lantern lighting up a storefront window. The air smelled like woodsmoke and winter, and Mick kept pausing to sniff it. My brain was playing a song that my dad had once sung to me when I was little—something by Don Henley with the name *Lilah* in it. The melody was a pretty blend of love song and lullaby, and my father said he had started singing it to me almost the moment I was born. So I walked along hearing the refrain of my own name, which was both comforting and disconcerting. We went around the block and returned home, where Mick ambled to his basket beside the fireplace for a little evening nap.

"Okay, buddy. I'm going out for a while, but I'll see you after bingo, okay?"

Mick gave a half nod because he was already dozing.

I went out and locked my door behind me. I returned to the car, where I had a Mexican casserole waiting, keeping chilled in the October air. This one was for Danielle Prentiss, who hosted poker parties at her house on Saturday nights. I drove to the outskirts of town, to Jamison Woods, a little forest preserve where Mick and I would sometimes go on a weekend morning to watch wildlife and enjoy nature. In Mick's case this often meant chasing things, and once it had even involved pursuing a young deer. He stayed on its tail as far as the tree line, and then they both paused, looking at each other. Mick finally peered back at me, confused. He wasn't sure what in the world he was supposed to do with this animal. I laughed and took pictures on my phone; eventually the deer ambled off, no longer afraid of my big soft-hearted puppy.

I pulled into the empty parking lot; no hikers were visible on this particular day. Dani showed up in her station wagon with the wood-look sides, seeming as always like a throwback from the seventies. She climbed out of her car and met me at the back of mine. "Hey, Lilah. Thanks for meeting me at our little rendezvous point." She grinned at me and blew out some smoke; only then did I notice the cigarette in her hand, although I shouldn't have been surprised—Dani was a two-pack-a-day smoker, and her raspy voice told the tale.

"Sure. I made this one with some extra onion and cheese, as your patrons requested," I said, pulling out the box that contained the glass baking pan. "I think you'll like it even better than last time. I put in a new and wonderful spice."

"What?"

"Just a little cumin. Not enough to change anything—just to enhance it."

She looked at me, dubious. "I really liked it the old way."

"You'll love it. Have I ever given you anything bad?"

She shook her head. "No. I love your cooking." She grinned at me. "And my poker pals love mine!"

"That's right. And when they ask you why it's so extra delicious, say it's cumin."

I set the box in her arms and slammed my door.

"Money's in my jacket, hon," said Dani, sniffing the box.

A little white envelope jutted out of her pocket. I took it out; it smelled like smoke.

"Thanks, Dani. Just e-mail me when you need another dish."

"You got it, hon. Hey, your hair looks pretty. I like it in a braid like that. It's so thick." She sighed. "I always wanted blonde hair, like a Disney princess. Instead I got boring brown, and then it turned gray. What're you gonna do?" she asked, and laughed.

I laughed, too. "Thanks, Dani. For the job and the compliment. See you soon!"

I climbed into my car and sighed deeply. My day's work was done, and now I could relax. With my mother. At St. Bart's bingo.

Some Saturday nights were more exciting than others.

ALSO FROM

JULIA BUCKLEY

The Big Chili

An Undercover Dish Mystery

Lilah Drake's covered-dish business discreetly provides the residents of Pine Haven, Illinois, with delicious, fresh-cooked meals they can claim they cooked themselves. But when one of her clandestine concoctions is used to poison a local woman, Lilah finds herself in a pot-load of trouble ...

After dreaming for years of owning her own catering company, Lilah has made a start into the food world through her covered-dish business, covertly cooking for her neighbors who don't have the time or skill to do so themselves, and allowing them to claim her culinary creations as their own. While her clientele is strong, their continued happiness depends on no one finding out who's really behind the apron.

So when someone drops dead at a church bingo night moments after eating chili that Lilah made for a client, the anonymous chef finds herself getting stirred into a cauldron of secrets, lies, and murder—and going toe-to-toe with a very determined and very attractive detective. To keep her clients coming back and her business under wraps, Lilah will have to chop down the list of suspects fast, because this spicy killer has acquired a taste for homicide...